THE LAST SANCTUARY

BOOK 3 OF THE SANCTUARY SERIES

NIKITA SLATER

Dear readers,

Thank you for purchasing The Last Sanctuary! I really appreciate your support and hope you love reading this book as much as I enjoyed writing it. If you haven't read Sanctuary's Warlord and Sanctuary on Fire, you'll want to go back and read those first as this series must be read in order for the full reading experience. I've enjoyed creating the Sanctuary world so much that I've decided to add two more novels and a prequel to the series. I promise that this book, The Last Sanctuary, won't end on a cliffhanger. I fully intend to wrap up Taran and Diogo's story, though they may show up in future novels as side characters. Thank you for following me on this incredible journey!

Love always,

Nikita

PROLOGUE

It's 2074, the world, already an apocalyptic nightmare, is on fire. Nuclear power plants all across the eastern side of the continent are melting down, the subsequent fallout driving Primitives toward our only hope for survival, sanctuary cities. As they overrun each city in a desperate need to feed their hunger, they drive the survivors further and further west.

In New Tucson, in our Sanctuary, rebels have taken to the streets protesting food shortages, lack of resources, and their unfair treatment under an authoritarian government. Brutality is clashing with good intentions until nothing remains but ashes. Hope has been lost, and, as our city falls from the inside out, waves of refugees with Primitives close behind are begging Sanctuary from us. Sanctuary that we cannot possibly provide until we solve our own problems first.

Our situation has become bleaker than ever. Friends, families, allies are all crumbling under the pressure of a city divided. Our only hope is to unite, to strengthen our walls, rebuild our homes and face the threat coming our way.

My name is Taran and I've lost nearly everything. My parents, my grandparents, new friends, old friends. I even lost the sister I was reunited with for a few brief hours. My home is burning, my loved ones are trapped and I'm clinging to the edge wondering if I will see my husband again. I am forced to make the decision between staying with him or saving our unborn child.

As I take this leap into the darkness, I can't help wondering how can I, how can any of us, survive a world on fire?

ONE

TARAN

Heat blasts me from below as smoke rises to sting my eyes. I'm clinging to the side of a building, 7-months pregnant, with tears streaming down my face. It isn't just the smoke making me cry, but the gut-wrenching choice I've just made, leaving my husband, best friend and others behind, trapped in a burning building.

I try to concentrate on the task, climbing from the sixth floor down to the ground. I'm not safe yet. I remind myself that once this task is complete, I can cry all I want for Diogo, Emery and Grayson. Right now, I need to pay attention, pick out a path, make my way through the flames. Save my baby.

Just as I reach the fourth floor, the sound of shattering glass followed by roaring and intense heat startles me. I cling harder to the windowsill, hugging the building, remaining motionless until the worst of the heat passes. I look down. One of the windows about ten feet down was blown out by the pressure of the fire, and now flames are licking the side of the building. The path I'd carefully picked out to the ground has become cut off.

I search desperately, squinting through the smoke and choking back my coughs. I breathe a sigh of relief when I see that there's still a clear path down if I crawl sideways about twenty feet. I move as quickly as I can with my protruding stomach bumping into the side of the building. Luckily, I'm not showing as much as I thought I would at 7 months. But I still have a healthy sized belly making the climb feel far more awkward and difficult than it would have been in the past.

Exhaustion beats at me competing with the adrenalin rushing through my system. I feel myself growing weaker with each step, the strength draining from each part of me. My hands are sore, my legs shaky and my lungs on fire with lack of oxygen. I promise myself, and the baby, that if we reach the ground, we can sleep for a week after this.

My bare legs, arms and feet are scraped raw from sliding down the exposed concrete. I'm only wearing one of Diogo's shirts. I didn't have time to change after the bomb went off in the bowels of the building waking me up in our high-rise apartment. Diogo grabbed me and rushed us into the stairwell.

A shot rings out somewhere on the street and I shudder, trying to scan the streets below. They're shrouded in smoky darkness, night having fully taken hold in the past few hours. As I continue to climb, I wonder who's winning the fight on the ground; the city forces or the rebels. I pray it'll be Diogo's men I encounter when I'm finally down.

I can no longer pretend that I'm a rebel. I understand their cause even if I don't condone the extreme actions taken by some, but now I have a better understanding what it takes to make a Sanctuary city successful. And though I don't agree with all of Diogo's policies, I do believe that he's the best Warlord for our Sanctuary. He's a thoughtful man, even if he's not a kind or forgiving one. He doesn't have the luxury of such things.

I see this now, better than I ever have, as our city burns from the foolishness of a lost cause. Lost, because if the rebels somehow win this war, they will bring our city down in the chaos they have sown.

I can't tell how far I've climbed, but I would guess I'm somewhere between ten and twenty feet to the ground. The shouts and gunshots are getting closer, clearer. I hear the word 'Authority' shouted, the sound echoing across the buildings. My heart sinks as I realize it must've been a rebel. Though the city forces are Authority, they don't refer to themselves that way. Only the rebels will shout the word with derogatory intent.

Just as I'm dropping into a crouch, sliding my fingers down the concrete, about to take a new handhold, a window bursts right next to me. The fire roars in my ears and the heat is so intense I'm forced to let go of the ledge and fall in a controlled drop, my fingers sliding down the side of the building, more windows shattering all around me. I manage to catch myself on another ledge, but I can't find a foothold.

I'm dangling above the street, gripping a window ledge with the last of my strength. God only knows how high up I am! I can't look over my shoulder or I'll lose my hold. I try lifting my leg, scrambling for a hold, but my bare foot just slides down an unbroken pane of glass. I'm not tall enough to reach the ledge below me.

The fires are burning all around me, scorching my hands and legs. I can feel the heat from inside the building. I probably have seconds before the window I'm dangling against explodes.

"Oh god, I'm so sorry!" I cry out.

I tried to keep our baby safe, tried to do what Diogo

asked, but I'm about to fail. If I don't die in the fall, the baby probably will. Tears streak down my cheeks as hopelessness takes hold. There's nothing I can do, nowhere I can go. There are no more moves left for me. I only pray that Diogo somehow makes it out of the building alive.

As I lose my grip the window explodes, fire bursting out. I scream as I fall through the flames, shattered glass following me down, fire licking at me.

"Taran!" My name is bellowed into the darkness.

Softness envelops me, cradling me as I fall into the black reaches of my mind.

TWO

DIOGO

The moment I hear her scream, I shout her name, my voice echoing through the night. I'm frantic to reach her, to dive from a sixth-floor window and rescue my wife. Arms reach for me, pinning me, holding me back. I turn to beat at them, to force them back, but Emery shoves herself into the fray.

"Don't!" she snaps, gripping my arm. "The last thing she'll want is for you to fall and kill yourself."

"She needs me," I snarl in Emery's face.

She shakes her head. "She needs you alive, Warlord."

I try to shake my men off, but they've managed to get a solid hold on my arms and shoulders while Emery speaks. Grayson has somehow inserted himself between me and the window. I will throw him out that window if I have to, but Emery's words are starting to penetrate the black haze that took me over when I heard Taran's frightened scream. I concentrate on Emery's voice and force myself to internalize each word.

"Think about what she would want. If she thought you could escape through the window, she would've insisted you go with her, but you aren't capable of making that climb any more than I am. Only Taran. And she might be hurt, the baby… " Her voice trails off for a few seconds as the words choke her. She closes her eyes for a moment, and then continues, "They'll need you if she fell. She could be hurt and she needs you alive if she's to recover. We have to be smart, use our heads. Now, tell me Warlord, how do we get out of here? We need you to guide us."

Finally, I nod. "Enough." My voice comes out sounding as tired as I feel. "I won't jump."

I shrug the hands off me and pace away from the window. I need to clear my mind of Taran if I'm to help the people still trapped in the building. There are five of us left. Five lives depending on a solution. Depending on the man who leads them, who dictates their futures.

"We need to go back up," I decide. The fire is still below us. If it hasn't consumed the stairwell, we can still climb up to the floors above in an effort to get away from the smoke and flames. If the building collapses we're fucked anyway and the safest place to be in a collapse will be the reinforced stairwell. We'll either die by fire or by building collapse. Neither prospect sounds pleasant. "We need to go higher."

The man closest to the door checks it for heat and then wrenches it open. He jumps back as a blast of hot air and smoke pours through. He covers his face with his shirt and peeks into the stairway, then jumps back coughing.

When he can speak, he says, "It's hot and there's almost no visibility, but I think we can still get through. As far as I can tell, nothing's blocked."

"Cover your faces and run up as fast as you can. There are missing windows on floors ten and twelve. Stop there and take a breather if you need to." I bark the instructions through a throat ripped ragged from smoke inhalation and coughing. "Don't stop unless you have to."

Emery looks at me with fear in her eyes. She's smaller and older than the rest of us. We're built for battle, she isn't. I stride toward her, taking her arm in a firm hold. "You'll stay with me. Be sure to keep up."

"I don't think I can," she says, her voice thready.

"You will." I pull her toward the stairwell.

"Deep breath," I instruct and then drag her with me into the smoke-filled landing.

Without pausing, I start running up the stairs, taking them two at a time. Emery runs as fast as she can, her face buried in the crook of her elbow, tears streaming down her cheeks. Tears prick my own eyes as smoke fills the air all around us. My heart is pounding and my lungs scream for relief. I embrace the pain, looking past it toward the goal. Pain is life. As long as we hurt, we are still alive.

Emery starts to stumble, lagging behind, my arm stretched out behind me as her weight drags me back. I haul her back up and tuck her into my side, half dragging her with me as I climb. I can hear my men clattering behind us, one of them so close he'll pass us in a minute.

I lift my face and shout, "We'll stop on twelve."

Two more floors. Every part of me is screaming for oxygen and Emery is nearly limp in my arms, her feet tripping over each step. She's almost as light as Taran, having spent years starving on only half her food rations. But as small as she is, I'm still struggling, the energy I'm expending to carry her while running is depleting the last of my strength.

My man edges out in front of us, shooting past as we near the twelfth floor. He flies through the door, sprinting for the windows just as the floor begins to shake and a rumbling sound goes through the building.

"Get back here!" I shout desperately, trying to call him

back. It's too late. As he turns to look at us, the floor collapses out from under his feet and he disappears.

I look up and to my horror, the ceiling is collapsing, the floor above falling into the one we're standing on.

"Get back!" I fling my arm out, smashing it into Grayson and throwing him back.

I pick Emery up and fling her against the inside wall of the stairwell, flattening her against the concrete, protecting her with my body. The terrible roaring of a building collapsing all around us is the last thing I hear as something sharp hits my head and the world goes black.

THREE

TARAN

"There, do you feel that?"

I move Diogo's hand on my belly, mine pressed over his, my fingers linked with his. I press the palm of his hand against the fluttering. I smile through the tears slowly rolling down my cheeks, dripping off my chin and landing on our hands. The tears have been coming for three weeks, since I escaped a burning building, leaving my heart behind.

Leaving him to be crushed by the concrete shell that fell on top of him and the others.

"There... right there," I whisper, bowing my head as the baby kicks into our combined hands.

I should be out of tears. I should have moved past this grief, but I can't. Maybe I'm not strong enough. My city still burns, only the actual fires are gone.

The door opens behind me. I brush away my tears, as much as I can, and twist around. Emery comes through the door, her arms full of supplies. Gratitude rushes through me as I set Diogo's hand back on the bed and push myself clumsily to my feet. We're in my old bedroom in Emery's house, the best place we could think of for Diogo to recover.

"Let me help." I reach for one of the sacks.

"No, I'm fine," Emery says, moving past me with her burden.

"Emery, you have a broken arm," I scold, moving forward to at least help her set her packages down. "I'm carrying less than ten pounds of baby. I can help."

Emery smiles ruefully as she turns to me. "May I?" she asks, and at my nod she runs her hand over my bump, searching for the seemingly never-ending movement of my cartwheeling baby. I yearn for the days when the turnip wasn't making itself so known. Her shoulders relax and her smile becomes less forced when she feels the movement. "Our future Warlord is a strong one."

I laugh and shake my head. Emery insists on believing that the child will be a boy. She chatters to Diogo about how strong and handsome his son will be. I think, in a way, she's almost as heartbroken over Diogo's condition as I am. He saved her life, protecting her with his body as the Tower collapsed. Thank goodness, only half the building collapsed, or there would've been no survivors, let alone the three pulled from the rubble.

"Did you get what I asked for?" I turn back to the table and start digging through the packages.

Emery laughs, the sound warm and comforting, moves my hands away and reaches into one of the sacks. I sigh happily as she pulls a straight razor out and hands it to me.

"Oh, thank goodness."

She shakes her head. "Of all the things we need to survive right now, you decide a razor is the most important."

I glance guiltily toward Diogo and lower my voice. "He's such a handsome man, Emery. But with that scruff all over his face and neck..." I eye him doubtfully. "Who would've thought it could grow so fast."

She crosses her arms and looks down at my husband. "I think he looks just as fine as he did before. You know, men with beards is perfectly natural. You should get used to it, learn to enjoy it."

"No," I shake my head and try to speak past the lump that has suddenly leapt into my throat. "I want him to look the same as before."

Emery curves her hands over my shoulders and puts her cheek against the side of my head. "Then we'll do what we can to get our Warlord back."

She means more than his appearance. She means his body, his spirit, his grim determination. Everything that made this man our leader. Because our city is falling apart under the leadership of another. It's being consumed by a man hungry for power. A man who too easily stepped into the shoes of his Warlord and is now reigning his brutal brand of justice down on the slums. Sanctuary won't last much longer without Diogo at the helm.

Almost the moment The Tower fell, Jorje Cruz, Diogo's right hand man and elite military advisor, stepped in as the new Warlord. It became quickly clear that he'd been taking steps to maneuver the city into his care, to undermine Diogo's leadership. He leaked information to the rebels and set up the final standoff that resulted in the burning of my home and nearly destroyed my small family. For that alone, I will never forgive him, but for the things he has done to our Sanctuary since he took over, I will stand against him.

"I would give anything for him to open his eyes." I brush impatiently at the tears that begin once more. "Or the twitch of a finger. Anything. I just want him back. I can't stand the thought that he might never wake up."

Emery nods, her face touching mine. "Doctor Bishop

said he may still recover. He's breathing on his own and the swelling has gone down. There's still hope, sweetheart."

Diogo suffered trauma to the head when he was hit by falling concrete in the building collapse. His brain swelled within his skull and possibly even bled. It took hours to dig him and the others out of the rubble. We lost precious time that we could've used trying to revive him.

Doctor Bishop started working on him the moment he was rescued from the building, stitching up the gash across the back of his head and trying to reduce the swelling. The Doctor says that there's no way to tell how much, if any, brain damage has occurred until Diogo wakes up... if he wakes up.

I try to retain hope in the small victories. Diogo's heart is beating strong. It hasn't once faltered since his ordeal. And his body is in remarkable condition considering a building fell on top of him. Besides the blow to the head, he didn't suffer more than a few scratches and bruises. Emery had a broken arm and Grayson, the other survivor, had a concussion and two cuts deep enough that they required stitches.

I walked away without a single injury, except for a few small cuts and burns from the climb and the burst window. Someone on the ground saved my life. He reached up into the darkness and caught me as I fell. I don't know what happened after, since I woke up in Bishop's clinic while he was tending me.

I did discover who caught me. He's dogged my every step since, watching me with an intensity that makes me almost uncomfortable, his eyes following my every move. I don't understand why he's suddenly acting this way with me, but he refuses to leave my side. He only leaves when I ask him to, but I can tell he doesn't want to go. His strange new devotion is unquestionable, but his motives are unclear.

Stryker.

My saviour… but also my stalker.

"I'll get some hot water." Emery interrupts my thoughts. She leaves, going into the main part of the house. I can hear her banging around as she fills a pot with the water we reserved for drinking and bathing. I'm grateful. I know that we need to conserve every drop, but I'm desperate to see Diogo's face. To touch the cheeks and lips that are familiar to me.

When she comes back, she sets the pot down on a wooden box next to the table. Then she crosses to Diogo's other side and sits down on the bed next to him. She helps me apply a soapy lather to Diogo's face. Then I dip the razor in the hot water and start scraping away the scruff that has taken over. I begin on one side of his face at the top of the cheek, shaving in slow even strokes with the grain, holding the blade at a slight angle. I'm confident in my ability with a straight razor as I've been using one on my legs for years. I won't nick my husband.

Emery gently tips his head back, exposing the skin under his jaw. As I continue my even strokes, I brush the edges of my knuckles against his smooth skin, reveling in the texture. Even though Diogo is unconscious, and my best friend sits on the bed with me, the moment is intimate. Nothing in the world exists except me and my husband, my hands on his skin, my gaze taking in his beloved face as the hair is scraped away and each part of him is exposed.

As if sensing my mood, Emery remains silent, helping when she sees a need.

I am careful as I maneuver around the scar on his cheek.

He hadn't told me where he got it, and I didn't ask. Now, I want nothing more in the world than to know how he got it. It's old, the edges are white, but the cut had gone deep, the skin around it still puckered. In my eyes, the scar doesn't detract from Diogo's natural masculine beauty, only enhances the Warlord.

I finish the last stroke, sweeping away the last few coarse whiskers and washing them in the pot of water. I set the razor down next to the pot and pick up a warm, wet washcloth, wiping the soap residue from his face.

"There he is," I whisper.

"I'll leave you alone." Emery stands and when I snap out of my moment, I reach for her, about to stop her. She smiles and shakes her head. "I need to get some dinner going. I think we're having company again."

We have company almost every night. Along with the family that moved into Emery's place after she moved into the Tower, Grayson, Stryker and sometimes Bishop make their way to Emery's kitchen. She's a good cook and everyone is contributing to the food stocks in her kitchen, trying to sustain us until Diogo is well again.

Where the food shortages used to be due to overpopulation and illegals filling the slums, now we're experiencing a genuine lack of food. In order to control the rebellion, the military has stopped almost all rations from crossing into Sector 13. Now our food supplies come from the few gardens people have planted in Sector 13 and illegal hunting.

When the door closes behind her, leaving us alone, I stand and stretch my legs. They cramp easily when I sit for too long. Of course, the movement reminds me that I have to pee. The baby seems to enjoy sitting right on my bladder.

If it weren't for my need to be near Diogo, I might consider living in the washroom.

I relieve myself as quick as I can and return to Diogo's side, crawling into bed and curling up next to his body, moving until I'm pressed full length against his side. I drag his arm across his body and settle his hand on my stomach, linking our hands once more. If there's any chance he knows what's going on, I don't want him to miss a minute of being with me and the baby.

I wish I'd thought to pull the blanket over us before settling in, but now it seems too far out of reach. Things that were once easy to me, things I took for granted, have definitely taken on new meaning with this pregnancy. Now I weigh each decision, big and small. Some things aren't worth the energy, while others require reserves of energy. I'm not really that cold, I don't need the blanket.

I talk to him as I wait for sleep to claim me. I've been napping a lot lately, trying to sleep when my body asks for it. When I'm awake, I keep vigil over Diogo. Bishop told me it would be good for Diogo to feel my touch, that I won't hurt him by laying next to him.

"Grayson says another wave of refugees from the eastern Sanctuaries arrived last night. He thinks there are around 8000 or so outside our walls." I yawn widely and try to choose my next words carefully. I don't want to lie to Diogo, but the truth is bleak. The truth is, our interim Warlord has refused all entry, supplies or security. The refugees are forced to remain outside the wall, trying to defend themselves as more and more Primitives show up. "Most of the refugees are fleeing into the ruins of Old Tucson and setting up a makeshift line of defense around the encampment."

If I wasn't pregnant, I'd be trying to find a way to

smuggle supplies to the newcomers. And though Diogo has always taken a hardline on immigration into the city, he has a heart. He would take them in. I know he would, he'd find a way. He just needs to wake up and resume his role, put his city back in order.

"The baby is as healthy as it can be," I whisper, tipping my head back to look at him. "The space in my womb is tight now, so he's slowed his movements." I catch myself referring to the baby as a him. Emery's influence. I know Diogo won't mind though. He doesn't care if it's a boy or girl, he just wants a healthy baby. "Bishop says that he could come any day now. That my small size increases the chance of an early birth. He doesn't think it'll be a problem though. The heart is strong and he's a good size."

I press my face against his ribcage and inhale, his scent hitting me with such a hard longing that my body instantly melts against his. Though he's lost some muscle mass, laying in a bed for three weeks, he's still a big man. Still very much the Diogo I married.

I drift to sleep, the memory of our old camp bed on top of the Tower terrace flashing in my mind. In the image, Diogo's arms are wrapped as tightly around me as mine are around him. He's stealing kisses and telling me that he'll keep me safe forever. Only this time, instead of chafing at his protectiveness, I'm reveling in his overbearing attitude. In his strength and determination.

When consciousness comes to me again, the heavy languid feeling pinning me down tells me I'd been asleep. I'm warm, the heat from Diogo's body seeping into mine. I shift against him, snuggling closer. His hand slides gently over my belly. His heart beats steadily against my ear where I'm using his chest as a pillow. Something brushes against my cheek, moving the hair.

"Mmmm..." I don't ever want to relinquish this feeling. I'm safe, content, in love. When I open my eyes, everything will change. It'll go back to the hopeless pit of hell our lives have become. "I love you, Diogo."

"I love you too, baby."

Taran screams and bolts upright, despite the burden of her midsection getting in the way. I try to grab her arm to prevent her from leaping right off the bed, but my own arm is weak and it falls back to the bed. She seems to understand, and relaxes back onto the bed, reaching for me, touching me with shaking hands.

"Emery!" she shouts, her eyes glued to me, expressions of panic and happiness duelling for supremacy on her face. "He's awake!"

Something clatters outside the room and feet hit the floor in a dead run. I watch in consternation as the door is thrown open and a stunned Emery flings herself into the room. She looks at me as though seeing at a ghost. Our eyes meet and hers fill with tears. She falls next to Taran on the bed and reaches for me, grabbing hold of my hand.

What the hell is going on? Since when have Emery and I been on touching terms?

As if understanding my confusion, Taran takes a couple of deep breaths, trying to calm herself, and then starts speaking. "You were unconscious, Diogo. You were hit on the head when the Tower collapsed. We... we didn't know if you were ever going to wake up."

At first, I can't make sense of her words. Hit on the head? Tower collapse? Then memory begins to return, at first in sluggish flashes, then in a rush of images. An explosion. The fire. Taran crawling out the window, Taran's scream, running up the stairs, watching my man fall through the floor. Throwing Emery against the wall and covering her.

Despite the weakness in my body I force myself up, grab hold of Taran's arms and pull her toward me until our faces are nearly touching. "You fell." The burn of fear rises up inside me as I try to imagine what happened to her.

She touches my cheek, running her fingers down my scar and resting them on my jaw. "Yes, I did. The window I was holding onto blew out from the force of the fire. But I didn't fall far, maybe ten feet. Stryker was underneath, he was fighting the rebels. He caught me."

I groan and wrap my arms around her, holding her close against me with all my strength. Luckily, my strength is not much or I would crush her. She pulls away to look into my face, tears sparkling in her eyes. She touches me again, stroking my cheek as if she can't believe I'm here with her.

Finally, she pulls back and shakes her head as if to clear it. She turns to Emery and says, "Can you go find Bishop? I think he's doing rounds over at the old elementary school. He'll want to see Diogo right away."

When Emery leaves, Taran explains. "The school was turned into a makeshift hospital. There've been casualties. Bishop offered his expertise and the rebels were in no shape to argue. He seems to have proven himself to them, they ask him to come over almost daily."

I try to make sense of her words, try to understand the

meaning behind them. I look around and realize that we're in Taran's old bedroom, in Emery's house. I'm deep in rebel territory in Sector 13.

"Why am I here?"

She seems to understand the wider meaning to my question. "After we pulled you and the other survivors out of the Tower – "

"Who?" I interrupt.

She shakes her head, her eyes distant. "Just you, Emery and Grayson. Only half the Tower fell and the stairwell was mostly protected. But the rest of your men were…" She stops speaking for a few seconds. Then she looks at me. "The Tower fall seemed to end fighting in the area. I think the seriousness of what'd happened struck both the rebels and the city police force. They stopped fighting and started looking for survivors. When they dug you out, they brought you to Bishop. That's where I'd been taken."

"You're okay?" I demand, touching her stomach. "The baby?"

She puts her hand over mine and presses it against her belly. A shock of familiarity runs through me, the sensation telling me she's done this before while I was unconscious. The baby kicks against my hand, strong and hard, harder than before the building collapse. I automatically yank my hand away in disbelief before replacing it just as fast to catch the next kick.

Taran laughs. "We're both fine. He's a tough little guy."

"He?"

She shrugs. "Until we find out the sex it helps calling him something other than it."

We sit in silence for a few minutes, her hand over mine as I feel the strong little kicks. I'm filled with awe as I feel a tiny fist or foot press against Taran from the inside. The sensation can't be comfortable, but she just continues to smile and experience the moment with me, her eyes soft and her face peaceful. More peaceful than I've ever seen it. I can tell that she's come to terms with the imminent birth of our child. There doesn't seem to be any hesitation about her anymore. I'm happy that she's doing so well, but disappointed that I missed even a moment of our time together.

"How long have I been out?" I finally ask the question that needs to be asked.

She hesitates for a moment and then says, "Twenty-two days."

I'm shocked by the number. It seems impossible that I could've missed three weeks of my life, but it does explain the weakness in my limbs. The pain in her voice tears at me as she recalls the days that I was out, the waiting and wondering, hoping and despairing. I would bring the world to her feet if I thought it would make her happy, but there's nothing I can do to reclaim our lost time, or the pain it has caused her. She opens her mouth to continue speaking, but chokes on the words, blinking rapidly, trying to stop the tears that threaten. That's my Taran, trying to be brave despite her pain.

"We're okay," I tell her, gathering her close again. "All three of us."

"Yes," she whispers, clutching me.

We stay like that until the shuddering of her body passes and her breathing returns to normal, her emotions under control. I tip her face up and ask, "Why am I here, instead of the military compound or Bishop's office?"

I suspect I already know, but I have to ask. The details will help me create a plan for moving forward.

She settles back on the bed and tells me, an edge of anger to her voice, what's been happening in my city. "After the Tower collapse, it became quickly clear that your position was being threatened, almost like he was waiting for you to fall. We were afraid you'd be executed in the new Warlord's bid for power, so we decided the best course was to tell everyone you'd died and move you into rebel-held territory. Our lie was not a strong one since we couldn't produce a body, but no one thought to look for you here. Since you weren't seen alive or dead, news of your demise spread through the city. So far our plan has worked. You've been safe to recover for as long as it takes."

"There is only one Warlord," I growl, the idea of another usurping my position sparking anger. I shouldn't be surprised by the coup. Though I'd held strong to this Sanctuary, it is a universal truth that when one Warlord falls, another will rapidly step into his place. And someone was taking steps to weaken my hold on the city before the rebellion had even reached its peak. "Did no one think to connect you to me? Follow you back here to see if I was hiding out?"

She shakes her head, her eyes shadowed as she lifts them to mine. "We spread the rumour that I died as well. We said I went into early labour when I found out you'd been killed, and I hemorrhaged after some complications. I haven't left the house since we went into hiding. Only those who are completely loyal to us are allowed here."

She finishes her little speech in a rush as though she knows the effect her words will have an me. And she's correct. The thought of anything happening to her sends an icy bolt up my spine toward my heart. The vivid images she's painted, a reality that is all too possible in our world, are threatening to send me into a rage.

I clench my fists and breathe through the fury squeezing my chest. When I get my hands on the usurper, he will die a slow and extremely painful death. And I don't have far to look, I know exactly who has caused this pain. Who's sown the seeds of destruction throughout Sanctuary. I should've seen it earlier, but his solid, unquestioning presence at my side never set off any inner alarms. I believed him to be a good man, if somewhat cold and unapproachable. All of my soldiers are built that way. It takes a certain personality to survive the elite military, and he has every quality. Including a thirst for power. One I should have seen sooner.

I grip the edge of the bed and force my weight up, standing on uncertain feet. I rock back and forth for a moment as my center of balance adjusts. Pins and needles rush through my body as it slowly comes back to life, reminding me I've been comatose for over three weeks.

"What are you doing?" Taran asks, her eyes wide and her voice sharp with worry.

I look down at the beautiful face of my wife, taking in the healthy glow in her now rounded cheeks. I will do anything to protect her and our unborn child, even the things she doesn't want me to. A mantra I've often thought to myself. She deserves the world, so I will seize it. Take it back and place it at her feet.

"I'm going to kill Jorje Cruz and take my city back."

FIVE

TARAN

"The fuck you are!" I snap, pushing myself awkwardly to my feet. My back groans in protest but I ignore it. This is more important. "You are in no condition to do anything, let alone challenge some dumb fuck that doesn't know what to do with the city he stole."

He looks down at me, shocked, then his face splits into a grin. He's amused, either by my words or my profane language. Well, that makes one of us, I'm less than amused at the moment. He sways on the spot and I grab hold of his arm.

"Sit your ass down, Warlord, and let me explain a few things so you don't go racing into headquarters without any kind of a clue as to what's been happening."

Diogo studies me, his brow furrowed in concentration as he makes a decision. He's a strong man, a proud man. I just hope he sees the value in my words. I bite my lip as I wait for his response.

Finally, he nods and allows me to help him sit back down. He sighs in relief as his body folds into the bed. I fluff the pillows behind him and then push him, a hand against his chest, easing him back against the headboard. I'm under no illusion that he will do what I want if it isn't also what he wants.

"Fuck," he groans and runs a hand over his face and hair. "Don't think I could've even made it to the door."

"Bishop said you'd be weak if... when you woke up. He said you'd need a few days to recover your strength."

He gives me a frustrated look.

"This will give us time to plan." I try to reassure him. "Cruz's hold on the city isn't strong. He's making some pretty colossal mistakes. Once we fill you in, you'll have a much better chance at retaking the city."

He shakes his head, his dark eyes sharp with determination. "It won't be chance," he growls. "I *will* retake this city, and I will decorate the walls with his intestines."

His referral to the insides of a person coming out makes me a little queasy. I stopped throwing up several weeks ago, for the most part, but sometimes certain words or smells trigger a disgust response from my turnip. I make a face at Diogo.

"I don't really care what you do to him, I just need you to get better before you do it. I need you to trust us right now. You're used to being the one in charge, but you've been out for three weeks and a lot has happened. We need to fill you in."

He searches my face and then nods and reaches for my hand, holding it tight. "Of course, my wise little wife is correct. I won't leave this house until I've regained my strength. A day should do it. I just need to walk around and get some food in me."

I smile my relief at his capitulation. "Two days. You need to give yourself more time to recover."

He pulls me down in top of him and then holds me just

right, cradling me so I don't feel the pressure of my belly against his. He lifts his head to meet mine and says, inches from my lips, "36 hours."

"48," I counter, fanning him with my breath. I know how much he loves it when I do that.

He chuckles. "I don't think you understand how negotiation works."

I grin at him and lean over, breaching the last inch, pressing my lips to his for the first time in weeks. I hadn't the heart to do it while he was unconscious. I wanted Diogo's response, the feel of his excitement, his dominant presence as he took my lips in return. And he does, without reservation. Cupping the back of my head, he holds me tight against him, taking my lips with his, my tongue with his, my mouth with his.

The kiss is like coming home. The re-merging of our hearts, the perfect symphony of our souls. He takes over completely, kissing me as though doing it for the first time, stealing my every gasp and sigh, exploring me and savouring my taste. I grip his arms, while his hands span my waist, curving around my rounded middle, his palms protecting the life within, his fingers lighting up my body with need.

I'm happier in this moment than I've ever been. I know what I lost, and I know what I've somehow found again. A love so unique, so fragile, we'll have to spend a lifetime nurturing it. We could have lost it, crushed under the rubble of a city on fire. Instead, we've been given another chance. A chance to fight for Sanctuary.

Diogo spends the next few days recovering and consulting with his advisors: me, Emery, Stryker, Bishop, Grayson and some of the rebels that swear allegiance to their old Warlord. The current state of the city has convinced many former rebels to renounce the rebellion and back Diogo's claim.

Diogo walks the length of the house, back and forth, lifting objects that are progressively heavier, rebuilding his strength. Grayson, Stryker and a couple of former rebels, stand around him, working on their plan to get Diogo into military headquarters. As they speak, Stryker's eyes are on me where I sit in one of Emery's old armchairs, sorting and folding baby clothes donated by some of the refugee families.

"Stryker, I need your attention. You'll be crossing the checkpoints with me," Diogo snaps, drawing the man's glare. Diogo is torn between his gratitude over Stryker's saving my life, and his annoyance over his man's new obsession with me. Stryker doesn't even try to hide it, his eyes constantly following me. If I move, he moves. If I go into the washroom or bedroom, I have to tell him to stay behind. He grumbles when Diogo sends him on a mission and insists that Grayson is my bodyguard, not Stryker.

I shudder at Diogo's words. I'm terrified that something will happen to him as he retakes the city. It's one thing to know what his job entails, it's another to be privy to all the details. As his wife, I don't want to know that he's entering into battle zones with every intention of firing on the enemy, drawing fire back to himself and his men. I worry that this plan is being set in motion too quickly, without being fully thought through. Diogo insists there's no time though. He needs to retake Sanctuary so he can get to work on the problem of a potential nuclear meltdown. So he can deal with the masses of incoming refugees and hordes of Primitives.

The sheer amount of problems facing us is staggering, but my husband is willing and ready to face each one head on. Eager even, to take back his title so he can start resolving the issues threatening our Sanctuary.

I sympathize with Diogo's need to move on the new Warlord, I'm also a person of activity and action. I don't like sitting restlessly, waiting to hear news. The baby has tied me down more than just physically. Now, his welfare is more important than anything else. And while I certainly don't resent the little turnip, at least not anymore, I do feel the need to take part in Diogo's plan. To watch over him and step in if I think he'll need my help. I wonder if this feeling is universal to all parents and caregivers, the internal fight between protecting our children in the immediate present and the need to do what it takes to ensure their future. Between Diogo and I, we will do both. I will continue to protect the baby by protecting myself, and he will go out into the dangerous city and ensure the stability of a future for our family.

The front door slams open and a cold, wet Doctor Bishop steps through. The weather has been unseasonably bad for the desert, with unprecedented amounts of rain. We fear this is a product of fallout from the nuclear reactor meltdowns. I labour to my feet, reaching for him. He's been coming home later and later, spending most of his time at the makeshift hospital.

"Come sit down, I'll get you some food."

He shakes his head and turns to Diogo, interrupting his planning session. "We need to talk."

Diogo lifts a brow. "I'm listening."

"Dee sent me a message at the hospital. She got it through the checkpoint herself, so we can be certain it's accurate."

Dee, Bishop's nurse and receptionist from the clinic, has been aiding us every chance she can, sending supplies and information. She's been using Jorje Cruz's wife, Milla, to get her supplies through the checkpoints. Though loyal to her husband, Milla has a big heart. She's been sending as much aid as she can into the slums to help mitigate some of the damage her husband has caused. Unfortunately, there can be no happy end to their love story. Cruz will have to die for his betrayal.

"What's going on?" Diogo demands.

"They're getting set to publicly execute your top advisors in the morning, Bossman included." When Grayson looks to speak, Bishop holds his hand up and continues. "After the execution, Cruz intends to lead the military into this sector to clean it out. They're gunning for the rest of us; Stryker, Emery, Dodge, me. According to Dee, they intend to use brutal force, leaving only women of a certain age and children alive. All undocumented refugees will be gathered up and expelled. Any known rebels will be executed on the spot."

I gasp and clutch the arms of my chair so hard my knuckles ache. I'm not surprised by this news. In fact, we've all been expecting it for weeks. But hearing the brutal reality spoken out loud in stomach churning detail is another thing. I look at Diogo. "Is there anything you can do?"

He nods slightly. "We can go in tonight, take HQ, free the political prisoners and turn the military back to me." His eyes are on me as though no one else in the room exists. Just the two of us caught in a private moment. "Do you release me from my promise?"

I give him a rueful look. He'd promised to rest for 48 hours before making any move to retake his city. He's been recovering for less than 30 hours. If he goes in tonight his strength won't be what it should be. Though I know he will do as I ask, my happiness meaning more to him than anything, I can't be the cause of more death. Not if there's anything we can do to stop it.

"Go get your people," I say softly. *And hopefully stop a massacre.*

SIX

DIOGO

We decide to make our way boldly into the heart of the city. No subterfuge, no stealthy takeover. I've never been one to hide and I'm not about to start now. Though weak physically, I feel the rush of power as I make my way through each checkpoint, gathering people as I go. Soldiers and police abandon their positions as they follow the Warlord they've sworn allegiance to. Few are loyal to the usurper, though enough that he has been notified of our imminent arrival.

They run ahead to inform Cruz of what's heading his way, determined to reach HQ before we arrive. He can attempt to fortify the building, to hide from my wrath. It won't work, I'll take him and his followers and show them the justice of disloyalty.

A body hurtles toward us out of the rainy darkness. Stryker lifts his weapon to shoot them down, but I hold a hand up, staying him. I look at him strangely. He's never been trigger happy, not until he sees the face of his victim. What's changed?

A woman steps out of the darkness. Milla Cruz. The usurper's wife.

She steps nervously toward me and stops a few feet away. I take in her tear-streaked face, the hood that covers her blond curls, the darkness of her clothes, disguising her body. She left her home tonight seeking me. I know what she'll say, the life she'll beg for. Sadly, though I'll accept her offer, her sacrifice doesn't matter.

"Please," she says tremulously. "I don't want him hurt."

"I know you don't."

"I'll go with you," she begs. "Use me to get him to surrender peacefully. He's a hard man, but he'll do anything to keep me safe. I promise, we'll cooperate if you let him live."

I nod toward Stryker who takes her arm. "Keep her safe behind the lines, cover her if anyone shoots at us. Bring her forward when it's time."

"Thank you, thank you so much, Commander," she cries gratefully as Stryker pulls her to the back of our group, out of harm's way.

We continue moving, advancing our way from checkpoint to checkpoint, picking up more people along the way. We only stop when we face the checkpoint leading into Sector Two where HQ, the police station and other key buildings lie. The guard at the gate looks at me as though seeing a ghost, his eyes travelling to the people at my side and my back. Men and women, elite and poor, military and civilian, have banded together to retake our city.

The guard opens the gate, steps to the side and says, "Welcome back, Commander Fuentes."

"Fall in, soldier," I say as I pass him. He joins the forces at my back and together we make our way to HQ, the home of my elite military. The building housing my enemy.

We encounter minimal resistance at the front doors. Men either join us or abandon their posts. Only a few are foolish enough to take us on, pointing their rifles and sidearms, wasting precious bullets before they're cut down by our weapons. Angry frustration wells within me at the pointless waste of good men. Cruz has built a small following. He's cultivated my men, probably over the course of years, ensuring their loyalty not just to me, but also to him. Now they are put in a no-win situation. Unfortunately, I don't have the luxury of time to convince them to turn back to my side. Nor would I, even if there was time. I can't have men at my back whose first loyalty can be corrupted. Their deaths are preferable.

Once we've cleared the door, I instruct the civilians to stay in the lobby while my men fan out, methodically searching the building for the usurper Warlord who is about to become deposed. "Stryker, you're with me. Bring his wife."

Milla sobs softly between us as we move through the building. There's the possibility that he fled when news of our imminent takeover reached him. He has to know that he doesn't stand a chance against me, or anyone loyal to me. Cruz was a good man, a good soldier, but without an army at his back he is just one man.

"The war room," I growl, hunching my shoulders, trying to keep my body as low as possible in case anyone manages to get off a stray shot. The lack of noise in the building tells me our counter-coup is meeting almost no resistance.

We round the last corner, and shove the door open to the war room. Bullets fly through, whizzing past us. Stryker picks Milla up and lunges to the side, while I hit the wall on the other side. Bullets continue to slam into the wall opposite.

They stop and movements from within the room indicate he's reloading his weapon. "Surrender, Jorje. You're surrounded, the building has been taken back. You have no moves left."

"Then I'll fucking die," he yells. "You're not making an example out of me."

I look to Stryker and nod my head.

"We have your wife," he snarls. "Stop shooting unless you want to put a hole in 'er."

"Fuck you!" Cruz yells back, his voice muffled by the thick wooden table. He must've tipped it on its side so he could use it for cover. He can reach over to shoot at us, but our bullets won't penetrate the thick wood. "Milla is somewhere safe where you can't get at her."

"You're wrong," I shout back. "If you want her to stay safe, you will surrender."

"You're lying!" Fear for his wife penetrates his tone.

I look to Milla. "Talk to him, convince him to lay down arms."

She shakes her head frantically, her eyes wide on my face. "You said you wouldn't hurt him!" she hisses, appalled.

I didn't promise her anything, just agreed to use her as a talking point for her husband. Splitting hairs aside, using her this way doesn't sit well. Still, it should prove to be the method that sheds the least blood. In the short term. I need Cruz to surrender, to come out alive. We'll deal with the rest later.

I nod toward Stryker. "Show him."

Stryker shoves her into the doorway, his hand still on her arm. She shrieks and cringes back before Cruz can let fly another round of bullets.

"Milla!" he bellows. "Milla, talk to me, tell me you're okay!"

Stryker gives her another shake and she lets out a squeak before taking her hands off her head and saying, "I-I'm okay, Jorje."

Silence for a moment, then, "You swear not to hurt her if I come out?"

"You have my word."

The clatter of a rifle hitting the floor heralds his surrender. I glance around the door cautiously in case he has another weapon. He stands slowly, his hands behind his head. He looks rough. His cheeks are hollowed, almost as gaunt as mine had become after a three-week coma. His clothes hang on him, the shadow of a beard now graces his usually clean-shaven face, and he looks like he hasn't showered in a while.

"You can have your city back." His voice sounds defeated, but almost relieved too. "I couldn't force the loyalty that you somehow managed to wrest from them when you took over."

"Loyalty should be earned," I say, stepping into the doorway and advancing into the room. "Did you learn nothing from the rebellion, the people whose loyalty I hadn't earned? You can't demand fealty, not when you give nothing in return. Turn around."

He turns, fingers lace together at the back of his head. I pull the handcuffs off his belt and bring one arm down at a time, cuffing his wrists behind his back. When I finish, Stryker allows Milla to join her husband. She clings to him, sobbing softly against his chest, her fingers clutching his arms.

"Th-they said if I came with them, you'd be alright." She sniffles and swipes at her face with a sleeve. "They can't hurt you, they won't."

My eyes meet Cruz's. His are faded to grim acceptance.

We both know she's wrong. Not only can we hurt her husband, but we must. The man who tried to wrest power from my regime cannot be allowed to live. It would encourage others to foster hope that the mantle of Warlord can be taken from me. There could be more threats to my leadership. This will be the first and last attempt at my position. With his execution I will make it known throughout my territory that my power is unquestionable.

Cruz knows this, knows he won't survive longer than I need him alive to use as a prop as I finish reclaiming my city.

"Take care of her?" he asks, the strength that had been in his voice now replaced by begging.

This is a man in love with his wife, willing to give up his pride to ensure her safety. A year ago, I would have scoffed at his weakness, killed him more brutally. I probably would have killed his wife too. I don't owe either of them anything. The love of my wife has taught me that there is no end in what I'm willing to sacrifice for her. I would also sacrifice pride to ensure her safety, especially if I was facing certain death.

"She will be taken care of," I assure him, then nod toward Stryker, asking him without words to take the usurper from my presence. "Interrogate him thoroughly, find out if he was behind the rebel leaks. He could've been sowing discontent in an effort to weaken the city for his coup attempt."

"Commander." Stryker takes Cruz in a hard hold and pulls him out the door, a sobbing Milla hanging off her husband.

I look around the room, my war room. It's a mess of papers, broken and overturned furniture and blood. At least one person died in here. Probably one of my own soldiers, refusing to promise loyalty to Cruz. Exhaustion hits me hard as I wonder who I've lost and who I'll have to sacrifice. It will take days, if not weeks, to discern truth from lies as I sort my loyal supporters from the weak-willed men who followed where they shouldn't have.

More than twenty years ago I took this city in a bloody battle. I will take it again, spilling blood to prove that it belongs to me once more. I will not tolerate disloyalty. Not from my own soldiers, not from the citizens and not from the rebels. I will remind this city who it belongs to. This Sanctuary belongs to the Warlord and will be mine until the day I die.

SEVEN

TARAN

"Please, you have to do something!"

My heart bleeds for Milla as she paces the floor in front of us, begging us to talk Diogo into freeing her husband. Even if I could convince him, it's too late. Jorje Cruz's execution has been scheduled for 3pm. Only a few minutes away.

He's being publicly executed for the crime of treason; plotting against and moving against his Warlord. There are a multitude of other charges that have been laid against him, but the crime of treason is what he's being executed for.

"You were charged with treason, yet you still live," Milla cried turning on her heel and pointing at me.

I open my mouth to speak, to defend myself. I didn't hurt anyone when I was acting as the Desert Wren. I certainly didn't try to take over an entire government or overthrow the Warlord. There's no point in arguing though. Milla is grieving. She's very much in love with her husband, would do anything to save him and has tried over and over, begging us to help and trying to get past the guards. In her place I would be frantic to save my husband too.

I don't know what to say to her, how to make this better for her. This is an impossible situation and there's no changing the outcome. But despite that, she seems to think there's hope to the end. I can't reassure her that she should hold onto any kind of hope. I know my husband. He will execute the man he considers a usurper. He will do it coldly and dispassionately, as he would any duty that befell his office.

There's nothing I can say to Milla that she'll accept right now. My husband is about to kill hers. Emery crosses to her and wraps an arm around her shoulders, squeezing and leading her to a couch. They sit together and Emery holds Milla while she weeps and begs for the life of her husband. Dee sits down on Milla's other side and leans against her, offering support.

This is why we've gathered together, so we can surround Milla with support during one of the worst moments of her life. By banding together we're showing her that no matter what's happening to her husband, she will be loved and supported. She will not be shunned or left to fend for herself. I glance toward our guards, Grayson and Stryker. Grayson's eyes are on Milla, filled with empathy. Stryker's eyes are on me.

I shift uncomfortably, trying to escape his burning gaze by standing and heading toward the kitchen. In Emery's small, warm kitchen I prepare drinks for everyone. The least I can do in such desperate circumstances. Though I'm no good at offering support to a grieving soon-to-be widow, I can make a cup of tea.

I groan at the ache in my back as I bend, reaching into a lower cupboard for the tea kettle. I jump as a hand settles on my back, rubbing the exact spot that aches. I straighten and whirl to face Stryker.

"Let me help," he murmurs huskily, his eyes dropping to my belly.

"I can do it!" I snap, edging sideways, trying to get away from his touch.

He stares at me, his eyes never leaving me as I move rapidly away. His over-attentiveness is driving me crazy. I don't get it. A few months ago, Stryker was indifferent to me, perhaps even somewhat hostile. Now, he acts like a doting father-to-be. Only he isn't the father and I'm the farthest thing from his bride as I can get. His constant presence has become more than annoying, it's creepy. I thought about bringing my concerns up with Diogo. He's definitely noticed Stryker's odd vigilance around me but believes it to be harmless. From the moment Diogo woke up from his coma he's had his plate full. I can't bear to add one more thing. Besides, if he finds out Stryker is bothering me he'll overreact and who knows what he'll do.

"You need to relax, Taran," Stryker says calmly, holding his hands up. "You're perfectly safe with me. I won't let anything happen to you."

Of that, I have no doubt. As my constant shadow, a person would have an immensely difficult time getting through Stryker to me.

"Don't tell me to relax," I say sharply, lifting the kettle to fill it with water. He reaches past me, takes the kettle from my hands, shuffles me aside and fills it, as though I'm incapable of handling the few pounds it'll weigh once it's full.

I grit my teeth and close my eyes, wanting to scream at him. I remind myself of all the reasons I should remain calm. Stryker thinks he's helping, he's just being protective. He saved my life once already. I should trust him. I don't want to upset Milla or Diogo. I don't want to be the reason

Diogo loses another of his men. And I know how he'll react if I tell him Stryker is upsetting me. The older man will be lucky if he's only banished from the city. Diogo has become more protective than ever, his entire focus on my safety when he's not trying to bring his city back under his rule.

When Stryker sets the kettle on the stove and lights the gas, I murmur my thanks and keep my eyes lowered so he doesn't see the blaze of fear and anger. I tell myself I'm being hormonal again, that he wants nothing more than to help. I know it's bullshit though. My instincts have never been wrong, and they're telling me that something has driven Stryker off a psychological ledge. Something that has landed his focus entirely on me.

"Can you please go see if any of the women want a snack?"

We both know the answer to this. Who would want a snack at a time like this? The city is starving and one of its most prominent soldiers is about to lose his life. Still, Stryker nods and goes to do my bidding. I sigh my relief, glad that I'm finally getting a few seconds to myself. Not only has Stryker become an annoying constant in my life, but I'm now sharing a tiny house with several people. Not to mention the sheer number of rebels and refugees that come and go from the premises.

Diogo asked me if I wanted to move back into Sector One, find a new apartment building and furnish it to make it our own. The offer is tempting, who wouldn't want an entire apartment building to themselves? But I refused. I want to be near Emery when the baby comes. I want to be in the only place I've been able to call home since losing my grandparents. The slums hold a special place in my heart, and now that the rebellion has been quashed, I can feel safe in Sector Thirteen once more.

"No snacks," Stryker says somewhat dryly, as he settles himself against the doorframe to watch me.

I ignore him and go through the motions of making the tea, pouring the hot, boiling water over the dry tea leaves, stirring them, leaving them to steep. I watch the hot water turn a clear dark red in the pot. The smell of chamomile and rosehips touches my nose, giving me a kick of nostalgia. This is the tea Emery serves me when I'm feeling down.

I set the pot of tea, some cups with a jar of raw sugar and a small pitcher of cream on the tray. Diogo insists that we take advantage of some of the food sources he's cultivated, even though we inhabit a home in the poorest sector of the city. It's hard to argue with him when fresh cream makes its way to our doorstep. I remind myself that he's the Warlord, it's okay to take advantage of some of the perks as long as we're still working toward the greater good of the entire city.

No one touches the tea, not even me, as we watch the clock, tracking time until 3pm arrives. Milla's sobs grow louder, filling the room. A tear tracks down Dee's cheek as she leans her head against Milla's, holding the other woman tight. Emery continues to speak, her calm, quiet voice, a reassuring constant in a chaotic, violent world. I sit clutching a cup of cold tea, my own eyes wide and dry. I have no more tears. Maybe I've spent them all. Maybe I don't know how to cry in a moment like this. Milla's husband betrayed mine. I have sympathy for her, but not the man that would've killed Diogo while he was at his weakest if we hadn't done a good job of hiding his whereabouts while he recovered.

Finally, after endless minutes pass, the seconds ticking by with agonizing slowness, Emery says, "It's over."

Her eyes meet mine and I nod. It's over. Diogo has officially retaken his city. He's killed a man who professed loyalty and then turned on him. Blood stains his hands once more. A justified sacrifice, so the next man that thinks to take him on thinks twice.

Not long after Bishop arrives. He was the one to oversee the execution. At his Warlord's insistence, he was to declare Jorje Cruz' death in front of the citizens of Sanctuary. His dark, empathetic gaze sweeps the room, landing on Milla. He crosses toward her, drops to a knee in front of her, gracefully for his age, and speaks quietly, his words directed to the new widow. He tells her of her husband's swift and painless death.

Her cries grow louder and she reaches for him. At first it looks as though she's beating at his shoulders, then she collapses against him, falling to the floor against his knees. He gathers her and holds her tightly while she cries. I look away, unable to handle the emotion in the room. It could have too easily been my husband, me in Milla's spot, if Diogo had been discovered before he woke from his coma.

"Come, let's put her to bed." Emery rises from the couch.

I look up, catching Stryker's eye. He hasn't stopped watching me since I reentered the room. I'm not even sure he knows what's happening. "Carry her to the bedroom," I direct him, nodding toward Milla.

Stryker's eyes flick to the dramatic scene playing out in the room and for a brief moment his lip curls in disgust. A flash of the old Stryker. All practicality, no compassion. He nods, and goes to Milla, bending to scoop her up. With Emery's help, the doctor is able to climb back to his feet. He picks up his medical bag.

"I'll heat some more tea," I murmur absently, my eyes

following Stryker and Milla as she's carried into Emery's bedroom. "The chamomile... it might help her sleep."

Bishop stops beside me, placing his hand on my shoulder and squeezing. He has a soft spot for me. I'm not sure why. I'm useless in situations like this. I don't know how to be a comfort to anyone and I'm more likely to say the wrong thing. Yet, I'm grateful for his friendship. His calm, selfless presence, that allows me to be myself.

"Yes, tea is an excellent idea." He releases my shoulder and heads to the bedroom.

I stand and turn toward the kitchen. Seconds later Stryker is on my heels once more. I do my best to ignore him as I reheat the kettle and put new tea leaves in the pot. The man is seriously testing my sanity. I'm getting ready to lose my cool on him, when the front door opens and, with a whoosh of cool autumn air, Diogo strides in. He searches the room until his eyes settle on me standing next to the stove.

I silently question him with the lift of a brow.

"It's done," he acknowledges.

I let my breath out on a long sigh. I watch him, looking for a reaction. Today he had to execute a man he considered a friend. Despite his tough exterior, I know how these things affect him. Diogo is a man of deep thought. Though he sometimes moves like a bulldozer when he's directing the lives of others, where he can, he contemplates each move with careful precision. Jorje's execution wasn't something he took lightly. Inevitable, perhaps, but not without a lot of thought and some amount of sorrow. Despite Jorje's defection, he was a good man when he stood by Diogo's side.

"Milla is resting," I say quietly, ineffectually. Her wails can be easily heard from every part of the house. The walls are paper thin.

"She'll need to be moved," Diogo says, coming to stand at my back, his arms curving around my waist.

I hadn't thought of it, but of course he's right. We can't live in the same home as the wife of a usurper. The wife of a man my husband executed with his own hands.

I lean back against Diogo's chest and sigh deeply. "Maybe it's time for us to move. Right now, Milla needs Emery more than we do. Let's look for a new place to live. Give her some peace, if she can find it."

"If that's what you wish then I'll have some of my men scout out a place for us tomorrow."

The thought of leaving the home I'd spent so many of my formative years in causes an ache in my chest. I don't want to leave. I want to be surrounded by the familiar. But I also recognize the impossible need for what it is. The desperate wish to cling to the past, the things I love and don't want to lose. As much as I love my husband, in this uncertain world, it can be difficult to forge a path forward through the constant trauma.

I nod and look up at him, over my shoulder. "Yes, I'd like that. Emery can visit as often as she wants?"

"Of course," Diogo says, his deep voice promising me anything I want as long as I'm happy.

Happiness is an elusive emotion, not something I fully understand, or ever thought to find. Still, being with Diogo is as close to happiness as I've ever managed. I'll cling to it with every fibre of my being if that's what it takes to hold onto this feeling. I stand on my toes and kiss the edge of his jaw.

He turns me toward him, cradling my stomach. His serious eyes lift to mine. "It's time to deal with the situation arising at the nuclear power plant. There won't be a future for Sanctuary if we allow it to be taken by the Primitives."

I nod and hide my face in his shoulder so he doesn't see the fear and disappointment. Of course he's right. The spectre of a nuclear meltdown has been haunting our territory for almost a month, since the waves of refugees have shown up. Luckily, one of Diogo's last orders before the coma was to send some of his men out to protect the facility. But news has reached us, and it's bad. His men are falling, tired, overworked and unable to hold back the onslaught of what seems to be Primitives organizing themselves to take out one of the last remaining power plants.

"I know," I whisper, trying to be brave. My husband intends to go out to the plant himself, to bring an historian, someone capable of shutting it down safely and making sure it stays offline. He will face a horde of Primitives intent on stopping him. Not just hungry Primitives trying to bite anyone that gets in their path, but beings intent on destruction for an unknown reason.

He hugs me tighter against him, his big hand sliding through my hair and cupping the back of my head. "I have to go."

"I know," I repeat.

"It's a delicate situation, has to be handled carefully. I can't just pass this off to another. It'll be my job to protect the historian and ensure the success of this mission. Take him to the power plant and back."

I lean back, take his face in my hands and give him a stern look. "I know, Diogo."

He smiles grimly and kisses my forehead. "I don't want to leave you right now. What if something happens?"

"Nothing will happen to me, I'm completely fine," I assure him. Then I bite my lip and glance away.

"What is it?" he demands. "What's wrong?"

"Nothing important," I try to reassure him.

"Tell me," he insists.

"I just..." I start and then stop, trying to figure out how to phrase what I want into a question. Then I give up and simply say, "My sister."

He understands. His gaze softens and he runs his hands down my arms. "Baby, you've been so patient. You must be frantic. I should've thought of her sooner. I'll find your sister, if she's out there. I'll make it a priority, before we head out on this mission."

My heart beats hard against my ribcage. Tears, the elusive wetness I'd been unable to find only moments before, prick my eyes. We'd only exchanged a few words about my sister after Diogo woke up. He asked if I'd had any contact and when I said no, he kissed me and promised that he would do everything he could to find her for me. After he retook his city.

Now, Sanctuary is his again. And while I desperately want him to find Skye, his other priorities are more important.

"We can find her after you get back. I can wait."

He shakes his head and touches a hand to my cheek. "Do you trust me, baby?"

"Of course," I answer immediately.

"Then trust me to find her."

EIGHT

SKYE

The road to hell was cracked and dusty with many detours to get around collapsed bridges and blockages. We've been here for two weeks. On the outskirts of Tucson Sanctuary, clinging to what meagre hope we need to stay alive. The outcome is starting to look grim. Life as I know it has been smashed to pieces leaving something unrecognizable in its place. And I am not unique. We're all suffering in ways we've never before experienced.

"Reload." Wolfe hands his rifle to me and pulls his sidearm. He turns and aims over the rubble surrounding us. We're crouched within the broken confines of a fallen building. Old Tucson. Or that's what the locals call it. I call it our last stand. The bodies are piling up, our situation becoming bleaker with every passing hour. Old Tucson is going to be our graveyard.

I flex my stiff fingers and breathe warm air on them, then work to reload the rifle. Except for the occasional crack of a gun going off, the morning is still, cold and empty. Once the gun is loaded, I set it next to Wolfe. At first, I'd complained about his taking point and me assisting, but when he handed me a gun and pointed over our makeshift protection, I'd nearly gotten us killed by wasting two bullets before a zombie launched itself at us. Wolfe had made quick work of the Primitive, cutting its head off for good measure. Then he silently took his weapon back and started taking out the continuing threats with calm, cool precision.

We've been doing this same routine for almost the entire time we've been here. Organizing in teams to protect the refugees crowding into the ruins of the old city. It won't matter for much longer though. We have no food, except what we brought. The Primitives and the constant boom of our weapons is scaring away any prey we could hunt. Our situation is rapidly becoming dire.

When we first arrived, I'd been angry at our lack of reception into the city. We were promised Sanctuary, yet the big gates remain firmly closed against us. Then rumours started filtering through. Rumours about the city falling apart from the inside out. A rebellion, a takeover, a fire that killed the Warlord and his family. I'd been stunned by the news. We came to this Sanctuary because my sister is here, yet she supposedly died. I refuse to believe it until I see her dead body. I thought she was dead before, when we'd been separated in Las Vegas over a decade ago. Then she magically appeared on my doorstep in Santa Fe. Taran is resilient. If anyone can survive a city on the verge of war, it's my sister.

Then, just this morning, news leaked about a new development. The Warlord, Diogo Fuentes, has risen up, stronger than ever, to take his city back. I hope this means that Taran is still alive and we'll soon hear news. Not just because I want my baby sister to be alive, but because we can't last much longer. With each passing day our situation grows grimmer. Though the waves of refugees begging for

Sanctuary has become a trickle, the Primitives are relentless. They come at us constantly. Whenever we kill them, more replace the dead. Our ammunition is running out along with our food supplies and our will to survive. Taran and Diogo are our only hope.

"Relief is here." Wolfe's low grumble snaps me from my thoughts.

I shift my tired body to face him, looking up at his hard, chiselled face as he concentrates his efforts toward protecting the perimeter. Wolfe can shoot better than any other person on the line, despite only having one eye. We take turns protecting Old Tucson along with a few dozen others who can shoot and fight. Most are soldiers and police from their own fallen Sanctuaries. We've been at this for weeks and the group morale is wearing as thin as our supplies.

I nod toward Remi, short for Ramirez, the man who'll replace me and Wolfe on the line. He's looking worse for wear. The clothes that filled his broad frame two weeks ago are now hanging on him, giving him a lean look. Weariness has etched deep grooves in his face and dirt has settled on him like a fine blanket. All of us look the same. There's not enough fresh water for bathing so we make do with the few drops leftover after cooking and drinking. Even that's starting to disappear. Our path to the dam is dangerous, overrun by Primitives. Our trips are far and few between.

I accept the hand Remi offers me and stand. My body, stiff from crouching on a cold, hard ground all night, creaks in protest. Wolfe growls at Remi which has him dropping his hand from mine. I sigh and send Wolfe a small glare. I don't have enough heart to back it up though. I'm utterly exhausted, and if truth be told, I need a protector in Wolfe.

He's the strongest man in this ruined city. Without him I'd probably be raped, dead or zombified by now.

Still, Wolfe is a hard man to read. He seems protective and aggressive one moment and coldly detached the next. I don't know his story, but there must be one. We all have stories. Some are more brutal than others. I would bet that Wolfe's story is the stuff of nightmares. What I'd like to know, is he the good guy or the villain?

Without a word, Wolfe holsters his weapons and heads toward the barracks. A temporary residence on the outskirts of Old Tucson that we set up so we can be more easily at hand in case the Primitives break through our line. When we first arrived, Wolfe suggested I take shelter in one of the centres set up for women, children and elderly refugees unable to fight. I'd suggested he go fuck himself, that I'm perfectly capable of fighting with the best of them. And while I've proven to be a bad shot, I can still fight.

Wolfe silently allowed me to stay and has been teaching me how to use his guns, how to take a Primitive down and how to finish them. I shudder as I remember the Primitive he'd hauled over to me a few days ago. He'd held it down and insisted I stab it through the heart and cut off its head. Though I'd done the deed exactly as instructed, I haven't slept well since. I see his wild eyes and clawed hands every time I close my eyes.

We stop at the mess tent before entering the barracks. I'm so tired it takes me a moment to realize that its Scarlett handing me a plate. Her face is so dirty I didn't recognize her, but her dress is unmistakable, a garment I've only seen worn by the harem women from Santa Fe Sanctuary. Only three of us women, a handful of soldiers and about a hundred citizens survived the fall of our city.

"Thank you, Scarlett," I murmur taking the plate of steaming food from her hands.

"Make sure you eat it all," she says, eyeing my frame, thinner now from lack of food and hard physical labour. "Don't give it away this time. If you're going to be on the line then you need it more than the rest of us."

I smile my gratitude and move away from her as she turns to give a plate to the next person in line. I trail after Wolfe and take a seat next to him. We've been inseparable since the moment I told him I wouldn't hide with the children. I'm not sure why exactly. Maybe some unspoken agreement that I'm safer with Wolfe. Or maybe he won't let me go. Though I haven't tested the theory, only an idiot wouldn't notice the way he is around me. He moves when I move, listens when I speak, growls when people get too close to me.

I try to remember if he was this way back when we were home. I think he was, a little anyway. The fortress guards certainly weren't allowed to speak to me unless through him. At the time I'd thought it was an order from my husband, the Warlord of Santa Fe. Now, I think otherwise. Silas had been a kind, gentle man. The opposite of most warlords. Yet he was also thoughtful and measured in his actions. He had the ability to make the harsh decisions, though it often went against character.

My eyes prick with unshed tears as I think of my husband, dead now. Taken down when the Primitives attacked our Sanctuary. He refused to leave when the rest of us were escaping. I haven't found the time to properly grieve his death. Haven't cried once since I was forced to leave over Wolfe's shoulder.

"Let him go."

My head snaps to the side at Wolfe's gruff command.

My eyes clash with his and we wage a silent war, one that we've been committed to from the moment we were introduced seven years ago.

"Don't act like you know what I'm thinking." My words are venomous barbs. Everything I say to this man is rude, but I can't seem to help myself. It's always been this way. And now, in this new situation, our footing is more like quicksand than ever. Instead of growing closer we've grown more distant. We're in some sort of weird dance, trapped with each other, constantly near each other, but with a gulf of anger and distrust between us.

"Always know what you're thinking." He turns back to his plate, hunching over it and shovelling food into his mouth. When he stops and finishes chewing the bite he took, he adds, "You think about him constantly."

Though his words are cool, I sense the edge in them. My jaw drops. I'm caught between fury at his assumption and curiosity about why he cares what and who I'm thinking about.

"Even if I do think about Silas that's my business, not yours."

He turns slowly to face me until his broad shoulders fill my vision and block out the sunlight behind him. I have to check the urge not to cringe in my seat. Wolfe is the biggest, most intimidating man I know. I tilt my chin defiantly.

"It's my business now." His words are so matter of fact and inarguable that I have to remind myself that my business is, in fact, none of his. Yet, when Wolfe says something, it always seems to be final, even when I want to fight him on a point. "You aren't dwelling on the old Warlord because you loved him, you feel guilty."

I gasp out loud and then quickly glance around to make sure no one has overheard us. I don't need anyone else getting in my personal business. I turn back to Wolfe and whisper in a low hiss, "You don't know what the fuck you're talking about. I have nothing to feel guilty about. You forced me to leave him behind."

His dark eyes follow my angry movements. "Not guilty for leaving him behind, guilty because you're alive and he and Hannah are dead."

Tears prick my eyes once more and I look down at the now unappetizing bits of food left on my plate. I hate that Wolfe can read me so well when I can't read him any better than a stone wall. He's right, I don't just feel agony over Silas' death. Silas had been dying for a while before the Primitive attacks. I'm upset that he died the way he did. That I couldn't protect him from a horrible death. That Hannah stayed behind and did my job. She had sacrificed what I could not.

"I don't feel guilty," I snap, glaring at him. "I'm angry that you stopped me from doing what I was meant to do, protect Silas with my dying breath."

"Noble," Wolfe grunts. "And stupid."

"Why would my sacrifice have been stupid?" I demand.

"Would've been an unnecessary waste." He doesn't bother to explain what he means. Maybe he doesn't need to. I'm young, strong, healthy. The world needs women like me to stay alive.

"What about Hannah?" I demand. "She wasn't much older than me. She could've been the one to live. You could've grabbed her instead."

"It was her choice to stay."

"And what about my choices, don't they matter?"

He doesn't answer, doesn't apologize or try to explain himself. Just continues to eat, falling silent. Dismissing our conversation. I let it go. It really doesn't matter anyway, what's done is done. We all made choices. Silas could've killed himself instead of standing stoic in the face of the invasion. Maybe that's why I'm angry. He had a harem full of women who would have sacrificed themselves, but would he have sacrificed himself for us?

I stand and leave the table, leaving half my plate of food behind. Despite knowing how much my body depends on the nourishment, I can't swallow another bite. Especially with an unfeeling beast sitting right next to me.

He doesn't immediately follow me as I walk away, though I know he'll be close behind. He doesn't really let me out of his sight except for short distances. The fresh air slaps me in the face and I'm grateful the usual desert heat isn't so bad today. I shouldn't be so angry with Wolfe. He's keeping me safe in this nightmare we've landed ourselves in. I don't understand his motives, but his actions are clear.

I sweep the area with my eyes, and frown. The usual scattering of people are gone and there's some kind of commotion coming from the barracks. I glance over my shoulder. Wolfe is standing a few feet behind me, his gaze on the sleeping quarters.

We walk silently together toward the buzzing noise. Before we can enter the building, a man steps out, his broad frame filling the doorway. My breath catches as I recognize him. Diogo Fuentes, husband to my sister.

He glances around, his eyes narrowed, before his dark gaze settles on me. Wolfe takes a step closer, protecting my back as the big Warlord makes his way over to us. Hope and trepidation war within my breast, each clambering for a spot. I know better than to show emotion to a Warlord though. I watch him with cool disinterest.

"Skye," he acknowledges, stopping several feet from my position. He glances at Wolfe and nods his greeting.

"My sister?" I demand.

He studies me, his gaze taking in my tattered clothes, borrowed from some of the refugees here. My own flimsy gown hadn't made it far and was no good for spending time on the front lines defending the city.

"She's anxious to see you. If you'll collect your things, I can take you to her."

I breathe easier knowing she's alive. The urge to run and grab my few belongings is strong. The desire to follow Diogo into the safety of Sanctuary and reunite with my sister, possibly permanently, is nearly overwhelming. Then I look behind him, to the people who are watching us curiously. These people need us. They need leadership. They need Wolfe. And Wolfe goes where I go.

"No," I say to him, my heart pounding in fear that I'm making the wrong decision. "I won't leave unless you offer these people Sanctuary as well."

"How many?" he demands.

"10,000." Wolfe speaks from behind me. "Give or take. More trickle in every day, but we lose some to the attacks."

Diogo shakes his head. "The city can't accommodate that number. We've had our own problems. We can't take more than a few at a time or the city will be overwhelmed."

My heart sinks. I gaze around the immediate area. Curious faces watch us, wanting to edge closer, wanting to beg the Warlord for Sanctuary. They don't dare approach the fierce man and his bodyguards. And they'd learned the hard way never to speak to Wolfe unless he starts the conversation. Their faces are all the same shade of dirty, shoulders slumped in exhaustion and defeat. The same way I must look.

"I can't leave them."

Diogo studies me, then says, "You'll be sacrificing yourself out of some false sense of nobility. These are not your people, not your concern."

I shake my head. He doesn't understand. "I've fought with them, eaten and slept with them. These *are* my people. Besides that, some are from my Sanctuary. What kind of leader would I be if I abandoned them for my own safety?"

"You are not their leader. Self-appointed or otherwise. A woman can't be a Warlord, and if another Warlord rose to the fore out here, it would be my duty to eliminate him as a possible threat to my Sanctuary." Diogo's voice is harsh and uncompromising, his dark soulless eyes on Wolfe though he speaks to me. "If you stay, you'll die with them."

There has to be another way. I can't believe that Diogo would just allow 10,000 people to die. I can't believe his wife, my sister, would allow this to happen. From the brief moments I spent with them all those months ago I'd seen a deep love. She must have some influence over him. This can't be it.

I lift my chin and look him in the eye. "I'd rather die with them than hide behind a wall and not lift a finger to help."

Diogo's gaze falls back to Wolfe. "And you?"

I'm not sure if he's inviting Wolfe to take the Sanctuary he offered me or if he's asking Wolfe what he thinks of my decision. Either way, he doesn't know Wolfe the way I do. There will be only one answer from my fierce protector.

"I go where she goes."

NINE

DIOGO

Stubborn woman.

I could easily kill her man and force her into Sanctuary. Give my wife the gift of her sister. But looking at the determined tilt to her chin and the glint of defiance in her grey eyes, I decide to leave her alone for now. She is so much like Taran the resemblance fucks with my head. Not just physically, but in her compassion for others and her determination to help, even if she's on the losing side of that battle.

Skye is not Taran though. It's not my job to protect this woman. If she chooses a path that leads to her death, then that's her decision. I don't have time to deal with her right now, I have bigger problems brewing on the horizon.

I nod toward Wolfe. "What's your combat experience outside of a Sanctuary? You any good at fighting on the move? I've lost men recently and need some good people for a mission. I'll pay you in weapons and ammunition."

His gaze grows shrewd. "I was born and raised a warrior. Know plenty about battle in the field and behind a wall. I have experience with sharpshooting, explosives, mission planning and hand-to-hand combat."

Pretty much exactly as I'd expected. Wolfe is one dangerous motherfucker, but if his skills help the success of the mission then I'll use him any way I can. "You're hired. Meet me here at 05:00 tomorrow morning. I'll supply the vehicle and weapons. We'll be gone about two days."

Wolfe glances toward a frowning Skye and says, "Throw in some food resources and I'll do it."

"Done," I agree, hoping I'm not wrong in my assumption that this man will make an excellent asset to my team.

"What's this about?" Skye demands, interjecting where she shouldn't. Can't seem to help herself. She's a planner, a doer and a general busy-body. If she'd been born a man and had a little more combat experience, I'd be inviting her along too.

Without another word I turn on my heel, motioning to my men and head toward the vehicles. I'll fill Wolfe in on the situation in the morning. As for Skye, well, the refugees outside of Sanctuary don't need to know that their situation is even more tenuous than they thought. Their current predicament is grim and not looking to get better without intervention. I'll hold a meeting with my advisors, see what we can come up with. Maybe we can do more to help them.

When I arrive back in Sanctuary, I go straight home. Though I don't have the news Taran will want to hear, I can at least tell her I've set eyes on her sister.

She's been busy settling into our new home. Taran was disappointed that we left Emery's place, but she under-stands that we need to be in a home that's more central and secure. We've taken over a building in Sector One, not far from where the Tower used to stand. This one isn't quite as high or impressive, but it's somewhat newer and easier to secure. After the fire, I insisted we look at every angle and every possible danger when moving into a new place. This one has multiple escape routes. It also has a rooftop that's easily accessible from the penthouse suite. Something both Taran and I appreciate. The freedom of our rooftop Sanctuary was invaluable to us and, of everything we lost, our greenhouse and view of the city was the most devastating.

Our new home was once an upscale apartment building and it doesn't take much to put the place in order. Emery has been helping Taran make it homier by moving Taran's old bed and furniture over. They've also been setting up a baby room. In a few short days we've managed to create a place that's even better than our last one. A home for our small family.

I nod toward Grayson before entering the suite. His face is set in stern lines. He takes his job very seriously and only lets Taran out of sight when ordered. When he lost her in the greenhouse attack, and then again during the fire, he started questioning his ability as a bodyguard. Neither incident could have been prevented by him, but I won't complain about his hyper-vigilance.

I open the door and walk directly into an argument.

"This is none of your business," Taran snaps, hands on hips.

"The future Warlord is everyone's business. You need to rest more, take better care of the baby."

I look at Stryker in surprise. Since when did the big grizzled soldier care about babies? He seems to have become protective of Taran since the fire, but somehow his vigilance is different from Grayson's. Stryker hovers around Taran, watching, following and trying to direct her if he believes she's doing something she shouldn't. Though borderline obsessive, his behaviour hasn't crossed a line yet.

"The baby is my business until and if he decides to become Warlord." Taran is practically growling at Stryker in annoyance. Her tolerance for him has waned over the past few weeks. Again, I can't argue with the extra layer of protection Stryker provides for Taran, but I can't have him upset my wife.

"Get out," I tell him, jerking my head toward the door.

Taran heaves a sigh as he leaves and shakes her head. "I don't understand what his problem is."

"He feels responsible for you, that's all. When you save a person's life it creates a bond."

Taran shakes her head again. "No... there's something else. Something about this baby. He doesn't seem quite stable. Like something's set him off. He's always been argumentative with me, but this is different. As though he thinks he knows best and gets angry when I contradict him. He follows me everywhere. He doesn't even leave the room if I'm in it unless you order him out."

"Are you afraid of him?" I'll tear his head off if he scares Taran, I don't care if his attitude comes from a place of wanting to protect. If he's gone too far with her, I'll finish him.

She thinks about it for a moment and then says, "No, he's fine. I don't really get what his deal is, but he seems harmless."

I don't tell her that Stryker is far from harmless. I've seen him execute prisoners without blinking. He's fast and he's brutal. There's a reason he was selected for my elite military team.

"Just say the word if you feel uncomfortable around him. I can have him removed."

She nods her head and then asks the question she's been dying to ask since I walked in. "My sister?" There's a sliver of fear in her voice.

"Alive."

Her shoulders slump in relief. She's been intensely worried about her sister, but helpless to do much about it. She's been careful not to bring it up often, knowing I had to bring the city under order before I could go searching for her kin. The wait has taken a toll.

"I invited her into the city, but she's refusing to leave the refugee encampment. She's hunkered down in Old Tucson with some of her people." I try to keep the worst of it from her, but Taran is intelligent and intuitive.

"And the Primitives?"

I don't want to lie to Taran, but I also don't want to upset my very pregnant wife when she's so close to giving birth. I stand next to her and run my hand down her back, pressing my fingers into the spot just above her ass where she seems to get the sorest.

"They're attacking the encampment," I tell her bluntly. "A group of the refugees are holding a line on the front." I don't tell her that Skye is also fighting on the front.

She tilts her head back to look at me. Her eyes are reflecting alarm, but her face set in weary resignation. She's not stupid, she has to know what's going on outside the walls of our city. Primitives will take any opportunity to attack. A gathering of unprotected humans is a prime opportunity.

"How many people are out there?" Her voice wavers, as though she doesn't want to know the answer, but needs to ask.

I hesitate. Again, she's going to hate the answer.

"We figure around 10,000."

She flinches and repeats in a shaky murmur, "10,000 lives."

Her grey eyes search mine, pain reflected there. The odds of survival in such brutal conditions are already slim, between the attacks, the lack of food, hot daytime weather and cold during the night. The numbers will fall and as they fall, so will their defences. They'll become easier pickings for the Primitives.

"We can't leave them out there," she whispers.

I gather her against me and press her head against my chest, over my heart. Her belly is hard against mine, our child safe between us. I choose my words carefully, not wanting to flatly deny her. "We can't bring that many into the city. We simply don't have the resources."

She tilts her head up to look at me, her eyes distant, her mind whirring as she thinks through the problem. "What would it take to find the resources? What would we need to do to incorporate these people into Sanctuary?"

I thought she'd ask me to find a way or beg for the lives of the survivors from other sanctuaries. It dawns on me that she's starting to understand what it takes to run an entire city. I think about her question, taking it seriously. I don't want to be responsible for the deaths of 10,000 people. If we can find a way around this problem, it's worth exploring.

I pull a chair out from the table, sit down and pull her onto my lap. She curls against my chest, leaning into me. I press my chin against the fine hair on top of her head, enjoying the silky texture against my rough chin. "Food, water, housing and protection are the big four. After that we'd have to extend medical aid, waste control and policing. If we were able to manage all that, we'd then need to establish schools, long term food resources, jobs for the able-bodied adults, and more."

She nods thoughtfully. I can almost see her brain whirring as she picks away at the problem. "Food...." She draws the word out as she thinks about it. "The people of the slums have stretched resources many times to cover the refugee families coming in. It's entirely possible to do the same with the other sectors. If we extended the rations of our entire city of 200,000 to temporarily include 10,000 more, no one should go hungry."

I want to tell her that the rations we currently enjoy are carefully balanced to cover the city. It was never meant to extend to include the numbers we're talking about. But she has a point, the slums, though poor, have cobbled together a system that works. "It would be a temporary and unsustainable fix. How do we deal with the food shortages long-term?"

"The third greenhouse," she says decisively. "It's already most of the way finished. It stalled when Manuel Sharp was killed, and then again when the riots got bad. If we get that process restarted and work on a long-term source of food, the city rations should balance out again."

"I can't spare anyone to the effort," I tell her. "You would have to be in charge of the project. Find people to help build the greenhouse and do the planting."

"I can do that," she says eagerly, seeing a solution just within sight.

I don't want to burst her bubble, but if she's going to take on the role I have planned for her, advisor to the Warlord, then she's going to need to think about every possibility. "You won't be capable of managing a project this big until after the baby is born."

"Of course I can," she tips her head back to give me a small glare.

"But you won't," I tell her bluntly. "You need to concentrate on this baby. I won't have you stressing about anything city related until I know you have the strength to handle the problems that arise with managing large projects."

She sighs irritably. "Fine, Emery can manage the

project until we can find a more permanent solution."

"I've said no to this idea before, Taran," I tell her warningly. I don't mean it though. I want to hear what her agile mind comes up with.

She shakes her head, rubbing the top against my chin. "She's proven herself completely trustworthy. Not only did she hide you in your time of need, but she's been stepping up to protect the families in the slums. She's been taking on more of a leadership role too, convincing former rebels to find a more peaceful solution."

She opens her mouth to say more, to defend her friend and argue her points. I gently cover her lips with my palm. "Good enough, Taran. If she'll accept the responsibility then it's hers."

She tilts her head back again, her eyes sparkling and her mouth curving into a smile. "Thank you, Diogo."

I nod and press a kiss to the top of her nose. "I've noticed Emery quietly working toward a unified city these past weeks. Her efforts have convinced me she can handle more responsibility. You better check with her though. She's not young anymore, she may not want to take on a project of this size."

"She will, I know she will," Taran says enthusiastically.

We sit quietly, enjoying the warmth and hominess of our new dining room and kitchen area. Taran and Emery went to a lot of effort to create a home, adding softer touches here and there. A salvaged china unit with the original glass still intact sits in the corner, filled with mismatched dishware and cutlery. The furniture is also mismatched, the table created from salvaged wood and the chairs all different shapes and sizes. Somehow it works though. Our home is colourful, happy. I will do anything to preserve this feeling. To protect my family. If anything were to happen to them, to Taran and the baby, I would burn this world to the ground and follow them into death. They are my Sanctuary now and protecting them is my biggest priority.

After a few minutes of silence, I notice a shift in Taran's mood as she becomes thoughtful once more. "What about the other problem?"

"The power plant," I acknowledge.

It has become the elephant in the room everywhere I go. HQ, home, meetings. If we don't shut down the one plant that's relatively close and still online then we won't have a place to call home, let alone a city to rule over.

"One thing at a time," I tell her, trying to sound reassuring, minimize a potentially massive problem. "Right now the Primitives are occupied chasing the refugees. I've had reports from scouts that the guards on the plants are holding steady. We're still trying to figure out why or how they targeted the eastern stations."

"Maybe they've done whatever they set out to do."

Again, we fall silent as a chill settles over us. Primitives aren't supposed to be reasoning, thinking creatures, yet somehow, they worked together to bring the eastern power plants down. I have my theories on what's happening but won't be able to confirm until I gather more information about the actions the Primitives are taking.

"One thing at a time," I repeat. "You are not to worry about the Primitives. I won't allow them anywhere near you or the baby."

She laughs and shakes her head. "Trust you to order me not to worry."

I turn her on my lap and take her mouth with mine, my lips lingering over hers in a slow, sensual kiss. I breathe in her scent of wild sunshine, enjoying the weight of her on my lap. She's heavier, curvier, and she's all mine.

TEN

TARAN

I've been trying to seduce my husband for almost fifteen full minutes without so much as a single hint that he's interested. I'm starting to think that the hit he took to the head injured more than his skull. He's never once hesitated when it comes to sex. Granted, he's almost always been the one to initiate things, but I didn't think it would be this difficult to catch his attention.

I try to calm the insecure part of me that asks if maybe he's not attracted to me when my body is heavy with the baby and my bellybutton has been missing for weeks now. Then the reasonable voice jumps in to assure me he's just tired. After all, retaking a city, taking revenge on his enemy, settling refugees and figuring out how to head off a potential nuclear meltdown might be preoccupying him.

I'm wearing nothing but one of his new shirts. It lands about mid-thigh on me and I've left the collar open to well below my breasts. I sit down at my new vanity table and brush my hair, pulling the thick red strands out straight and then letting them bounce back into smooth waves. He loves watching me brush my hair, and he enjoys touching it, running his fingers through the freshly untangled strands.

I twist around on my seat and glance back at where he's sprawled out on the bed, propped up against the headboard, long muscular legs spread in front of him. He's opened the buttons of his shirt and kicked his boots off next to the bed. His gaze is focused completely on the paperwork in front of him, detailed turn-of-the-century plans for a nuclear power plant. He's trying to learn as much as he can before going in to shut it down.

I sigh and drop my hairbrush on the vanity with a clatter. Diogo's eyebrow barely twitches and he doesn't look up. I'm not trying to be pouty or detract his attention from an extremely important project... oh wait, that's exactly what I'm doing. But damn it, I'm horny.

Pregnancy has pushed my hormones into overdrive. The excitement of the rebellion and the imminent threat of nuclear disaster had pushed those hormones to the back burner, but now that I'm settling in my new home and building a baby room, I'm feeling them again. I want sex when I wake up, I want it when I'm folding clothes and planning our meals. I even want it when I really, really shouldn't. Like when we have a house full of soldiers meeting with my husband.

I feel like I'll burst if I don't get some Diogo cock, right, fucking, now.

I push myself to my feet, going for graceful and sexy, but landing on ungainly and a little tippy. I clutch the vanity desk until I'm completely upright. Then I make my way over to Diogo, trying not to look too much like I'm waddling. I stop next to the bed where his leg is crooked over the edge and nudge his knee with mine.

He reaches out absently and grips my hand, running his

thumb down the inside of my palm. Fire sizzles right through me at the contact of his skin on mine. Am I the only one that feels that instant and undeniable attraction from even this small touch? My nipples peak and I know I'm wet and ready for him.

He doesn't look up.

Alright then... drastic times call for drastic measures. I thank god that the only lighting in the room are the candles that Diogo lit for his reading. It's after dark and Diogo tries to preserve electricity produced by our generator as much as he can. I walk my fingers down the buttons of my shirt, undoing them one at a time. Not really trying to be sexy since he's not even watching, but going nice and slow in case he clues in.

Once my shirt, his shirt, is hanging open, I shrug it off my shoulders and let it slide down my arms, shivering at the contact as it brushes my over-sensitized skin. I stand proudly naked next to the bed, my newly full breasts jutting forward, the nipples peaked from the cool evening air. Finally, he looks up, his eyes lighting with surprise and pleasure as they take in my unexpected nudity.

"Taran, what are you...?" he trails off, his voice deepening before it drops away.

I smile at him and lift a knee onto the bed, then very carefully crawl over top of him. He's such a big man that I have to climb him like a mini mountain, careful not to stick a knee somewhere that might end this little interlude. Finally, he gets a clue, tosses his papers off the side of the bed and then wraps his big hands around my arms and helps ease the burden as I put the pressure of my pregnant body on my hands.

"Baby, you look so good," he murmurs his gaze taking in

all the nudity climbing around on top of him. "So fucking beautiful."

I grin at him. He's saying exactly what I need to hear. It's not easy feeling attractive when your body goes haywire on you. But Diogo has assured me over and over that he loves the way I look, loves that I'm growing rounder and lusher by the day. Hopefully that includes the inevitable stretch marks.

I finally reach his head, take his face in my hands and lean low to whisper against his lips, "I need you, husband."

He groans and reaches for me, one arm wrapping around my neck and the other around my waist. He turns us, picking me up with his ridiculous strength and gently placing me on my back on the mattress. He covers me with his body, careful not to put too much weight on my middle.

"I've wanted nothing more than to take you and fuck you silly, little wife. You've been teasing and taunting me with this gorgeous body, but I knew you weren't doing it on purpose, knew I had to give you time to recover from the fire and everything else that's happened."

I wrap my arms around his neck and force his head down to mine. "Very noble, Warlord," I say huskily against his lips. "I think I'm done waiting."

"Me too," he growls against me and then takes my mouth in a heated kiss.

Every particle in my body surges to the surface, clambering for him. I moan in protest when he breaks our kiss to trail his lips down my body. His face is rough with a few days grown of whiskers and the sensation of scraping along my skin nearly drives me crazy. I moan again and squirm as he plays gently with my breasts, taking each nipple deep into his mouth and lavishing it with attention.

The breath catches in my lungs then huffs out impatiently. I'm growing wetter and wetter by the second. If he doesn't continue his journey downwards, I may have to disgrace myself by begging for that most intimate kiss that he's teasing me with.

He lingers over my swollen belly, trailing wet kisses across it as he continues his torturous path lower. When he finally reaches my pussy, I nearly scream out at the first touch of his tongue lapping through my folds. It has been six long weeks since we were last together as husband and wife. And now I want nothing more than to make up for lost time.

He licks and sucks until I'm grabbing the blankets beneath me and crying out in a long continuous wail. My legs are shaking and my knuckles hurt from gripping so hard. Finally, that sweet, wonderful, crazy rush of orgasm washes through me. I keen my pleasure for the world to hear, any sense of time or space gone as I float with the best feeling in the world.

I barely notice as Diogo lifts me and turns me over onto my hands and knees. I twist around to look at him, watch as he quickly drags his clothes off his body. I giggle when he throws them around the bedroom, a sock landing on top of my vanity mirror. He climbs onto the bed behind me and I suck my breath in, waiting for that breathtaking full sensation when he finally enters me; the sweet pinch as my body stretches to accept his length.

He's so tall as he kneels behind me that he has to drag my legs up his thighs before he can thrust into me. I squeal, my body stretching to accommodate him. It's definitely been awhile, my passage has become more snug over the past weeks.

He runs a broad hand over my ass and up my back.

"Okay, baby?" he asks. I can hear the strain in his voice as he holds himself still, waiting for my body to accept him.

"Wonderful," I reply with a grin.

And I mean it. I haven't felt this good in months. Every part of me is lit up with pleasure as happy hormones rush through me.

"Good," he grunts.

Then he retreats and thrusts back in. I gasp at the sensations engulfing me and press myself back onto him. I lay my front down on the bed, easing the pressure on my arms and sticking my ass up even further. He runs his hands all over me as I lay beneath him taking his cock and basking in the warm glow of another orgasm building inside me.

He takes his time, helping me build toward another incredible crest. I'm amazed at his ability to hold his own orgasm back. The husband I'd become used to was anything but gentle. Yet, he's giving me time, flowing with my body's needs instead of dominating me and forcing my orgasm.

"Diogo!" I cry out as I come again, a rush of exquisite sensation bolting through me, then softening into an amazing afterglow.

He follows me over the edge this time, his motions becoming jerkier with each thrust, though he continues to hold me gently, easing in and out, prolonging his own pleasure. Finally, he pushes in one last time, his fingers digging into the flesh of my hips as he grunts his release. I feel the heated wetness of his seed bathing me.

He eases out and helps me lay on my side, then curls around me, his big body blanketing mine in a protective curve.

"How are you, baby, I didn't hurt you?" he asks huskily in my ear, kissing the sensitive spot behind it.

I shake my head and tilt my chin so he can see the grin stretching my lips. "I've never felt better."

He kisses me, lingering against my mouth, our breaths mingling for a moment. Then he drags the blanket up our bodies, tucking it around and between us. He holds me as I drift peacefully into sleep, my last thought that I want to capture this moment and hold onto it forever.

Wolfe sits beside me in the jeep and Stryker is in the back. Silence fills the miles as we make our way from Sanctuary out to the last working nuclear power plant in the region. A monumental and dangerous task faces us. Several other cars follow the wake of our dusty trail. Other soldiers, men who will hold off the Primitives once we arrive.

In one of the cars, buried in the middle of the pack is the most important member of our team. An eighty-one-year-old historian who worked as a nuclear physicist before the Great Fall. I've never set a lot of stock in hanging onto history and haven't offered many resources to city historians. I'm thankful this one somehow managed to stay alive as long as he has.

Silence rules our travels. In part because we're scanning the horizon for our enemy, watching for obstacles and conserving energy for an upcoming battle. But mostly we are a silent vehicle because Wolfe doesn't speak unless spoken to, and sometimes not even then. And Stryker is pissed that he was forced to leave Sanctuary for this mission.

His preoccupation with my wife is colouring his decisions and will soon make him a powerful enemy he is not ready to face. I've given him time, weeks of time, to come round. To do his job, which yes, sometimes includes protecting the Warlord's wife. But his constant need to keep her in sight is unnatural and causing friction between him and everyone around him. Even if I hadn't needed his sharp eyes and reflexes on this mission, I would've ordered him along just to give Taran a reprieve from his constant supervision.

"You ever done anything like this before?" I direct the question toward Wolfe.

He remains silent for a moment then, without looking at me, says, "The Santa Fe water supply was overrun with Primitives a few years back. We went in and cleared them out, stationed better patrols and Primitive traps."

I'd been fairly certain this man would have some expertise in driving the enemy out of key points. His quiet demeanour is a mask for the deadly, violent man lurking beneath. I recognize his true characteristics because they are a close match to mine. The biggest difference is he has no desire to seize power. Something that could have made us enemies if he'd pitted himself against me. I get no sense of deception from the man though. He is exactly as he seems. Quiet, deadly and protective of a woman he has yet to claim.

"If yer done jabbering up there, might want to check the road." Stryker's sharp assertion has me squinting into the distance. For an older man, his eyes are infallible.

It takes me a moment but I see it, a section of road missing leading into a ravine. We stop and get out of the car, the three of us gazing down into the impassible section of road. A big, dusty crack in the earth with no road for miles in either direction.

"We're not getting through this with the vehicles," Wolfe grunts, and moves to lean back against the car, arms crossed, casually bored as he awaits a decision. I've no doubt the man can come up with a plan of his own, but he's not offering shit.

The other vehicles stop behind ours and I turn to point at the middle one. The one holding our resident historian. He obediently, if a little stiffly, emerges from the car and approaches the ravine, his gaze on the distance.

"How far?" I demand.

He sighs heavily as though expecting this question. I get it. We're relatively young, most of us are soldiers, all fit for duty. He's an old man. Anyone with eyes can see that the road has become impassible by vehicle. We'll have to walk the rest of the way.

"About twelve or so miles in that direction," he says dismally, pointing.

I slap him on the back. "Good, not far then. We'll arrive before sunset."

He nods unhappily, his shoulders drooping a little. I'm not a needlessly cruel man, but I am a practical one. I've never had a use for a historian until now. And I don't antici-pate having a use for one after we're finished. It makes no difference to me if this old man survives past what I need him to do. A callous perspective perhaps, but a valid one.

"Gather your supplies," I shout to my men. "We're walk-ing." I turn to the historian. "Keep up."

He nods his head dismally and turns back to his car to gather supplies. I reach into the back of mine and heft my bag filled with water, food, an extra set of clothes and weapons. Any smart traveller knows to pack the essentials when leaving Sanctuary. You never know how long you'll be stuck on the road.

I head toward the ravine, not bothering to wait for my men. Wolfe and Stryker fall in beside me, packs strapped to their backs and weapons within easy reach. The going is rough since the ravine used to be an old riverbed that cuts deep into the valley. Climbing up the other side isn't an easy prospect. Many of us have to scramble for foot and hand holds while others remain on guard for any predators coming in for an attack. A group this large is going to attract Primitives.

Once we reach the other side, I don't grant my people a reprieve but start walking across the desert with our goal in mind. The faster we finish the sooner we get back to our families. Exposure in a Primitive-ridden landscape is asking for death.

Unfortunately, moving this many people is a slow prospect. The historian can only walk so fast and we need his expertise for the survival of our Sanctuary and all the people in and around it. Otherwise I'd leave him in the dust to fend for himself.

I grow more frustrated with each slow step. At the pace we're going, it'll be well after dark before we make it into the power plant. We've probably gone just over half the distance we need and some of my less fit men are falling behind. I'd leave them to the Primitives, but I need them once we get there.

Then the moment I've been expecting arrives. Stryker growls, "Heads up," which can mean only one thing. I pull my rifle from the holster across my back and check the ammo. Wolfe does the same, pulling his own gun and a knife from the leather sheath strapped to his thigh. I call a warning back to my men in case they didn't see the dust cloud headed straight for us on the horizon, essentially cutting off our path to the power plant. I'm not surprised by their presence, was expecting an attack since we know they're after the nuclear plants. Still, the sight of at least a hundred Primitives bearing down on our position is a daunting one.

"Let's dance," Stryker growls and starts shooting as he walks toward them, each bullet finding its mark deep in the skulls of our enemies.

I follow suit, lifting my own weapon and taking out the Primitives that pull out front of the horde, the strong ones. The survivors. The ones most likely to put up a decent fight and take some of my men down with them. Between the three of us up front we must take down fifty of them before the horde even reaches us. I'm impressed with Wolfe's extreme speed and accuracy with a weapon. He proves he's even better at hand-to-hand combat when the horde finally falls on us, running so recklessly hard they cut a swath into my forces.

Wolfe wraps an arm around the neck of the first to reach us, taking him down to the ground and stabbing him through the eye with his knife. He barely glances up as he shoots another in the head before it can even lay a finger on him.

I don't have time to further admire his combat skills as I'm set upon by a mini horde of three. I marvel at their organization, their predator-like behaviour as they circle me. The intent of the trio is to distract me long enough for one to sink his teeth into the back of my neck while the other two attack from the front. I duck the swinging arms, hitting the ground hard and rolling beneath my attackers, taking their legs out with well placed kicks. The first falls next to me and gets a bullet to the brain. The next falls on top of his compatriot and meets the edge of my blade across his throat. I roll as the third lunges at my back, swing around and shoot him through the heart. As he falls, I put another bullet in his head.

I leap back to my feet and swing around making sure my people are doing what I told them, falling into formation, taking out the Primitives with quick, concise maneuvers.

"Move out!" I shout.

We have no choice but to fight and walk. We will be attacked every step of the way. Our options are either dig in and fight every damn Primitive that shows up, which could be endless, or keep walking, keep making our way toward the threatened power plant facility.

I can't tell how many men are still with me or even if I'm losing people. The fray is too thick. I'm hoping my soldiers keep enough presence of mind to protect the damn historian or we're done before we even get started. The urge to fall back and check on him is strong, but I'm best positioned at the front where I can take out the threat before it reaches him. With that thought in mind I kill as many zombies as I can, taking them out before they can make it back to my men. Stryker and Wolfe follow suit.

Between the three of us we probably kill more Primitives than my entire military combined. There's no way to keep track of time as we move through the horde, but we finally make it to the facility, the bloody evidence of our journey littered across the desert behind us.

I swipe a hand across my forehead, slick with sweat and blood. Not my blood. I look around at the men who've made it to the power plant, doing a quick head count. We lost two. Not bad considering the numbers we were fighting. I search the exhausted, bloody and bruised faces of my men until they land on the historian who is hunched over, hands on his knees trying to catch his breath.

I make my way toward him and take his arm, helping him straighten. "Rest later. Right now we have to finish our job and get out of here."

He nods and uses my strength as a crutch as we make our way through the massive metal gates of the nuclear facility. Wolfe stops and turns to scan the horizon, his sharp gaze picking up several advancing Primitives. "This'll make a good choke point. I'll take out anything that approaches."

I nod toward a couple of my guys. "Keep him company."

The area inside the gates seems eerily quiet considering the horde that attacked us on our way here. Where are the Primitives? This is where I'd expected to have to make a stand, not out in the desert. The hair on my arms and the back of my neck is standing up, telling me there's something wrong here. Telling me the enemy is close. I always listen to my instincts, they've kept me alive for forty years.

"Commander." A voice draws my attention and I swing my rifle around to find one of my men striding toward me. I'd stationed him here along with several others to hold the facility until we could arrive with the historian.

"Report," I demand sharply when he stops in front of me. He looks exhausted, as though he hasn't slept in days, but his eyes and manner are still sharp. I'm happy with the care he seems to have taken here.

"We've managed to keep the horde mostly beyond the gates. We set up sniper positions on top of the buildings and take out the enemy as they approach. A few have gotten through our perimeter so watch your step once you're inside." He stops and rubs his brow before continuing, his voice heavy with disapproval. "I lost one soldier to negligence on his part. He didn't comply with the buddy system and was taken out when he climbed down from where he was stationed to take a piss."

I nod my understanding and praise his vigilance. "You've done well here. Make sure you and your men fall back into the ranks. You'll leave when we do."

"Yes sir." He turns and strides away, climbing a ladder to where I assume he's set up a sniper station.

"Let's move," I say grimly to the men I've chosen to accompany me inside. The main building is still locked up tight, even after all these years. I wave for one of my men to pry the door open. The inside is dark and dry as we pass through the doors, smells like old dust, a scent all of us recognize.

"This way." I keep the historian with me, covering him as we move. It's my job to act as his bodyguard until he finishes his job. We don't have anyone else who knows enough about these old nuclear facilities to be able to shut it down safely. We follow the labyrinth of halls, similar to the blueprints I'd managed to get my hands on.

I point at Stryker. "Take some men and cover the main door. Have some others spread out and make sure we aren't about to get ambushed."

Stryker nods and strides away, waving toward some of our men and giving them orders as he walks. It doesn't take us long to find the control room though the doors are firmly locked behind thick, heavy steel. It takes several more minutes to pry these doors open. My feeling of unease sticks with me the longer we go without being attacked.

Once we're in, I point at the control booth and say, "Get to work."

The historian sighs as he sits. "First we have to make sure the plant reverted to the backup system when it was abandoned."

"Wouldn't it have melted down by now if it wasn't?" Bossman asks from the doorway where he's covering the hall. Boss knows more about this shit than I do. He seems to understand how old technology works and is able to convert it for our use when we find something worth our time. He's also spent time with the historian, understands the man in a way the rest of us don't.

"Not necessarily. These buildings are meant to withstand a lot, including the prolonged absence of human intervention. For the most part a meltdown ultimately depends on the integrity of the building and the water surrounding the active rods. If containment isn't breached then theoretically these things can last for a very long time without melting down. That's why most of the reactors on this continent have maintained integrity. I suspect the Primitives have somehow learned how to breach that containment," the historian says matter-of-factly, working at the controls. He crows in delight, "Got it, the backup is coming online now."

All of us turn to watch as the computer system lights up under his fingertips, not something any of us have ever experienced. I've seen computers, but never one that worked. They require power and repairs, two things our struggling civilization is short on. When attempting to rebuild a society, the convenience of technology becomes unnecessary unless it's contributing to our immediate survival.

As he works, the historian continues to speak. "The interesting thing about the cascade failures on the east coast is the organization of them and the timing."

"What do you mean?" I ask impatiently. We're here for one single reason, not to jabber about how interesting nuclear power plants are.

He shrugs, his fingers tapping away at the keys. He hunches close to the keyboard squinting at what he's doing as he hits the buttons one at a time. Though he has expert knowledge on these things, it's been a long time since he's interacted with a computer.

"The pack behaviour of the Primitives, Commander," he says simply as though that explains everything. And maybe it does.

The Primitives are supposed to be unthinking, instinct driven creatures. When the cascade failures hit the east coast, we got an inkling of some kind of organization. But we've been bombarded by Primitive attacks since and haven't had time to examine the actual behaviour patterns of our enemy. I watch the historian as he works. Perhaps he has more worth than I thought.

"Got it," he says, pushing away from the desk.

"What did you do?" I demand. "I want details, so we know this got done right and the Primitives won't be able to take us down the way they took out every other Sanctuary east of us."

He shakes his head and eases himself out of the chair. "Although I do believe the Primitives are more evolved than we give them credit for, they won't be able to bring this place to the brink of meltdown unless they're able to get into the computer system and key in the correct sequence to bring this place back online. I have secured the control key and encrypted it," he explains calmly. "And I've shut down fuel movements. The reactors might need maintenance in the future to ensure containment remains stable, but at the moment this place is effectively shut down."

If the reactors require further maintenance, then how is the place shutdown? It sounds like the historian's definition of "shutdown" isn't the same as mine. I'm about to demand further explanation when a shout draws our attention. Bossman looks out into the hallway.

"Company's coming!" he shouts, raising his weapon.

I turn to the historian and snarl, "You sure this place is as safe as it can get? We can abandon it to the Primitives?"

He gives me a long look. "I wouldn't suggest just handing it over."

"Who would you *suggest* remains behind? You volunteering?"

He quickly backs up and shakes his head. "They can't do any damage. Not unless they're able to get into the system."

I'm about to ask how the fuck they managed to cause cascade failures if shutdown is this simple, when Bossman throws himself into the hallway, stabbing and shooting as he's surrounded by Primitives. I join him, picking them off one at a time and doing my best to protect the historian. Though he seems like an annoying, arrogant old man, at this point I believe he may have further use.

"Stick to my back," I shout at him, clearing a path through the hall.

We fight our way back to the main doors where Stryker is holding off the horde trying to make their way inside. It becomes quickly clear that the ones we were dealing with in the control room got in another way. Soon we're flanked and vastly outnumbered, exits cut off and our ability to fight hindered by being trapped indoors.

I'd anticipated an organized attack though. The Primitives outside the gates were the first wave, the guards. The ones inside were here for another reason. Maybe to take us out as we tried to thwart them from causing a meltdown or maybe to use us to get into the control room. Until we find out how they're causing the meltdowns we won't know.

If Primitives are organized enough to take our nuclear facilities, then it's not a stretch to imagine they've managed to up their attack strategies. So, I've upped mine as well, the new strategy being not to underestimate this enemy again. Soon, the men that I'd ordered into key positions have wrapped their way around the Primitives and are cutting a path toward us. We use their impulse driven nature against them. Distracting them with one human while the other gets them from behind. It doesn't take long before we've cleared out the immediate area and are able to make our way back outside.

While Stryker continues to clear the area of any stragglers, I give Bossman his orders. "You and three others will remain. Make sure this place stays offline. Get the information you need from your historian friend on what needs watching. When the area has been clear for a few days, lock it up tight and follow us back."

"Yes, Commander." I can tell by the glint in his eyes that Bossman relishes the idea of having an entire nuclear plant to himself for a few days.

We rejoin Wolfe and the rest of my men at the gates. Without a word, the big, scarred one-eyed warrior steps away from the pile of bodies he clearly enjoyed parting from their heads and strides into the desert, heading our team as we prepare to return home.

TWELVE

DIOGO

"Explain," I demand, for about the fifth time since requesting the historian's presence in my home.

"Diogo," Taran says warningly, turning a sunny smile on the other man. "Christian is trying to help. Let's keep the growling to a minimum or the man will think you aren't appreciative."

I reach out, snagging Taran's wrist as she passes, fussing with her tea set, a gift from Emery. It's chipped, cracked, and well used, but the damn thing means the world to my wife. "Sit," I order. She turns her serene expression down toward me, but I can see the glint of teasing mischief shining through.

She turns and sits on me. I pull her back against my chest and rest a chin on her shoulder, inhaling the mouth-watering scent of her hair. She calms me. I no longer feel the need to rip the historian to pieces and walk away. Most people have learned to check their arrogance around the Warlord. Clearly this man doesn't understand what's best for his health.

He clears his throat and continues to explain, his

approach slightly more humble than a few minutes ago when he tried explaining as if I was a particularly dense child. "If we take the power plant completely offline it's more likely to meltdown than if we leave it online and shut the reactor down. That's why I left it online."

"And you didn't think this was something I should know before we went out into the desert?" I point out the error in his thinking.

"I believed my Warlord understood what was needed to shut down a power plant." He speaks in a dull monotone.

I growl in response.

Taran turns to the other man impatiently and cuts right through his crap. "If the Warlord understood the nuances of nuclear energy, he wouldn't be asking you. You are lucky to be summoned to his presence, his way of trying to decide if you're valuable enough to advise him. Keep your ego to yourself and describe in detail what your Commander is asking for."

I don't stop or correct her. There was a time where I would not have allowed a woman to speak for me. But Taran has a way with the citizens of our city. She is both soft and smart, able to use the sharp edge of her tongue and then sooth the ruffled feathers when she's finished. She's made my job easier by recognizing talent and pursuing opportunities that will help our city with sustainability.

Christian nods and drops his gaze, a flush staining his cheeks. "My apologies, Commander."

"Tell me what I need to know," I ask again.

He proceeds to give us the rundown on nuclear energy and how he managed to safely shutdown our plant. By the time he's finished explaining I feel more confident that the Primitives won't find a way around his safeguards.

"I'll need you to prepare concise, but detailed instructions on how you shut down that plant. Then we'll call out to the other Sanctuaries with the solution. Hopefully we'll be able to stave off a potential mass slaughter if the Primitives decide to move onto other territory and try their trick with less protected plants."

He nods, paling a little. "Th-that's assuming they've evolved to the point where they're able to reason and plan," he says. "While I do think they exhibit some pack behaviour, I doubt they're capable of that sort of planning."

"You're supposed to be the most intelligent man in this city," I point out. "You tell me, if they aren't capable of this level of planning then why do we have a city full of refugees banging at our gates with hordes of hungry Primitives behind them?"

He looks like he wants to speak but is afraid of his Warlord. Taran shifts on my lap about to speak to him again, most likely on my behalf. Tell the man what a pussy cat I've become. I tighten my arm around her waist and interject before she can. "You may speak without fear. I won't harm a hair on your body." I pause and then add, "Today." There's no point in letting the man think he gets a pass to be rude.

He takes my words at face value and tells me what's on his mind. "Evolution, simple as that." He doesn't explain. Not that he needs to, I understand what he means. He thinks the Primitives have evolved into pack behaviour.

"I don't agree," I say simply.

He gives me a look somewhere between scathing and pity. It makes me want to pull out my knife and show him why I should be respected. I now understand why Taran chose her seat on top of me. She doesn't want blood stains in our brand-new living room.

Before the historian can say anything guaranteed to set

my temper off, I ask him, "What evidence do you have that the Primitives have evolved this so-called pack behaviour?"

"Well... well, they have apparently gone from not even being able to turn doorknobs or display any kind of reasoning behaviour to organizing themselves enough to cause nuclear meltdowns across the continent." He scoffs as he speaks, as though the answer should be obvious, and perhaps it is. But it also seems obvious that there is a deeper more complex explanation.

"Don't be stupid, man. Wild animals can't open doors, but they will exhibit pack behaviour. I didn't ask what Primitives can and can't do." I lean forward my chin grazing Taran's shoulder as she leans back to give me room. "I'm telling you, these creatures are capable of higher reasoning than we give them credit for. I don't believe they have evolved this way, not over the course of fifty years. That's not how evolution works."

The man looks offended that I'm suggesting he might not have a proper understanding of evolution. "Well, a different kind of evolving then," he defends. "More rapid, like the spread of the disease they carry."

"No, I think they were always this way. Talk to anyone who's had prolonged combat experience with these creatures. Talk to any of my men, the pack behaviour isn't new. Humans are too blinded by their fear of Primitives, and too many of our good minds have fallen for us to be able to look deeper into their behaviours. Something I'd like to remedy. I'm hoping the more we look at our enemy with an intellectual instead of survival-based thinking, the more likely we are to take the next step toward eradicating them."

He nods slowly. "Not a bad idea."

I grunt my less than polite response. Taran pats my

shoulder and turns to the other man, shifting on my lap. "It's all we have," she says softly.

His sharp eyes examine her until I'm ready to tell him to take his fucking gaze off my wife. Doesn't matter that he's older than dirt, his mind should be on nuclear power plants and Primitives, not Taran. Then he says, "Maybe not the only way."

Taran opens her mouth to reply, but I cut her off. "Explain." When he hesitates, my voice drops a few degrees cooler. "Explain now, historian."

He clears his throat again. "I'm only suggesting..." his eyes drift to Taran's neck, covered by a high collar, and I know exactly what he's suggesting. Someone has been loose with their tongue. "... a cure."

Taran doesn't even blink. She smiles benignly. "Well, until a cure presents itself, do you not think that studying the enemy will have some excellent benefits and give us a fighting chance toward understanding what we're up against?"

"Of course, Mrs. Fuentes." Then he seems to realize exactly why he's been summoned into the Warlord's presence. His demeanour changes from relaxed arrogance to fear. "How close would a person have to get to study them?"

Taran barely contains a laugh at his fearful inquiry. "Very close," she says cheerfully. "And we're hoping with your background and expertise you'll be the right person for the job."

"Well, I don't really think..." he protests.

"I'm not asking," I tell him bluntly. "You'll be paired with Bossman, one of my best men, for your protection. You can work out of Doctor Bishop's office since you two will undoubtedly be consulting. You can report to me at military headquarters once a week with your findings."

He tries again to protest his new appointment. "I'm an old man, Commander. Hardly capable of..."

"All those within Sanctuary must contribute, historian. You are no different. You will contribute your knowledge and skill or you will leave."

His mouth hangs open for a moment and then he nods and says, "I understand."

"Dismissed."

He stands stiffly and leaves. Taran attempts to rise, to show him to the door, like a polite hostess. I hang on to her. The old man can find his own way out. She sat on my lap, now she can pay the toll for such a bold action. I slide my arms around her and force her to face me. Her mouth is tight and disapproving but her eyes are sparkling with laughter.

"Do you have to be so short and gruff to all the people around you?" she scolds. "He might be arrogant, but I think he genuinely wants to help. You could try being a little more understanding. Ask instead of demand. You know, honey attracts more flies than vinegar."

"What you fail to understand, my sweet, is that the only creatures on this planet I care about are you and the baby. Nothing else matters. I will sacrifice the historian and anyone else that gets in my way if it means protecting you."

She smiles wanly and curves an arm around my shoulder. "I know how you think. You think you have to protect me and the baby. Well, I know what I think. And it's that I can use the Warlord's preoccupation to my advantage."

I squeeze her tight to my chest, careful not to put pressure on her midsection. "You think so?" I say, a dark edge to my voice. "That sounds very close to manipulation, my love."

"Exactly," she laughs. "Is it working?"

"Depends on what you're looking for."

She raises an eyebrow. "How about a kiss?"

"Done."

I tip her back in my arms, revelling in the way she moves with me, trusting me to hold her up and catch her if she falls. I touch my lips to hers, soft at first, exploring. Just savouring and breathing her in. She moans and tightens her arms around my neck, breaking through the dam of my patience. I devour her mouth, sweeping my tongue against and past hers, touching every part of her and lighting us both up with need.

I pull back just enough to say, "You can manipulate me any time you want, baby." Then I pick her up and carry her to the bedroom where I roll her underneath me and set to work making her body sing.

Considering how exciting life has been since I met Diogo, when I finally go into labour, I'm doing nothing more innocuous than washing clothes. As long as I don't lift the water myself Diogo allows me to do some light chores. I find the task is a soothing one. I enjoy the process and I enjoy the product at the end. Fresh smelling clothes.

I'm in the process of squeezing excess water out of one of Diogo's shirts when the first contraction hits. It's nothing much, so at first I think the baby is just being more active than usual. Then, several minutes later, another contraction bands my stomach. I gasp as I realize what's happening, drop the shirt back in the water bin, and make my way over to the couch. Slowly I lower myself.

I sit for several minutes, waiting for another contraction. When it comes, I know. I'm in labour. It feels like I've been waiting for this moment for years instead of nine months. I stand, head toward the bedroom, then turn around and sit again. Then I stand, head for the kitchen, then sit again.

Shit, I have no idea what I'm doing. All the planning

and discussion surrounding the birth and I've forgotten everything.

"Okay, Taran, let's go through the list," I say out loud to myself, my hand on my lower belly, rubbing the tiny flutters there. "Step one, tell whoever's babysitting me. Step two, go find Bishop. Step three, send someone to find Diogo. Step four, get someone to find Emery who can calm Diogo down. Step five, produce the baby."

Okay, we can do this, baby. Let's get born.

I get back to my feet, cursing myself out for pacing so much while I was trying to figure out what to do. My poor feet become swollen when they aren't raised up on a chair with a pillow underneath them. I work my way laboriously toward the door and open it.

I bite back the annoyed exclamation that leaps to my lips when I find Stryker on the other side. I've come to detest his constant presence and have asked Diogo to give him other duties. Cognizant of my exasperation toward the big grizzled soldier, Diogo has been assigning Grayson to me unless his presence is required somewhere else, which apparently it was. I don't even remotely understand Stryker's fascination with me, and I definitely don't enjoy it. He hovers, he argues, he gets in my space until I want to scream.

"The baby is coming," I tell him bluntly. "I need you to get Bishop."

His eyes widen and drop to my belly. I want to tell him that yes, it's still in there, but I keep the snarky comment to myself. No need to antagonize him when I'm essentially helpless and need him to help me through steps one, two and three.

Once he finishes processing my words, he quickly

shakes his head. "No, better that I take you to the Doc than bring him here."

I grit my teeth. Absolutely everything about this baby has been an argument with Stryker, and now, apparently, so is the birthing process.

"I'm having the baby here, Stryker. We've been planning this for more than a month. Diogo agrees, Bishop agrees, Emery agrees. I should have the baby here in our apartment." I speak slowly so he understands every word. "Now please, go get Bishop and bring him to me. He should be at the clinic, but you can radio ahead."

"He's not at the clinic," Stryker answers quickly. "He went to Old Tucson to help with the injured. That receptionist of his let everyone know where he went and that the Doc forgot his radio. Safest place for you to be is at the clinic, where at least the Dee woman has some experience with this sort of thing. We can bring you back here if the Doc is found."

I stare up at him in dismay. We had a plan. The plan was solid. Everyone knows the plan. To suddenly be told my birth plan isn't going to work plunges me into a pit of uncertainty. I've managed to keep myself from being scared of the birthing process by clinging to the idea that our plan would make me as comfortable as possible. I'd be surrounded by medical expertise and loved ones, while staying in my home.

"Okay..." I say slowly, taking a deep breath to calm myself down. "Can you please go get Diogo then? My husband can make the decision whether I go or stay."

Stryker eyes me for a moment and then gives a sharp nod. He lifts his radio and says, "Stryker to Warlord."

We wait several seconds but the only answer he gets is static.

"Please try again," I insist, attempting to keep the note of desperation from my voice. I don't want to have this baby without Diogo. I don't want to have it without the Doctor. How is it that the two I trusted most with my delivery have disappeared at the same time? I'm beginning to feel cursed with all the bad luck I've been having over the past year.

He tries to radio for Diogo again, and then for good measure, the Doctor. I can tell by the look on his face that mine is starting to reflect the panic I'm feeling inside. Now what do I do?

He hooks his radio on his belt and slowly, as though reaching toward a wild animal, puts his hand on my shoulder. His massive paw covers the whole thing as he gently squeezes me. "It'll be okay, girl. I'm not new to this sort of thing. Wife had a baby before she was... well, I know what I'm doing anyway. This part takes the longest. How far apart are your contractions?"

I shake my head, my arms wrapped protectively around my belly, my lips turned down. "I don't know!"

"You need to calm down and think. This is important, Taran. How many minutes are there between the contractions and how painful are they?"

I force myself to breathe through the panic and think. Stryker's right, I'm not doing myself any favours by freaking out. I think about the answer to his question. "Uh... I think they're about eight to ten minutes apart now. And there's no pain, just a lot of pressure. Like a band around my stomach."

"Good girl, you're doing real good here," he says, still in that calm voice like I'm some kind of frightened bird.

I narrow my eyes at him. "Okay, we've established I'm not about to give birth out here in the hall in the next few minutes. What next?"

He thinks about it for a moment. "We go to the clinic. I

think you should at least have Dee nearby until Bishop shows up." I open my mouth to protest, to remind him of the at-home birth plan, but he anticipates me. "If the Doc gives the okay we can bring you back here. No harm done."

I heave a sigh and lean back against the wall. Honestly, I'm too exhausted to fight him. And having Dee with me until I can have the Doctor is a comforting thought. "Okay, let's go to the clinic." I eye him up and down. "You're going to have to carry me down the stairs since the Warlord has decided we need to inhabit the eighteenth floor and the elevator lift hasn't been installed yet."

He frowns down at me. "You think I'm too old to carry a little thing like you? Even with that little bird in your stomach you'll feel like a feather."

I roll my eyes at his posturing and hold my arms out as he scoops me up. It feels bizarre to be in anyone's arms except Diogo's. Since we moved in, I either don't leave the apartment or Diogo takes me out and acts like some kind of mama bear every minute I'm out of the new Tower. It's sweet, and maybe a little stifling. Although, since my stomach has become so large, I've grown to enjoy his fussing. He rubs my back and feet, makes food for me and takes me up to the roof to see the new greenhouse he's building. All this while still rebuilding Sanctuary. I couldn't have asked for a more attentive partner.

"Do you have a car?" I ask worriedly.

"Course." I don't know if he's trying to be reassuring or if I offended him. Cars are status no matter where you live. Inside Sanctuary and out. I imagine they're probably important commodities elsewhere in the world too. They represent the ability to travel quickly. Only the elite have them. If someone of a lower class has one, it's either stolen or about to be stolen, because cars are worth killing over. It's why stealing a car from the military or the elite carries a death penalty.

Diogo mentioned that I should learn how to drive so I'm not left helpless if anything happens, like another fire. I just looked at him like he had a second head and shook my head. I've never driven a car and I have no desire to learn. They are fast moving death machines. I'd be crazy to want anything to do with them except the convenience of an occasional ride.

When we reach the sidewalk, Stryker carefully places me on my feet and opens my door. As I climb in, another, more intense contraction strikes. I grip my belly and moan. When it passes, I look up at him and what I see nearly drives me back into the building and the safety of my cozy apartment all set up for the birth of this baby. His face, his eyes, hold a crazy kind of glee, as though he's just barely containing his excitement.

Before I can comment, snap at him to back off and give me some space, the expression disappears into his usual grim stoicism. He steps back and closes the door once I'm in. Suddenly I yearn intensely for all the things I need in this moment and don't have; my husband, my doctor, my friend turned mother figure, the nursery. As we pull away from the curb, I can't help but feel as though I'm making a big mistake in going with Stryker.

Her face flashes with fear, but it doesn't matter. It's too late. I have her and I have the baby. Mine now. I saved her life, saved her baby, by snatching her out of the sky as she fell through the flames of a burning building. Her life belongs to me, both of theirs do.

Until that moment I'd thought her painfully useless, hadn't wanted anything to do with the Desert Wren. She was a nuisance at best and a dangerous distraction to our Warlord at worst. Her philosophies, her convictions and her actions are all hopelessly naive. I had thought that the best thing that could happen to our city, to our Commander, would be for her to die quietly.

But then she'd come to me, landed in my arms. I'd cushioned her as we fell to the pavement, taking her weight against mine. She'd passed out as I held her, looking down into her face, smeared with dirt and ash. She'd taken on a beauty I hadn't recognized before. Her hair, almost the same shade of auburn as my wife's. Her small body with the delicate bone structure and bird-like features, so much like Abrielle.

As I held her, cradled her and protected her with my life, I realized that I was being given a second chance to atone for losing my family. Through Taran, through the baby, I will find *her* again. I will do a better job of protecting them this time.

I will finally find the peace I have spent decades searching for, and I will find it in the haven of this woman and our child.

TARAN

It doesn't take me long to realize that Stryker isn't taking me to the clinic. I sit up straighter and look around when we clear a checkpoint and head into Sector Seven, a sector with more abandoned buildings than any of the others, with a wide swath of it skirting the wall.

"Where are we?" I ask sharply, still looking around, trying to familiarize myself with the area. As the Desert Wren I've been all over the city, climbing buildings and walls for fun and for work. Often refugees would hide out from the city forces in these more remote sectors.

At first Stryker doesn't answer, just focuses on the road and driving around the piles of garbage that build up in the lesser used areas of the city.

"Answer me," I snap, glaring across the car at him. "This isn't the way to Bishop's clinic. In fact, we're driving in the opposite direction."

Finally, he looks at me, his blue eyes shining with manic energy. I recoil back into my seat. The usual sarcastic grumpy Stryker has transformed into something twisted, frightening. I shake my head, hoping it's my imagination.

"Please, Stryker, I need Doctor Bishop. Let's go back."

"You don't need that old fraud," he growls, refocusing on the road. "You just need me, you've only ever needed me. You didn't see it, but you will."

"I don't know what you mean. But this is important, Stryker, I can't have the baby out here with just the two of us. Please take me back," I beg, trying to keep calm. His voice sounds different, almost unhinged. Terror starts to settle in a ball in the pit of my stomach. I've been through too much not to recognize an imminent threat.

He slams his fist into the steering wheel, causing me to jump. I grip the door handle so hard my knuckles turn white. "You do know what I mean! You were always so stubborn, wanting to be independent, do things for yourself. But you got hurt. Now it's my turn to take care of you, make sure nothing else happens."

Of course I'm independent! Anyone living in this post-apocalyptic nightmare knows that a person has to be independent and capable of caring for themselves. We all have to contribute to the greater good. Somehow, I don't think this is what Stryker means though. I'm starting to think he might not even be talking about me.

"Who was too independent, Stryker?" I ask quietly, though I suspect I know.

He confirms my belief when he answers, "My wife, Abrielle. Her stubborn need to take care of herself, take care of the baby, got her killed."

"I'm so sorry," I say calmly, hoping I'm making headway into whatever crisis he's working through.

"She didn't have to die," he snarls, but the despair is easily picked out.

I take a deep breath as another contraction squeezes me, this one strong and steady. They still aren't painful, but they're coming closer together. I don't want to give birth anywhere near Stryker on a good day, let alone when he's this unstable. I need to keep him talking, find out where his head is at.

"You did everything you could for her," I try to reassure him, though the contraction is still gripping me. I take quick, shallow breaths until it eases up. "But whatever we're doing now isn't right. I'm not your wife, Stryker. You don't have to save me. My husband will come and protect me when we get to the clinic. You're doing your duty just by taking me there."

I hold my breath. Did I say too much? He seems to be mulling over my words. Stryker can be hot-tempered, but he's usually reasonable enough.

Then he shakes his head. "No, he wouldn't have let you fall from a burning building if he'd been doing his job. He failed, showed his weakness when he let himself sleep through the takeover of his city. I had to catch you, save your life, protect you. I've had to watch you ever since that day, while he was incapacitated. And now, while he cares more about this godforsaken city than his pregnant woman."

I want to cry out in defence of my husband, but Stryker has become too unpredictable. I don't want him to focus his ire on me. At least for now he seems to want to protect me. I need to leverage that feeling, get him to listen.

"We don't have to involve Diogo then, but you know the clinic is the safest place to be right now. Let's go there and we'll sort everything out after." I lie to him, fully aware the moment I can tell my husband what's going on I will.

"No," he says simply.

I try to think of what I can possibly say to convince him. "Is this what she would've wanted? Would Abrielle have wanted you to take another woman away from her family?"

He slams on the brakes, sending me into the dash. He catches me before I hit and shoves me back into the seat. He twists around and leans over until his face is right in front of mine. I lean away from him, regretting that I set him off.

"My wife," he spits out, "didn't know what she wanted. Her bad decision led to the death of our baby. I won't let that happen again."

But I'm not her! I want to scream it, leap from the car and run away. I wouldn't make it two steps before he caught me and god knows what he'll do if I push him over the edge. I close my eyes against his words. They don't make sense. Something's happened to Stryker, something in his brain has shifted and he seems to be losing his grip on reality.

He resumes our trip and drives us right into the bowels of one of the most abandoned parts of Sanctuary. Despair beats at me as he takes me further and further from any hope of rescue. Diogo won't know where to find me once I'm reported missing. If anything goes wrong with the birth before I'm able to get to the doctor... I can't even think about it. Bishop assured me my pregnancy is textbook, despite my small size and narrow hips. He thinks I should be able to have a vaginal birth.

A few minutes later Stryker pulls the vehicle up to the entrance of an old house. At first glance it looks as dilapidated and abandoned as the rest of this part of the sector, but when I take a closer look I see signs of inhabitation. The never-ending encroachment of nature has been cut away from the front door and windows, and a path has been cleared from the road to the house.

"Where are we?" I ask hesitantly.

"Home," he says succinctly, and climbs out of the car.

He slams his door shut and rounds the car to my side. I hurriedly slam my hand over the lock button, but, as with so many mechanical objects, the locks are broken. Stryker sees my move and his brows lower in annoyance. He jerks my door open, grips me by the upper arm and pulls me from the car.

As I'm forced to straighten quickly a painful spasm hits me, first in my womb and then radiating outward. I cry out and bend over, my arms wrapped around my middle. Before I can straighten, I feel the warm trickle of my water breaking and leaking out onto my thighs. I'm wearing a loose cotton dress, far more comfortable against my sensitive skin than form fitting pants and T-shirts.

I lift frightened eyes to Stryker, a plea on my lips. The psychotic glee in his eyes stops my words. There's no reaching him now. He's gone too far. Diogo will kill him for simply crossing into another sector with me without permission. That he seems to have planned this abduction is enough to send Diogo into a blind rage when he finds out. A thought tickles my brain. This whole scenario feels weirdly planned out. How did Stryker happen to be my keeper at the moment I went into labour?

"How did you kn-know I would have the baby today? How did you get Diogo to reassign Grayson?"

"Didn't know the baby was coming today but knew it would be soon. Convinced the Warlord that Grayson was needed somewhere else. Kid has a very specific skill set, a mechanical genius. I told Diogo his ability to fix broken shit was needed on the wall lift. Without that lift my men can't patrol the wall properly and the likelihood of Primitives getting in becomes higher." He frowns in annoyance. "It still took some convincing, think maybe he doesn't trust me to watch over you the same as that kid."

I'm shocked by the level of Stryker's cunning and how well thought out his plan is. He's using Grayson and Diogo to get them out of my space, leaving me alone with Stryker for the inevitable birth. I'm not surprised Diogo didn't fully trust Stryker, I've been complaining about him for weeks, showing my displeasure at his presence. Unfortunately, I should have been more vocal in my complaints. Trusted my instincts and insisted that Stryker no longer be left as my only guard.

I shudder as he bends to pick me up, holding me against his chest as he kicks the door of his car shut. The tip of his long grey-blond beard brushes my face and I turn my head away. He carries me up to the door of the house and easily shifts me in his arms to open it. We're immediately assailed by the dank musty air of a place that feels abandoned.

Looking around I realize it's not abandoned though, just uncared for. A thick layer of dust has settled over everything in the home. A sofa, an old broken TV, the screen smashed out, a bookshelf with rotting books on it. I gag as we pass the kitchen. It's clearly been used, but the dishes and pots are piled everywhere, crusted with food that hasn't been washed away.

He continues down a long hall, bypassing an empty room with a master bed that looks comfortable enough. The dust has been cleared away from it. That room is definitely used by someone. He walks into the room at the far end of the hall.

I gasp as he sets me on my feet, a hand at my back to steady me.

"Prepared this room myself, just for you and the baby. I think she'll be happy in here, don't you?"

My mouth hangs open as the reality of my situation sinks in. I'm trapped in a house with a man who is clearly having some kind of mental break.

In front of me is the perfect, lovely and utterly creepy

room for a baby girl. It has been lovingly prepared and cared for. Not a speck of dust touches any of the shelves, the gorgeous handmade crib that occupies the centre of the room, or the wooden change table in the corner. Cloth diapers sit neatly folded on the shelves beneath the table. Unable to help myself, I reach out and touch a fingertip to the crib. Tiny animals have been crafted into the head of the crib. A hand knit pink blanket covers a mattress that looks new.

In the far corner of the room is a small, single bed, less beautiful than the rest of the room with its dull grey blanket and single white pillow, but still tidy and dust free. I suspect that bed is where Stryker means for me to give birth.

Another contraction hits me and I double over as the breath is forced from my lungs. Stryker hovers beside me and I tip my head back to look at him. His face is bordering on ecstasy, as though his dream is coming true in the form of the birth of my child.

I'm in very big fucking trouble and I have no one to rely on but myself.

SIXTEEN

DIOGO

"You're a cold-blooded asshole," Skye snaps in frustration.

I want to tell her that yes, I am a cold-blooded asshole, that her confirming that status won't change my mind on the waves of refugees filling Old Tucson. We've been negotiating on the timeline for integrating old Tucson into Sanctuary, and how to handle the refugees while they wait for our plan to unfold. She objects to the terms I've laid out for accepting some of her precious refugees into Sanctuary. Thinks 200 out of 10,000 is a weak number. She's not wrong, but then 200 lives is not zero lives. Those 200 people will thank their new Warlord while the rest will be left to fend for themselves for the next several months until we're able to take them in.

I remind myself that I'm here to negotiate with the self-appointed unofficial leader of the refugee camp. She is as self-righteous and annoying as the Desert Wren had been before I neutralized her and made her my wife. This thought calms my urge to rescind the offer and walk away. Skye is as passionately optimistic as her sister.

"200 lives, final offer," I tell her, steel running through my voice. "Choose carefully. We have a decent clinic, food supplies and shelter. Send only those that are most in need, but not your elderly or sick. Your choices must be able to contribute."

She struggles to accept my words, her gaze fixed past me on the door at the back of the tent as she contemplates her answer. I'd ordered it clear except for her and her man. Wolfe stands at her back next to her sitting form like a rock statue, solid and unmoving. He doesn't once submit an opinion. Not even a silent one by way of a glance or a facial expression. This man is a complete enigma. Part of me admires him, the other part wants to kill him so I can preemptively take out a potential threat before it materializes.

"Alright," she sighs in defeat, her shoulders slumping a little. "I will make the decision tonight on who to send. If I can have them ready, will you take them tomorrow?"

"Yes," I agree.

It's sooner than I'd planned, but Milla, backed by Emery and several of the city's elite women, has thrown herself into preparing for an influx of refugees. I suspect she's using the project to alleviate some of her guilt and grief over Jorje's death. She's being carefully watched by city police in case she holds a grudge against the Warlord and his family, but so far her motives seem pure.

"What about supplies?" Skye asks, straightening a little, her piercing grey eyes on mine. "We need blankets, medicine, food and clean water. And ammunition, as much as you can give us."

"I can arrange for some of everything except medicine. We're struggling to cover our basic medical needs within the city without giving away our supplies."

She nods decisively and stands. "Good enough."

I stand with her, somewhat amused that she seems to be the one dismissing me, rather than the other way around. Though I'm not convinced yet, I'm starting to soften toward the idea that a woman might be able to survive as Warlord. If anyone could do it, it would be this woman with her fierce shadow protecting her back. Of course, she couldn't take a position of such power anywhere near my city.

"Thank you for meeting with me." She holds out her hand and I shake it, squeezing her slender fingers.

Wolfe finally lifts his gaze, his dead stare clashing with mine. I drop Skye's hand and step away from her. His eye fixes on the wall once more and he goes back to ignoring us. He acts as though he could as easily kill me as look at me. Apparently slaughtering Primitives at my side hasn't softened him toward a new Warlord.

"When can I see Taran?" Skye asks eagerly as she walks with me to the door of the tent. "Is the baby here yet?"

I'm surprised it wasn't her first question. Then, Skye is a woman who can prioritize her needs. While she wants to know about Taran's health and the status of her new niece or nephew, she needs to deal with the immediate problem of what to do with thousands of starving refugees being constantly attacked by Primitives. Now that our negotiations are out of the way, she feels able to ask the burning question she's been wanting to ask from the moment I arrived.

"There is no baby yet. Taran seems to be going to full term as her doctor has predicted. Though she would love to have a visit from you. I can guarantee safe passage into and out of Sanctuary if you agree to come see her. We both understand your desire to remain with the refugees until they are safely integrated into Sanctuary. I will deliver you back inside your camp after you see her."

She mulls over my request, trying to decide if she trusts me enough to take me up on my offer. She's not wrong to worry. In this instance, I'm not above lying to get what I want, especially when it comes to the health and happiness of my wife. If Taran wanted it, I would feel no qualms about tricking Skye into Sanctuary and then forcing her to stay. Luckily for Skye, Taran is sympathetic and supportive of her need to defend the people of Old Tucson.

"Maybe you aren't as much of a cold-blooded asshole as I thought," she says, a small smile curving her mouth, relieving some of the exhaustion etching her features. "I think I will take you up on your offer. Tomorrow, I'll cross the gates with the 200 refugees. I will visit with Taran and accept a ride back before dark."

"I'll be coming too." Wolfe speaks for the first time. Once again, I'm struck by the man. He doesn't give a shit about the waves of poor, sick and terrified refugees. He has no thirst for power, if he did, he would remain and solidify his position. He cares only for Skye, and she seems blind to his regard.

She throws a glare over her shoulder at him, but his gaze remains fixed on the wall. "You will stay here and help on the line," she orders him.

His gaze meets mine once more, his one intense green eye speaking his piece for him. I know what he's going to say before he says it. "Where she goes, I go."

I nod my head, interrupting the angry tirade about to fly from Skye's mouth. "A car will be waiting for you at the gates, it will take you to Taran at the new Tower and after you've had a chance to catch up, it'll bring you back." I glance at Wolfe and add, "Both of you."

I turn and stride away leaving the woman to argue with her self-proclaimed bodyguard. I'm not interested in their drama. My own wife brings enough of that to the table for me. With a broad grin I get back into my car and head toward the gates of Sanctuary, eager to see Taran and hold her against me, reassure myself that she's real, alive, and unharmed.

I don't make it up to the apartment, don't get to see my wife, happy and healthy, bustling around our new home preparing for the baby. Instead, I'm greeted by a frantic Emery as she comes flying down the stairs toward me her face creased with worry.

"Diogo!" she yells, relief on her face as she catches sight of me.

I reach out to steady her when she stops abruptly. "What is it? Taran?"

"She's not up there, and neither is Stryker," she says worriedly. "I can't tell why she left and she was supposed to have the baby at home, so if she went into labour then where is she? We need to radio the clinic and see if she's there."

I lift the radio before the words are even out of her mouth. I have a bad feeling about this. Anyone who is on guard duty for Taran knows that they radio in her every move. There is absolutely no reason that I shouldn't know where my wife is. I pull Emery into the hallway of the floor we're standing on, the ninth. The radios get interference in the stairwell from the thick concrete.

"Fuentes to Doctor Bishop."

It takes seconds for him to respond. "Bishop here."

"Is my wife with you?" I demand immediately. "Is she alright?"

The only thing I can think of is that Taran went into labour or something happened to her that necessitated Stryker leaving the apartment with her in such a hurry that he couldn't radio in. But that scenario doesn't make sense, as he should've radioed the moment he got her someplace safe.

"I'm sorry, Commander, I haven't seen your wife. I've been here at the clinic all day. I was going to stop by your place in a few hours to check on Mrs. Fuentes." Bishop's voice holds concern. The two have become quite close in the past few months.

"Remain at the clinic in case she shows up."

"Of course," he replies. "Please let me know when you've found her."

I put the radio back on my belt and thrust a frustrated hand through my hair. Where the fuck is my wife? I look at Emery who's chewing on her lip, a look of suspicious concern on her face.

"Tell me what you're thinking," I demand.

She doesn't hesitate. "Stryker."

I nod. My thoughts were headed that way too.

"He hovers over her constantly, like a mother hen or something. I've often gotten the feeling he wouldn't let any of us near her if he could get away with it. He's been acting so strange, but not dangerous enough to worry."

"And yet we both suspect he's done something with her," I say, angry guilt making my words hard. "Obviously we did have something to worry about if we're both thinking the same thing."

She nods miserably. "Taran was uncomfortable with him always following her about, and so was I. I should never have left her alone with him."

I sigh heavily and touch her shoulder. "I was well aware of her feelings toward Stryker, yet still I insisted she stay with him. I should've listened to her, posted him somewhere else, kept a watch on him. This is my fault."

Emery gives me a grim but commiserating look. "You've had your hands full, Warlord. Watching after a man you trust isn't something you should've been worrying about."

She's not wrong. Bringing the city back under control and fighting with the forces outside the city has occupied my every waking moment. "It doesn't matter, we can sort out what went wrong when we find Taran."

I head out the door and hesitate on the landing. Maybe there's something in the apartment that can lead me to her location. But if I go back up there, I might be wasting precious time better spent searching. As if reading my mind, Emery shakes her head, grips my elbow and gives me a light push toward the stairs going down.

"There's nothing there but some half-washed clothes and a cold tea kettle on the stovetop. The apartment is empty. I tried the roof too, but it didn't look like anyone had been up there today."

I take her advice and start down the steps, taking them two at a time and leaving Emery to catch up or fall behind. To her credit she manages to keep pace, despite having to run to keep up.

"If she is with him, then I think we can assume that Stryker won't hurt her, at least not yet," Emery says as we descend. "He's been quick to anger with her if she does something he perceives as harmful to the baby, but he was never violent."

Her words echo the same ones Taran spoke to me weeks ago, and with a sinking feeling I realize that they are both wrong. Stryker is a very dangerous man, no matter who he is with. I trusted him with Taran because I thought he was in his right mind. However, if he's taken her to some undisclosed location without my express permission, then he's clearly having some kind of mental break. Which means there is a very big possibility he poses a danger to my wife and unborn child.

I grunt my acknowledgement of Emery's words but don't respond. She doesn't need to hear my doubts. She's a smart woman, if she can help me find Taran then we may be able to get to her before any harm falls on her or the baby.

The moment we're clear of the building I get on the radio and mobilize everyone I can, sending them out in a city-wide search for my wife.

I think long and hard about escape, frantically coming up with new plans and then discarding each one as too dangerous, too complicated or too likely to fail. I think about climbing out a window and then hiding out somewhere. I even try to pry the window open, but I'm stopped when a contraction hits and doubles me over. The cramping is even worse with the added physical strain of trying to find a way out.

Even if I somehow manage to escape the house, I would be walking so slow it wouldn't be long before Stryker discovers me gone and comes after me. I ponder the idea of incapacitating or even killing Stryker. The thought is a disturbing one and I'm forced to ask myself if I have what it takes to kill. I killed a zombie when it was attacking me in the church, but it happened so fast that I didn't have time to do anything but react.

My stomach twists in protest as I remember the way the gun felt as it went off, kicking in my hands and punching a gory hole through my attacker. No, I can't do that to Stryker, not unless my situation becomes truly desperate. Not unless he threatens the life of my child.

My only other option is to get him talking, see if I can convince him to take me back to my husband or the doctor. Instead of searching him out I wait for him in the bedroom. He seems to be doing rounds of the house, inside and outside. Securing the area. I'm not sure from what. Primitives? My husband? He should be afraid of Diogo. Once Diogo realizes I'm gone he'll scour every inch of this city. There won't be anywhere Stryker can hide. It's just a matter of time.

Time I don't have. My hand drifts down to my stomach. I need to relax, I can already tell that the stress of the situation isn't helping. My labour pains are erratic and becoming more painful with each one. I'm concerned that there doesn't seem to be a regular pattern. Sometimes eight minutes apart and sometimes only two or three. I hadn't discussed this with Bishop, have no idea if it's normal, but I'm worried that it means my rising blood pressure is affecting the birth.

I force myself to take deep breaths, in through the nose, out through the mouth, counting each second. Just the way Bishop and Dee showed me.

"What are you doing?"

I raise my head from where I'm standing next to the window, my shoulders hunched and one arm wrapped around my middle as I wait out another contraction. One hand rests on the window sill next the board I've managed to pry open. Stryker is standing in the doorway looking at me suspiciously. He's a smart man, he'll know all of my potential escape options even better than me since he's had more time to plan this out.

"I just needed some fresh air," I tell him and move away from the open window to sit on the bed.

He nods thoughtfully, his eyes lingering on the window before they fall to me. "Need anything else?" he asks.

I'm surprised by the question, that my kidnapper actually cares about my comfort, but the truth is, Stryker is confusing me with his wife, a woman he loved deeply. He wouldn't want her to suffer. In that, Diogo is much the same. Even when he's being his most brutal Warlord self he still makes sure I'm as happy and as comfortable as he can make me.

I'm tempted to tell Stryker that yes, there is something I need, my freedom, my husband, my doctor, but instead decide to take a more diplomatic approach. Things aren't desperate yet, there's no point in antagonizing a potentially unstable man.

"I could use a glass of water please," I tell him.

He gives me another long look before silently leaving the room. When he returns I accept the glass and drink thirstily. It tastes fresh enough, which means he must've brought it in recently. I'm struck again by the preparation that went into this place, this whole situation.

"You've been sending Grayson out on more tasks lately so you can keep an eye on me, haven't you?" I ask the question in a neutral tone of voice so I don't accidentally upset him.

He nods his head and leans back against the crib, arms crossed over his chest, facing me. "Though he works for the Warlord, he also works under me. I'm a Commander on the wall. It wasn't too difficult to send him to the wall while I took over as your bodyguard."

I'd known there was a hierarchy in Diogo's military, but I

hadn't realized Stryker was so near the top. It makes sense. He spends a lot of time around my husband and helps make decisions. Especially once Jorje Cruz was executed. This is two of Diogo's top men that've proven themselves to be untrustworthy, to have separate agendas from their Warlord. After this, I won't be surprised if Diogo becomes far more suspicious of his top people. A shame, because Grayson and Bossman are good men.

Stryker might still be a good man. He's not threatening me and despite his actions against the Warlord and his family, his reasoning isn't bad, just flawed. If I can keep him talking, perhaps lure him into realizing that we both need help, I may be able to convince him to contact Diogo or the Doctor. It's hard to tell how far into a mental break he's gone.

"Do you really think I'm your wife?" I ask him softly, cringing back into the bed a little as he straightens. Maybe I shouldn't have asked him that, but I'm straightforward, blunt. I say what I'm thinking. I don't know how to either play along with or resist his delusion.

"You aren't Abrielle," he says gruffly. "But you need saving just as much as she did."

"But why, Stryker?" I ask him. "My husband takes care of me, he keeps me safe. I'd rather be with him right now. I appreciate what you're trying to do, but it's not necessary."

"Your husband," he says scathingly. "So arrogant, so sure he can bring this city back into order, thinks he can deal with the outside threats and protect his wife at the same time. Well, he's wrong." The words are so emphatic, so sure, that I realize he's talking from personal experience.

"Where are you from?" I ask him gently.

"San Antonio."

I nod sympathetically. "San Antonio fell to the Primitives after the flu epidemic."

"Yes," he agrees. "We were in the city until the end. I was so fucking confident back then, sure I could take care of my city, my Warlord and my wife. I was wrong. Just like Diogo is wrong."

"Tell me about it," I invite him, keeping my voice low and soft, encouraging him to reminisce about the past. Maybe it'll help him see the present more clearly. "Tell me about your wife."

His eyes take on a sharp look as he gazes at me. I sense I'm skating a dangerous edge. What if he realizes I'm definitely not his wife, nor am I his second chance at saving her? What if he leaves me here to give birth alone? Or what if he just kills me, gets rid of the evidence and walks away. I have to hope that neither is an option for this broken man.

Just when I think he won't answer, he starts speaking. "She was beautiful, but more of a quiet beauty than obvious. Like when she smiled, her intelligence, love, hope, it all shone through. Kind of like you."

Despite the situation I'm flattered by his comparison. I've never dwelled on my looks, there was too much else going on around me. But like every woman, I've had moments where I wonder if I could be prettier, more delicate, more desirable.

"She sounds wonderful," I murmur.

"She was," he agrees. "She was also stubborn as a mule and refused to listen to anyone if she thought she was right. When the flu came to San Antonio, I begged her to leave with me. She was pregnant and vulnerable. But she dug her heels in, insisted she wanted to have the baby in her hometown, near her family."

"I can understand that," I say a little drily. I'd also planned on having my baby near the only family I know: Diogo, Emery and Bishop. My sister too, if I could've gotten her into the city in time. A shaft of pain slices through my heart as I think about Skye on the other side of the wall with the other refugees. Diogo had been trying to get her into the city for tomorrow morning. Tears prick my eyes when I realize that if she agreed to come, and I was still at home, she would get to see her brand-new niece or nephew. Now, well, now I don't know. Don't know where I'll be or if my baby is going to be okay...

Stryker doesn't notice my sudden distraction, he keeps talking. "Most of her family fell to the flu. Took out three quarters of the city until our defences went down."

Same story as Las Vegas Sanctuary and a few dozen others. Flu ravaged the regions, taking out humans and leaving the Primitives to pick off the rest. Of course, knowing this, I know exactly where his story is going next.

"After her parents died, along with her siblings and their families, she went into early labour. Had the baby in our apartment while I was out on the wall. Didn't even radio for help, just gave birth right there in our bed."

He sounds both admiring and frustrated. The more he talks about Abrielle, the more I feel a kinship for the woman. She also found herself pregnant and about to give birth while under extremely difficult circumstances. She was probably terrified but did the best she could with what she had.

His voice takes on a strange faraway quality as he continues. "I was terrified that either she or the baby would get that flu. I wouldn't let her leave the house. Cleaned every part of my body and clothes when I came home from wall patrol. I was so fucking careful, but it made no difference."

"There's nothing you could do," I say quietly. He doesn't hear though, he's lost in the past. His fingers clench around the wooden bars of the cradle as memory assails him.

"We were overrun while I was on the wall. I fought harder than I've ever fought in my life, my single goal to reach Abrielle, pack her and the baby up and escape the city. I wasn't far from her position, but I just couldn't get back to her. Every time I killed one of those fuckers, another ten leapt into place. By the time I made it back to her it was too late."

A wave of sympathy rushes over me as I listen to his story, as I watch the creases in his face deepen with grief and guilt.

"There's nothing you could've done," I say again. Maybe if he hears it enough he'll finally be able to let go of the guilt that has been riding him since Abrielle's death.

He shakes his head, his voice hoarse now. "The baby... the baby... she was only a few weeks old, she was... they..."

Nausea wells up and another contraction squeezes me. "I know," I choke out. He doesn't need to explain what happened. Babies are vulnerable. They're too fragile, too soft. The skin just... I shudder at the thought of dead babies.

I breathe through the contraction and nausea, asking, "Abrielle was bitten?"

He nods and drops his chin to his chest as he remembers. "She was covered in blood, crumpled on the floor, surrounded by zombies when I arrived. Thought she was dead, but she was in the middle of the Turn. I fought them with everything I had, cut them down as a group, determined to follow her into the grave if I found her dead."

The contraction passes and I relax back against the wall. "She wasn't dead though, was she?"

"No," he agrees. "She was just coming out of the Turn when I reached 'er. I wrapped my arms around her, tilted her head back to look at 'er, but she was already gone. Eyes wild, nails turned to claws. She launched herself at me, tried to tear my throat out. I pushed her away, but I couldn't... I just couldn't."

He couldn't kill her. Of course he couldn't. I don't think I'd have it in me to kill someone I loved either, even if I knew it's what they would have wanted.

Silence falls between us as he remembers and I'm left with yet another horrific story of the lives and loves lost to the Death Kiss.

"Should've finished her," he finally says.

I shake my head. "You did everything you could, Stryker. You have to trust yourself."

He looks up at me, his eyes glowing with the ghosts of his past. "I don't trust anyone, but this time'll be different. This time nothing will happen to you or the baby. I'll make sure of it."

"Stryker..." If I'm going to reason with him it has to be now. The contractions are too close together. If I'm going to get out of here, have the baby someplace safe, it has to be now.

He takes a step toward the bed and reaches out. I flinch back, but all he does is touch his fingertips to my forehead and brush my hair to the side. "I'll do for you what I couldn't do for her, for my Abrielle."

My heart breaks for him as he turns and strides away.

NINETEEN

DIOGO

"Commander, we've temporarily shut down all sector checkpoints and the main gate. We've deployed people throughout Sanctuary with orders to watch for Mrs. Fuentes, Stryker and Stryker's vehicle. I'm confident someone'll report their position soon." Bossman follows me out to my car, giving me the rundown on the search for Taran.

I don't know how long she's been missing, I don't know if she's safe or in danger. I can't imagine Stryker would do anything to hurt her, but I don't know his reason for moving my wife without permission. He can't be in his right mind. He has to know that his actions today have essentially signed his death warrant.

"I should've seen this coming," I mutter my frustration as I open the door to my jeep. I'd tried remaining in one place, in my office at HQ, but the inaction was killing me. I can't remain sitting while my wife and unborn child are missing.

"If you don't mind my saying, you're only one man, Commander."

I look at Bossman, lost in my own thoughts for a moment. Then I clue into the meaning behind what he's saying. He's right, I am only one man. I can't keep one hand on the city and one on my wife. I'd tried to protect her, tried to give her around the clock protection detail when I wasn't available. I trusted the people around me. I trusted Stryker with Taran's life. He never gave me a reason to doubt him. This is on Stryker.

"Thank you," I say to Bossman, climbing into the vehicle and slamming the door shut in his surprised face. I smile grimly. Thanking one of my men for putting things into perspective isn't something I normally do. Taran is changing me, changing the way I look at things.

Before Taran, I was a good leader, strong and capable. I held the city with an iron fist because it was what I knew, it was how I kept stability. Now she is teaching me to rule with fairness, with an open mind. We don't always see eye to eye, but she makes me think long and hard about my decisions. Make me question my assumptions and look at things from different angles.

I don't just need Taran, all of Sanctuary needs her too.

TWENTY

TARAN

I bite down on my lip so hard that a sudden burst of blood hits my tongue as I try to keep myself from crying out. I breathe heavily through the pain, trying to do as Bishop told me, taking air in through my nose and then steadily breathing out through my mouth. Concentrating on my breathing, on getting through each contraction is distracting me. It's hard to concentrate on the problem at hand; Stryker's intentions.

It's clear he plans on keeping me here until the baby is born. But then what next? Is it me he wants or the baby? Or both?

I'm laying on the bed he'd prepared for me, in the corner of the baby's room. I want nothing to do with this creepy, weird scenario but I'm about to give birth, I can't exactly be picky at the moment. There'll be time later to mourn the loss of my home birth plan, with my husband at my side and our doctor attending. For now, all I care about is that me and the baby survive whatever Stryker has planned.

I really, really don't want to have to get Stryker's attention. After leaving me in the bedroom, he went out into the main part of the house "to tidy up" before the arrival of the baby. He mumbled some kind of apology for the abysmal shape of the rest of the house. Said he's lived the life of a bachelor for too long.

Still, I have no choice but to call out to him. My contractions are only a few minutes apart and I'm starting to get the urge to push. "S-Stryker?" I call out tentatively. When he doesn't answer I call louder.

Seconds later he's standing in the doorway. I squeeze my eyes shut for a moment, trying to centre my thoughts. I have about two minutes to get organized before the next contraction hits.

"Stryker, I need your help," I tell him, though it costs me to ask this man for anything.

"Of course, Abrielle, anything," he drops onto his knee next to the bed and takes my hand in his.

I stare at him in shock. I knew he was mixing real life with delusions, but if he actually thinks I'm his dead wife, we're talking a whole other level of risk. He's already unpredictable without some kind of fantasy guiding his actions. I can fight twisted logic, I can't fight full on delusions.

"The baby is coming soon," I tell him hurriedly, trying to get the words out fast as the muscles around my womb start to clench once more. "We have to get ready."

The pressure hits followed closely by pain. This time I don't bother hiding the pain, I shout in agony reaching out to grip a fistful of bedding. Stryker takes my hand and holds it while the pain goes on and on. Finally, it releases, and I'm left sweating, shaking, gasping for air. I yank my hand from his, unable to stand his touch.

He frowns and reaches for me. "I'll take care of you, don't shrink away from me." His voice is a demand and I flinch.

I don't know the best course of action here. Do I play into his delusions, pretend I'm his wife? What happens if he snaps out of this brain fog and realizes I've been playing him. What if he attacks me while I'm too weak to defend myself? But if I don't play along, is he even more dangerous? Will he kill me for the crime of not being his beloved wife?

I want to sob at this impossible situation, but I don't have time. I have to keep my shit together. When I'm back safe in Diogo's arms, then I can fall apart, then I can cry at the injustice of a world that takes away everything from everyone, sending a tough man like Stryker into a delusional spiral. I can cry about the constant waves of misfortune that happen to me and my family time and again. To every family. But for now, I have to deal with this or risk losing the one thing I can't lose, my baby.

"Stryker... honey." I take a risk and try sounding like a devoted wife. I wait a beat for his reaction. I'm relieved when his face lights up in happiness. "I need you to get me some things. Quickly now."

"Anything, baby, anything for you." I nearly gag at being called baby. That's what Diogo calls me. Stryker just ruined the endearment for me.

I force a strained smile to my lips. "We need more blankets or towels, fresh sheets, hot water."

He climbs to his feet, leans over and kisses my head, his dirty blond beard brushing my skin. I shudder and close my eyes, trying to banish his image. I just want him to go away so I can deal with the next contraction on my own.

"I'll be back as soon as I have the stuff," he assures me and heads for the door.

"Stryker!" I call out before he can leave. He turns and looks back at me. "A knife, we need a sharp knife."

He frowns, his eyes growing sharper and I hold my

breath waiting for him to snap out of his delusion and realize where we are. Best case scenario, he changes his mind and takes me to Bishop and then Diogo. Worst case, he kills me and hides the evidence of his crime.

Before he can ask, I say, "We have to cut the umbilical cord."

He nods, his eyes refocusing with the same manic energy. "Of course."

Once he's gone, I do the incredibly difficult task of lifting my dress to pull my underwear off. Agony grips me with each move I make. Thoughts are bursting through my brain at lightening speed. Questions, answers, worries. I feel nearly as off balance as Stryker. Is this really happening? Is it possible that I'm about to have my baby in a creepy little room inside of a hovel?

And how do I go about doing that? I don't want Stryker to touch me, but I don't think I can give birth alone. I'm going to have to swallow my disgust and allow him to put his hands on me, in places I would never allow anyone but my husband and my doctor to touch.

"Fuck!" I shriek as another contraction seizes unexpectedly fast and hard. The urge to bear down is almost impossible to ignore.

As Stryker comes flying through the door to check on me, I yell at him, "Get the stuff, Stryker! Wash your hands with soap, this baby is coming right fucking now!"

"Remember this room, Abri? You remember how much we loved picking out the little animals for Lilly?"

Stryker is sitting next to me on the bed, pointing out various aspects of the room he's created for the baby. I realize he's built an exact replica of his dead baby's room. If I weren't so utterly creeped out I might be more sympathetic. But, right in this moment, I'm not. If this birth doesn't happen seamlessly, both me and the baby could die right here in this horrible little room.

"Tell... tell me about her?" I ask through gasps, my arms banding my middle as it contracts.

The contractions are so close together that one is nearly indistinguishable from the next. I try to mitigate the terror by telling myself everything is going textbook the way Bishop assured me it would. I'm healthy, I'm strong and everything seems normal.

Stryker frowns down at me. "You want to know about Abrielle or Lilly?" he demands, his sharp eyes refocusing again. Shit. I keep trying to say the right thing but talking to him is like trying to avoid land mines. Yet, when I don't talk to him, he gets agitated.

"Tell me about our baby," I gasp, gritting my teeth through another wave. My hips are on fire and unbearable pressure is attacking my entire lower body, threatening to tear me right apart. "Please, Stryker, tell me about Lilly."

He grins suddenly and stands, pacing away from me. He runs a hand over the fine woodwork of the crib, touching his fingers through the animals carved into the headboard.

"She loves her mama," he says, his mind firmly entrenched in the past, his gaze far away. I lean painfully over, reaching down the side of the bed. I saw Stryker put a butcher knife on the floor next to the bed. I feel around for it as he talks, ignoring the tightening in my groin as the waves keep hitting. "Whenever she saw Abrielle she would light up and wiggle with happiness."

I touch the edge of the blade and feel my way carefully down the knife, reaching for the handle. Every muscle in my body feels terribly strained as I reach, but I can't stop now. I have to have a way to protect myself and the baby if Stryker snaps.

"What else does she like?" I ask softly, straightening and shoving the knife under the pillow next to me. Stryker found several house items from scavenging through this house and the ones surrounding it. He admitted that he found most of the baby stuff from other places, but he built the crib himself. I breathe through the dizziness swamping me as I straighten my body.

"She smiles and sometimes she laughs. Abi thinks she has gas, but I can tell when my little girl is looking at her daddy and smiling."

"That's beautiful," I murmur, settling my back against

the pillows and pulling my legs up. "Stryker, honey, it's time for me to push now. I need you."

I'm not lying, either about thinking his story is beautiful, or that I need him. Finally, as the birth of my child approaches a wave of peace settles over me. There's nothing I can do now. I'm not an expert in psychology, I don't know what Stryker needs from me, and right now, I can't think about it. I have one task to concentrate on and that's where every last ounce of energy needs to be focused.

He runs his hand over my head, and I close my eyes, picturing the face of my husband. Of Diogo's broad hand running over me, soothing and calming me.

Stryker positions himself between my knees, pushing the skirt of my dress back. Tears of pain and terror leak from my eyes as I push.

"I can see the head, baby, keep pushing!"

I grunt, grip fistfuls of blanket and bear down, pushing with all my effort. My heart is racing and my face feels hot, each push makes me feel dizzier and dizzier. I haven't eaten yet today, haven't had enough water. What if something goes wrong? What if I hemorrhage? Oh god, I can't think about it.

The pain is unbearable. My screams rip through the room as I feel something tear in my vagina. I'm sobbing now, while Stryker remains concentrated, one hand on the inside of my thigh while the other guides the baby. I pull myself up on my hands at the same time as giving one last huge push. A godawful, painful tearing sensation grips me, then something sliding from my body. Wetness soaking the bed beneath me.

I'm dizzy and sobbing. I've never experienced anything so painful in my life. I don't know if I'm okay. My thighs are wet, the bed, the blankets, everything. Water, blood, after-birth? I don't know.

I reach for my baby, now cradled in Stryker's massive hands. He has stolen this moment from me, from Diogo. I feel a powerful dislike for this man as I reach out and snap, "Give me the baby!"

He's frowning down at the infant. It's not crying and I'm gripped by panic as I fear something is wrong. Why isn't it crying? Aren't newborns supposed to cry?

"Stryker!" I yell, terrified.

He looks at me, his eyes wild and unfocused and deep frown penetrating between his brows. "It's a boy."

Then I realize the arms and legs are moving. He's alive. My baby is alive.

"Give him to me." I'm crying in earnest now, elated, frightened, horrified.

"It's a boy," he says again. "Lilly... she was a girl."

I realize what's wrong, why Stryker is just sitting, holding the baby, not moving. He's crashing back into reality, realizing that I am not his wife and this is not his baby. Despite the painful gripping sensation in my middle, I lunge for him, snatching the baby. I try to be careful as I grab my son, but he's slippery and nearly falls as I pull him to my chest. Stryker lets him go. Just sits staring at us, then around at the blood and gore from the birth.

"What have I done?" he whispers.

I swallow hard. This is what I was both afraid of and hopeful for.

"You helped me give birth," I tell him, reaching slowly under the pillow next to me and gripping the knife. The one I'd told him was meant for the umbilical cord. He seems to have forgotten about it. I slide it out cautiously while holding my tiny son against the now soaked front of my dress.

He shakes his big grizzled head. "No... he won't see it that way. I'm finished." His voice is filled with despair and tears glitter in his crystal-clear blue eyes.

I look down at my baby for the first time, terrified of what I'll see. But he's perfect. Tiny, red, his face screwed up as though he wants to cry but can't. I realize I need to clear his mouth. Maybe he has some mucus or something in there. But I'm afraid to move, afraid to draw Stryker's focus.

Stryker stands abruptly and reaches down to touch me, his fingers moving the sweaty hair from my forehead. His eyes are sharp and intense, his delusional world having vanished for now. I shake, staring up at him open-mouthed. He can do so much damage if he wants. I've never in my life been this vulnerable.

He slides his hand down my shoulder toward my wrist. I realize he's reaching for the knife and I swing it out, intent on threatening him to get him to step away from me and the baby. But he doesn't try to take it away from me. Instead he leans over me and brings my hand up with the knife in it.

"No!" I yell, my voice already hoarse from screaming during the birth. I flinch expecting to feel the bite of the blade as he kills me.

He holds it still between us, inches from my son's face. His eyes are intent on me and for the first time I see a completely different emotion in them. Pity. He pities me. "He doesn't deserve you," Stryker growls. "He doesn't know how to love you the way you need to be loved."

"Stop this," I sob. "You don't have to do this, Stryker."

"I do, I need to be with Abi and Lilly now," he says and then points the blade at his own chest and thrusts.

I scream again and try to jump away as blood gushes

from the wound. He's too strong though, even wounded, his grip is unbreakable. His expression doesn't change. He watches my face as the light slowly fades from his eyes.

"Taran," he gasps my name.

"Stryker," I sob, my mind spinning. I wanted to be free of him, but I didn't want this. I didn't want more death. He was confused, living a different reality. He didn't deserve this.

"You're in love with a monster." His words are slow and slurred, it takes me a moment to understand what he's saying. "A... a murderer. He k-killed your husband."

My mind whirls as I try to follow, finally landing on who he could possibly mean. "Xavier? Do you mean Xavier?"

"Yes."

"But Xavier died in the desert," I protest, but Stryker is already shaking his head.

"Died in the jail, stabbed through the heart. Same as me," he chuckles at himself, then he looks at me, his eyes penetrating mine. "I cleaned up the body myself. Diogo... got rid of him. Didn't want... a... martyr."

With the last word he slides from the bed, his hand finally releasing mine, the knife sticking out of his chest. I stare at him as his eyes fade and the lines of his face smooth out. Dead.

As Stryker takes his final breath my son lets out his first cry.

TWENTY-TWO

OFFICER GILLERT

It's been hours since we got the call to search for the missing Mrs. Fuentes. I've been assigned one of the most deserted sections of the city, Sector Seven. It's close to the wall and far from the city resources so many of the buildings were left abandoned as people moved into the slums and closer to city centre.

It's unlikely the Desert Wren would've made her way over here. She's a busy-body, has her hot little hands in everyone's business, from refugees, to the illegals, to the city elite. She's probably holed up with a new man somewhere in the slums. It doesn't hurt me none to imagine what the Commander will do to her once he finds her.

I've been told she might be in the presence of Stryker. Now he's a man that deserves a little respect. Not because I actually respect the guy, but because he'll rip a person's head off and shit in the neck hole as soon as talk to them. I've steered clear of that guy as much as possible. When he comes into the police station, I'll usually head out on patrol.

Now, if the little urchin turned Warlord's wife took off with Stryker, that'll be an interesting predicament. Between

Fuentes and Stryker, I don't know who I'd lay money on. Both men are deadly, both accurate and both power-thirsty.

Not me. No, I'm mister status quo. I'd rather live a comfortable life flying well below the radar. It's why I picked up a job as city police. The job is interesting, not very dangerous since the Warlord keeps a tight city. I get to exert my own brand of power and then go home and forget about work after a long day. Even this search for the Warlord's wife, a good time waster in my opinion. It took him years to get his hands on her in the first place, if he can't keep her nailed down she'll disappear and never come back.

I'm about to radio into HQ that the search of Sector Seven is a bust when something catches my eye. A car. Vehicles are rare enough as it is but seeing a road-worthy one in a nearly deserted place like this is definitely unusual. I get out of my own police issued cruiser, a car I share with a few other guys on the force, and walk around the other vehicle.

"Fuck me." This car definitely belongs to Stryker. The mismatched scavenged parts had been painted a bright cherry red except the hood, which is a dull black. The paint is chipped and rusted out, but the car is still recognizable.

I hadn't actually thought I'd find the pair, am not prepared for any kind of fight. Stryker can kill me six ways to Sunday before I could get off a single shot, and even glancing at the Warlord's wife is risking life and limb. This is not how I saw my day going.

I unhook my radio from my belt and lift it slowly, hesitating. I could just walk away and pretend I didn't see a thing. It'll be far safer for my health if I don't confront Stryker without backup. Then again, if anyone finds out they're out here and I was the one assigned to this sector, it could mean more than my job.

Maybe they won't ask me to go in?

"Officer Gillert to Commander Fuentes."

It takes seconds for an answer to come back. I haven't talked directly to the Warlord since he brought his Desert Wren in for police processing over a year ago. His voice still gives me the chills.

"Fuentes here, report," he demands.

"I was told you were looking for Mrs. Fuentes," I say hurriedly.

"Do you have her?" he barks.

"No, sir, but I have Lieutenant Stryker's car. It's sitting outside of a property that could contain your wife."

Seconds pass, then, "What Sector?"

"Seven, Commander."

"Fuck, I'm on the other side of the city." Another moment passes in silence, then the words I dread hearing, "Listen to me carefully, Gillert, because if you fuck this up, I'll have your balls and then your head."

"Yes, sir."

"I want you to go into the property and search for Taran. You will go in with your weapon drawn. Stryker is a dangerous man, you don't want to go in unarmed. If he's threatening then you shoot to kill. Don't wound him, that'll just piss him off."

That's what I'm afraid of.

"Be careful, Gillert. Find my wife. Make sure she's safe."

I swallow and lift the radio, "Yes, Commander."

"Report back the second you find out what's going on in there."

"Yes, Commander."

"Fuentes out."

I should've volunteered for another section of the city.

Hell. I should've volunteered to man the wall. Right now, the thought of taking out a Primitive horde seems easier than taking on Stryker by myself.

I draw my weapon and approach the house cautiously. Like many of the homes in Tucson Sanctuary, it's bungalow style with a front entrance that opens into a living room and kitchen area with the bedrooms toward the back of the house. The door is unlocked and opens easily under my hand. I'm sweating profusely now and have to pass a sleeve over my forehead before I can continue.

If I survive this, I think I'll retire and do something less dangerous, like wall construction, or waste removal. Anything other than police work. Anything other than dealing with the Warlord's hellion bride. She's not worth the trouble.

I pass into the front room, sweeping it at a quick glance, my weapon out in front of me. I put my back to the wall and glance quickly around the kitchen. Clear. The entire house is weirdly silent. Dust has settled over almost every inch, though there is still evidence of recent occupation. Dishes piled up, the trail of a fingerprint through the dust, and a man's coat laid out across one of the chairs. Someone's here. No one leaves behind clothes, not when they're still useful. Good quality items are hard to find.

I want to call out, ask if anyone is there. Human nature to see if an answer comes. But police training tells me to keep my mouth shut. Don't give away my position.

I make my way slowly down the hall, back to the wall, glancing into each room as I pass. The master bedroom catches my eye. The blanket has been pushed back as though someone sleeps here. I go in, give it a quick look around. Hasn't been occupied in a few days, but this house is definitely not abandoned.

The hairs on the back of my neck prickle and I swing around, lifting my gun. An apparition stands in the doorway, blocking the hall. Beautiful, pale, ghostly, long red hair tangled down her back and a bloody gown clinging to her legs and stomach. My mouth goes dry and my hand shakes.

Her eyes are dull and the hollows beneath give her a stark appearance. But the strangest thing about her is the bundle held tight to her chest where her dress is pulled down and her breast exposed, the nipple pressed to the tiny mouth sucking greedily.

Slowly I lower my weapon, my eyes still wide and mouth hanging open. Totally lost for words I just stare at her as she looks me up and down and then gives me a pointed look that gives her opinion loud and clear. She definitely remembers me as the man who arrested her during the food riots.

"Gillert," she sighs.

I continue to stare for a moment, and then finally manage to blurt out. "Stryker?"

"Dead," she says matter-of-fact, then walks toward me. My hand twitches on the gun, but she just passes by, stumbling toward the bed. She eases in, the baby still clutched tight to her breast. When she settles she looks at me. "Well don't just stand there like you've seen a ghost, please get the Warlord on the radio."

TWENTY-THREE

TARAN

I'm sitting calmly on the bed, holding the baby to my chest when Diogo bursts in. The relief that crosses Gillert's face is almost laughable. I suppose it's rather poetic that my old police nemesis is the one to find me, to call Diogo. Gillert was the one to arrest me during the food riots, he was the one to process me when Diogo arrested the Desert Wren. Now, he is the one to help reunite me with my husband.

"Taran!" Diogo kneels on the floor next to the bed. He reaches for me but pulls back when he sees the bundle in my arms.

As angry as I am with my husband, as betrayed and hurt, I will still always cherish the look on his face as I reveal our son to him for the first time. Gently I move the blanket away from his face so Diogo can see him. The tiny red face screws up in annoyance as the cool air touches his cheek. He turns his face back toward my breast.

"A boy," I murmur.

"A boy," Diogo repeats my words, his own voice holding the awe I'd felt when I first saw our child too.

"Do you want to hold him?"

Diogo doesn't move, the stunned look on his face telling me he's processing slower than normal. I shift my body slowly, painfully aware of my need for medical attention. I'm bleeding, I'm torn and I'm weak. But this moment is more important.

I slowly move the bundle away from my chest, though it pains me to do so. Every cell in my body wants to snatch the baby back when he turns his face toward me, seeking the warm comfort of his mama. "Hold your arms out," I instruct Diogo. When he doesn't move, I say his name louder and nudge him with my foot.

Slowly he reaches out, sliding his arms along mine and taking hold of his son. As he takes the baby my heart skips a beat. I want him to love the baby, I want the baby to recognize him. But I'm also angrier than I've ever been at Diogo. I want to scream at him, cry and demand an explanation.

Why did you kill my ex-husband? Why did you murder Xavier? Why didn't you tell me?

A hollow ache fills my chest as I hold in the questions. There'll be time for that later. All the time in the world for accusations and apologies. Now is for us. To reunite, to meet our son, to bond as a family.

Diogo holds the baby against his chest, cuddling him close, his eyes glued to the tiny wrinkled face. His big hand slides up, his long fingers engulfing the tiny head as he cups it. My throat aches as I hold the tears in. Tears of terror, loss and anger, yes, but also tears of happiness and relief. We're okay; me and the baby.

"We need to name him," I whisper, and Diogo nods without looking up.

We'd talked before about what to name our baby but we didn't get far in the conversation. We'd been too busy saving Sanctuary, rebuilding our home and dealing with the nuclear power plant situation. Now that we know the sex of our baby, now that we're finally meeting him, it's time to give him a name.

"What was your father's name?" I ask curiously. Maybe Diogo had a connection with his family that he wants to carry on.

"Hernando," he replies shortly. "And my grandfather was Francisco, all of us named after famous Spanish conquistadors."

I swallow, imagining the expectation of generations of men living up to their names. I don't want my son's future decided for him. What if he doesn't want to be a conqueror, or a Warlord, or anything else too big to imagine? Before I can voice my doubts, Diogo puts an end to any possible debate on the subject of naming our child along the lines of his family tradition.

"No, we won't be naming him after any Spanish conquistadors. Not with the Desert Wren as his mother." Diogo looks up at me, his eyes warm with love and appreciation. Again my heart skips in confusion, anger and love warring for supremacy. My husband killed my ex-husband and lied about it. He lied to me when he said he never would. But he also loves me more than his own life. More than the lives of others.

"No conquistadors then," I agree shakily.

He continues to touch his son, to run his finger over the tiny brow, cheeks, lips and chin. His finger lingers over the ever so slight crease in the baby's chin, the exact same as Diogo has.

"You had a brother?" Diogo asks.

The tears I've been holding in start to flow as I realize what Diogo is saying. I blink rapidly but they continue to fall, wetting my cheeks. "Yes," I choke out. "He was a child when he died of the flu. He was amazing, so brave and adventurous, but also kind. Always helping around the house. Cheerful to the end." A moment of silence passes as I sniff back my tears. We both stare down at the baby. "His name was Blaze."

"Earth, fire and air."

"Yes." I smile as he connects our names: Taran, Blaze and Skye. "My father was quite poetic. He wanted his children's names to mean something. Our planet is still here, still going strong, despite the damage humans have done to it. Our names are a reminder that the planet will survive, even if we don't. Elements are forever."

Diogo nods. I wonder if the names are too poetic, too unsubstantial for the name of a Warlord's son. But then he surprises me by saying, "Your father sounds like an intelligent man."

"Yes, he was. The child of farmers, he was simple in the way he lived, but complex in his thoughts."

"Blaze is a good name," Diogo says decisively. "Strong, representative of a new generation. One that will be stronger than previous generations."

Blaze.

We look down at our son as he settles against Diogo, his eyes shut tight, his mouth set in a little rosebud, a tiny puckered frown between his minuscule brows. His black hair is short and fuzzy, dry now and standing on end where the blanket has moved back away from his head. He's stolen my heart and I'm pretty sure he's stealing Diogo's with each new breath he takes.

This child is our loving burden, the thing we must now protect with everything in us. He is our tears, fears and future happiness. I feel something shift within me. A different purpose has fired deep inside. I created this being, he belongs to me and I will do everything in my power to raise a man worthy of my brother's name.

After several moments in silence, Diogo finally looks at me. "Stryker is dead."

He's not asking. He must've found out from Gillert.

"Yes," I respond.

"How?"

Pain blossoms with the memory of the knife buried deep in Stryker's chest. A man I hadn't known well, despite our close proximity to each other for so many months. He was complicated, he was gruff and rude, but he was also a loving husband. Right to the very end.

He died of a broken heart.

"He stabbed himself."

"I'm so fucking sorry I left you alone with him." The pain and self-blame is evident in Diogo's voice.

I want to tell him it's not his fault but the words stick, the same words I'd said to Stryker over and over while he described how his wife and daughter had died. Maybe it is Diogo's fault, maybe we're all to blame. We hold ourselves together physically in a world that constantly beats us up. But what about our mental health? We don't talk about it, we just keep going. We ignore the problem because each passing day is reserved for survival. It's time to look at people as individuals that require more than just the basic physical needs met.

I don't say anything to Diogo. There's nothing that can be said right now. Stryker is gone. Even if he was still alive, I'd have to convince Diogo to spare his life, to get him treatment. Not something my husband would consider. Kidnapping the wife of the Warlord is a death sentence.

Bishop arrives moments later, his face creasing into a relieved grin when he spots the baby. Diogo is reluctant to give Blaze up to the other man but must realize he doesn't have a choice. Making sure our child is in good health is the top priority. Bishop sets him on the bed next to me and gently unwraps him like he's made out of the most precious glass.

He goes over the baby from head to toe, examining every inch, counting fingers and toes, looking in his mouth, eyes and ears. Finally, as the baby wakes up and begins to fuss, Bishop bundles him back up and hands him to me announcing, "Perfect, simply perfect. Well done, Taran."

I grin at Bishop, completely agreeing with his assessment. I did create a perfect baby.

"And what about his mother?" Bishop asks seriously, his eyes drifting down the front of my body. I'm covered by my bloody dress and the blanket. "How are you doing?"

I smile wanly. "There was some tearing when he was coming out, and now a trickle of blood."

"The placenta?" Bishop asks the question matter-of-fact, but I still blush, still hesitate to speak about such an intimate thing. Especially around Diogo, my ultra-masculine husband.

I shake my head, indicating it hadn't come out yet.

Bishop nods. "We'll get you back home right away, take care of the afterbirth and get you stitched right up. I imagine you're feeling pretty uncomfortable."

I let out a sigh of relief at his words. I am extremely uncomfortable, my entire vaginal area is on fire and the perineal tear stings like a motherfucker. The worst is that I'm going to have to pee soon and I'm terrified of doing that in my current state.

"Thank you," I say with heartfelt gusto. I'm so ready to leave this horror show of a house.

"I'll carry you," Diogo says, standing to his full height.

As he bends over to scoop me up, I hold out a hand, stopping him. "Don't touch me," I say calmly, moving back against the headboard. "I can walk."

I push him and he moves back away from the bed. Of course, he wouldn't move if he wasn't prepared to move. Maybe surprise at my words forces him back. I clutch Blaze to me as I slowly, gingerly slide off the bed and get to my feet. Bishop takes my arm as I sway for a moment. Then I look at him and nod, prepared to walk out and never come back.

"'Taran," Diogo says from behind me.

I turn to look at him.

The question is in his eyes, he doesn't understand why I've suddenly become so cold. Doesn't understand that now that he's met his son, named his son and seen to his family's safety that I'm through with pretending. He betrayed my trust. He kept a secret from me.

"You killed Xavier," I say simply and turn to walk out.

Before I make it two steps out of the bedroom, Diogo is behind me, scooping me into his arms, holding me with the baby in between us. I glare up at him. "I don't want you to touch me."

He stares back, his eyes blazing emotion and anger of his own. "Fuck that," he says simply and strides out with me in his arms.

"Talk to me, baby."

I'm damn near ready to get down on my knees and beg. It's been two weeks since I found Taran in that Sector Seven hovel. Two weeks since she's spoken to me. I'd taken her straight home where Doc Bishop did a full exam, stitched her up and examined the baby. She'd refused to look at me, refused to speak to me, refused to acknowledge my existence after our initial meeting.

She knows about Xavier, knows that I killed her ex-husband. I'm not sorry I did it, and if I could go back and make the choice again, I would make the same one. Xavier Gunther was a traitor to his city, he needed to die, and I needed him to do it quietly. But this is not a choice my wife can understand, not one she will ever be in the position to have to make, so I can understand her feelings. To an extent. But this cold war our marriage has turned into must end. I want my wife back.

I've tried talked to her about Gunther's death, explaining myself, giving her the opportunity to clear the air. No amount of explaining, apologizing or demanding can get her to budge on the issue. She is pissed off and not talking to me.

I now inhabit a home with a silent wife who has made it abundantly clear that she would move out if I let her. Of course, I won't. She belongs to me forever. Even if that means we spend the rest of our marriage never speaking to each other. At this point, I would welcome her vitriol, would enjoy her words of hatred and accusation if she would just open up and speak to me. Somehow she knows though that her words, any words, will be cherished. And so she gives me what she knows I hate, nothing. Not even an acknowledgement that I've spoken.

I've gotten so used to her silent condemnation that I'm almost shocked into silence myself when she whirls around from where she's standing in the baby room next to the cradle, her arms wrapped protectively around our son. "Don't ever call me baby!"

I raise a brow and hold a hand up. "I've always called you that, you didn't mind before."

She turns back to the crib, giving me her back. "Well, I mind now."

Her words seem to indicate dismissal, but this is the first time she's spoken to me in weeks. I'm not willing to let the topic go if it keeps her talking. I stalk toward her and turn her around to face me, a hand on her shoulder. Mindful of our son, I gentle my touch and my voice.

"Explain it to me."

She glares up at me, allowing me to see the fire in those grey steely depths. My patience is ebbing. I want to shake her, force her back to the way things were. We've never been given the opportunity to be a happy family, not with a city at war, but we found a deep and abiding love in each other. And though it's my action against Gunther causing the rift, I need her to find a way past it, a way to be happy with me. Because there is no other option. Happy, miserable, angry, sad, she's mine no matter what.

She blinks a few times and then pointedly looks at my hand on her arm, silently telling me to remove it. My fingers flex involuntarily and once more I am forced to shove my anger into a deeper, darker place. I will not treat my wife the way instinct is driving me to treat her. I've been taught to respond to reticence in a prisoner with aggressive, brutal tactics. I remind myself that Taran is not my prisoner, even if she acts like one.

When she realizes I have no intention of moving away until she speaks, she grits her teeth, baring them at me a little before saying, "Stryker called me baby before he died. I can't stomach the word now." Her voice wobbles a little on the last few words and I realize she's serious.

I'm frustrated all over again by Taran's silent treatment over the past weeks. I should've known this detail, should know all the details. If she won't talk to me, then how can I possibly understand the depth of damage Stryker did to her when he took her? If he hadn't died there, in that dingy little house where Taran was forced to give birth to Blaze, I would resurrect him and kill him all over again. I would make Gunther's death look like child's play in my quest for vengeance against the man that took and terrorized my wife, forced her to give birth to our child without the comfort of family and home nearby.

Not only did he take my wife, but he put her through hell. He terrorized her in a new way, one that will leave lasting scars on her psyche. I long to gather her against my chest, to run my hand down her smooth red hair and reassure her that I will scare away all of the ghosts. That I'll never let a bad thing happen to her again.

Of course, not only would she reject my assurances, but we would both know I would be lying. It's impossible to promise a future in such an unstable world. But Taran and Blaze give me reason to work harder than ever to ensure stability. To at least work toward giving them the world they deserve.

With that thought in mind I do what I do every day when Taran refuses to speak to me, to open up, I dig deep for patience. She's healing, both physically and mentally. As much as I'd like to, I can't force her to open up to me.

I sit in the rocking chair and I watch her. I watch the way the sunlight filters through the glass windows and casts shadows across her beautiful face, caressing each perfect feature. Her freckles stand out against her pale skin, across the tops of her cheeks and sprinkled over her nose. Her lips, the bottom slightly fuller than the top, curve in a partial smile she reserves specially for Blaze. A smile that she can't hold back, like a glow that bursts forth every time she looks down at him.

Her brow wrinkles a tiny bit telling me that as much as she wishes me gone, she's aware of my presence. We will always be this way with each other. There is too much chemistry, too much passion for her to ignore me entirely. This fact gives me hope. Because eventually I will lose patience, I will force her to accept me back in her life. There is no alternative. And she may end up hating me even more than she does now.

"We took in another 200 refugees this morning." I give her my daily update on the state of our Sanctuary. She may not be speaking but she's certainly listening. "Your sister is one hell of a negotiator. She's managed to weasel more out of me than anyone else ever has. Of course, she looks and sounds like you, so I'm more inclined to give her what she wants. Maybe she knows and that's why she pushes."

Taran doesn't say anything, but she inclines her head toward me, her subtle message that she's listening to my words. I've blocked access to her sister, another thing for her to be angry about. Skye is a born leader and has the potential to even further destabilize my marriage and if she puts her mind to it, my city. If she decides my wife isn't being treated fairly, she will become a thorn in my side. Work to get her sister out from under my care. I haven't told Skye the full truth of Taran's ordeal, partially because Taran hasn't told me herself, and because I don't need Skye breaking down the gates to my Sanctuary to get at her younger sister. She's enough of a handful on her own when she isn't pissed off. I suspect if she decides to go up against me, challenge my leadership, I'll have to put some real effort into keeping her in her place. Not something I want to do. Not right now, not with Taran's only surviving kin.

"She's getting impatient though, she wants to see you," I tell her, watching carefully for a reaction. "All you have to do is say the word."

My Taran has grown more stubborn than ever. We're deadlocked over the issue of her sister. I thought I could use Skye as a bargaining chip to get Taran to speak to me again, but she's proven herself more stubborn than that. As much as she wants to see Skye, she's angrier at me, not willing to give even an inch.

She sends me a small glare to reiterate her stubborn stance on the subject of her sister. I decide to move on.

"Within the city we're negotiating with any non-residents that were living here before the influx. They'll be given the opportunity to swear allegiance and apply for citizenship through the proper channels." Taran nods a little, telling me she's listening carefully. The fate of our Sanctuary's refugees are a topic near and dear to her heart. She spent years as the Desert Wren, a rebel hell-bent on saving the lives of everyone that asked for sanctuary, whether they were granted official documentation or not. "I feel bound to give Sanctuary to those actually living within the city first, before I offer it to the others coming in from the fallen Sanctuaries."

She comes to stand beside me, Blaze cradled securely in her arms. She stares at me pointedly until I move. I almost laugh out loud at her audacity, but keep it in. She's such a tiny little combatant. Her fiery anger would be almost cute if it weren't directed so firmly at me. If her anger weren't impacting the first weeks of our son's life.

As soon as I stand, she sits, taking the rocking chair I'd just warmed for her. She pulls the top of her shirt to the side, one of my collared shirts, and bares her nipple. Blaze hungrily sets about his supper as we watch him together. I share his hunger but for a much different reason. Her breasts are fuller now, begging for my touch. I long to worship my wife, explore the new curves that come with motherhood and kiss each new mark, memorizing her all over again.

When it became clear that Taran wasn't going to give an inch on her anger, I'd had no recourse but to go to the Doctor and make sure both she and Blaze were doing well. Bishop assures me that both mother and child are not only doing well, but exceeding expectations. Blaze has almost doubled in size in just a few short weeks. Taran has had her stitches out and is healing very well, all things considered. According to Bishop, the physical trauma she'd suffered after being taken by Stryker was normal for a woman who gave birth, and Taran was healing particularly well.

Perhaps it's my relief at her current condition that has made me more willing to give her leeway in her anger.

I watch my wife feed our son for a few minutes before I continue speaking. "The third greenhouse is finished and supplies are being shifted so we can get the planting done right away. Of course, pumping in water from the dam is another issue we'll have to deal with."

She looks up at me and opens her mouth, a comment on the efficiency of pumping water on her lips. I think she's almost ready to start talking again, but instead she shrugs and lapses back into silence. It doesn't seem to matter how big the issue, whether she has a solution or not, she refuses to talk to me. Every day my frustration grows. It's just a matter of time before it finally blows.

A sharp knock interrupts my thoughts. We both look up as Grayson opens the door and steps into the baby's room. His gaze immediately clocks his surroundings and the safety of his charges, lingering on Blaze. Everyone who meets this baby seems to develop a soft spot, including Taran's big immovable bodyguard.

"Your appointment is in twenty minutes." He directs the comment to Taran, giving me only a cursory nod. My wife's pique seems to have extended to her personal bodyguard, a somewhat amusing development. The only thing saving Grayson from a real ass chewing and a lesson in hierarchy is his utter devotion to Taran and Blaze.

"What appointment?" I demand.

Taran ignores me, leaving Grayson to answer the question.

"Bishop wants to see the baby," Grayson finally answers, his eyes on the wall behind Taran. He might have to speak to me because I'm his superior officer, but his real loyalty is becoming abundantly clear.

I frown. "I thought he saw the Doctor a few days ago."

Grayson becomes visibly uncomfortable. He shrugs and looks toward Taran for help. She stands and reaches for her bag containing everything Blaze needs while she's away from the apartment. "I'm ready," she says softly.

I growl and step in front of her, blocking her path to the door. Cool grey eyes meet mine and she cocks a brow, daring me to stop her.

"Explain," I demand.

She looks past my shoulder and nods at Grayson, as if giving him permission to speak. My man, my soldier. And my petite stubborn wife is giving him permission to speak to his superior officer. Real, unamused anger now beats at me.

As she steps away from me and pointedly stares at a wall, Grayson answers the question. "Blood testing."

Comprehension hits me like a brick to the head. Blaze is old enough that his blood can be drawn. Immunity to the Death Kiss can be determined and Taran decided to go ahead with the testing without even speaking to me. Pain and anger wars within me. She just took our cold war to another level.

I look down at her with hard eyes, and then take her arm, pulling her from the room as carefully as I can, aware of our son cradled in her arms. "I'll take them," I say to Grayson as we pass him. "You can provide backup."

TWENTY-FIVE
TARAN

We drive to Bishop's office together in the jeep, neither of us speaking. Diogo drives ridiculously slow, to the point that I almost think he wants me to break my vow of silence and berate him into driving faster so we can actually get to the appointment on time. But he's not trying to get to me, he's taking extreme caution with Blaze's safety. Our son is cradled in my arms as we drive and could be easily hurt if Diogo were to hit something. Though he'd scoured the city for child safety seats, he'd come up empty-handed. So few people drive, that there's just no reason to keep them around.

When we finally arrive, I reach for the door, eager to get inside, but Diogo says, "Don't move." His voice is hard and implacable. I can feel him reaching the end of his patience with me. Actually I'm pretty impressed with his patience so far. Or I would be if I wasn't so furiously angry at him.

I could've handled it if he'd had Xavier executed through the proper channels. I wouldn't have been happy, I would've tried to argue Diogo out of doing it. I'd have been angry, but ultimately I would have understood. Xavier was planning a coup, he was leading the rebels into extreme behaviour that put the entire city at risk.

No, I'm angry that my husband lied to me, especially after telling me many times that he does not lie. He told me Xavier died in the desert. For weeks after he told me about Xavier's death, for months even, I'd had nightmares about Xavier's violent murder at the hands of the Primitives. Nightmares about predators picking away at his flesh until he was nothing but a pile of bones. No, forgiving Diogo for that lie feels impossible. I've come to the conclusion that I'd much rather a brutal dictator for a husband than a deceitful, back-stabbing liar.

He opens the door for me and takes my hand as I stand with Blaze. I pull my hand away as quick as I can and step away from the car, away from Diogo. His anger beats at me, like a wave of heat. Well two can play that game, I turn and glare back at him. He takes my arm in a tight hold and pulls me up the steps to the clinic.

When we enter, we're immediately greeted by Dee, who jumps up from behind her desk and rushes around with her arms held out. I laugh and give her what she wants; Blaze. She's made it abundantly clear that her number one priority is always going to be the baby if there's one in her vicinity. She holds him against her chest and coos at him.

"Who's a good little baby Warlord!" She grins down at Blaze and rocks him in her arms, dancing from one foot to the other. Diogo stares at her like she's grown an extra head and I'm hard-pressed not to giggle at the whole scene.

Dee looks up at me with a smile. "Follow me."

I walk with her into the back offices, ignoring Diogo who trails behind. This is his first doctor's appointment since the baby was born. He's usually working hard at this time of day, ensuring a safe and stable Sanctuary. Despite my annoyance over his whopping lie, I can't blame him for trying to create a better city for our child.

We pass by Christian, the historian, on our way to the back office. He looks up and nods guardedly when he catches sight of the Warlord. I smile sunnily and pat his shoulder on my way by. From what I've seen in my visits to the doctor, he's thawed considerably, unable to hold up a coolly professional distance with the friendly Doctor Bishop. Now, he seems to enjoy his work and enjoy his time spent in the small clinic.

Bishop looks up as we enter his domain and gives me a genuinely warm smile. He stands carefully, his joints stiff with age and fatigue. I worry about how thin he stretches himself, between catering to the elites, making contacts within the slums and attending to the refugees in Old Tucson. He's not a young man, he shouldn't be working as hard as he does.

Bishop pulls me in for a quick hug and a kiss on the cheek. He smiles broadly past me and greets Diogo. "Ah, Commander, it's good to see you. Your son is quite a strong little man, you should be proud of his progress."

Again, I almost laugh out loud as I feel Diogo's discomfort. A practical man, he probably doesn't see how he should be proud of an infant not yet able to lift its own head. Instead of pointing this out though, he says, "I'm proud of my wife. She gave birth to a strong son and she nurtures him so that he will grow stronger with each day."

Tears flood my eyes at the praise. Diogo is not one to hand out compliments, and when he does, they mean something. He is genuinely proud of me for carrying, birthing and caring for his son. I want to thank him and to return the favour and tell him that Blaze wouldn't be here if it weren't for Diogo's dogged determination to keep us both safe. But I stop short of speaking to him. He doesn't value human life, only mine, and now Blaze's. His attitude is unfair and dangerous.

Ignoring Diogo I smile at the Doctor. "He's doing so well now. He's sleeping more than I thought he would at this point, so I've been able to grab a little more sleep myself. He eats regularly but goes right back to sleep after. He doesn't cry a lot and isn't very fussy."

"You haven't been sleeping?" Diogo demands darkly.

I stare pointedly at the Doctor, ignoring Diogo, and continue speaking as if he weren't in the room. "He watches my face and he's making more sounds now, besides crying. He gurgles and coos. His lips twitch too, so I don't think it'll be long before he's smiling at me."

Bishop grins back. "It'll be a few weeks yet before he's ready to smile on his own." Bishop takes Blaze from Dee's arms and lays him on the exam table. "He's a strong little guy though, I don't doubt he'll be ahead of the curve."

Diogo grabs my arm before I can step toward the exam table. "You haven't been sleeping?"

I'd requested a bed put in the baby's room after the birth. In part to escape having to share a bed with Diogo, but also because it's just easier to be close when Blaze needs me. Newborns need to eat a lot, and they need to eat often. Though a good, fairly quiet baby, Blaze is no exception to the rule. During these past few weeks I've been on a regular rotation of waking every few hours to feed and change my new little man. Diogo wouldn't know because he's been in his own room, sleeping soundly and waking early to attend to his Warlord duties. Perhaps if I was still speaking to him I might've told him about nights with a baby.

I ignore the question and try to shake his hand from my arm to join Bishop at the exam table. Finally, fed up, Diogo growls, "Tell me, Taran, and don't think to leave out any details."

I stare up at him keeping my gaze frigid. I hate the idea of keeping even a moment of his son's life from him, but I won't budge on this issue. My Warlord husband made a major misstep when he killed Xavier and had the body disposed of. Just the thought makes me feel queasy. Xavier had been my husband and lover. Though we were very different people, and in the end, I'd lost a lot of respect for him, I didn't want him dead. And I especially didn't want him dead the way Diogo did it.

Sensing our standoff, Bishop decides to take pity on his Commander. Or perhaps, he doesn't want a bloodbath in his clinic, which tends to be the result when Diogo gets pissed off. "Babies get hungry and need feeding every few hours. Their bodies require a lot of high fat energy in order to maintain a rigorous growth schedule. Your son is no different. He's been keeping his mama here on her toes."

Diogo turns a dark glare my way. "You were struggling and you didn't feel that I should be informed. You didn't think I would help."

I sigh. Of course, I was struggling. Sleepless nights are the curse of every new parent. And, of course, I know Diogo would've helped. He may be a ruthless Warlord, but he's made it abundantly clear that his family will come first every time. The cauldron of emotions I'm feeling right now, particularly toward Diogo, prevent me from asking for help.

Instead of answering, I turn to Bishop, my hand on

Blaze's waving fist. "Once you take the blood, how long before you know if he has the same immunity I do?"

"Ah, well, that's a complicated question. I still haven't determined what it is about you that makes you impervious to Necrotitis Primeval. What I really need is to examine your sister, compare samples, and try to figure out what causes this immunity." Bishop has mentioned this before, but it was never really a possibility. Now that Skye is within driving distance, bringing her into the city for an exam shouldn't be too much of an issue.

Before I can answer, Diogo says, "I'll have her delivered to the clinic within the next twenty-four hours."

I grit my teeth, annoyed at the way he discusses Skye as though she's a piece of furniture that needs delivering. I want to yell at him that this is part of his problem. He treats people like commodities, moving them about like pieces on a chessboard. My sister is as human as I am and should be respected.

Instead, I ignore Diogo's comment and say, "I'm sure she'll do it, but I think it would be best for me to talk to her first, maybe get her used to the idea of testing before we ambush her with a bunch of needles and questions."

"Good idea. Once she's ready, bring her on by," Bishop says, ignoring the undercurrents of tension running between me and Diogo. "With both of you as baselines for the immunity, I should be able to determine if Blaze has it too." Bishop looks past me toward Diogo. "It would help if you could find someone knowledgeable in medicine, especially the field of infectious diseases. There may be someone useful in the refugee camp."

"I'll send out some men to question the people in the camp. We should document skillsets, anyway, see if we have anyone that'll be more useful on this side of the wall."

I gasp and turn to Diogo, a retort about the cold calculating way he thinks of the people fleeing for their lives, leaving their homes behind. He lifts and eyebrow as if waiting for me explode at him. I realize he's purposely baiting me. Clever. I swallow the impulse to argue and give Bishop my full attention once more.

He finishes Blaze's exam, draws blood and asks me a few more questions about my own health. I answer truthfully, tell him that I've been feeling better and stronger with each passing day. As we're wrapping up the appointment, Diogo speaks.

"When can she have sex again?"

I gasp, feeling the redness creeping up my neck and flooding my face. If I wasn't super pissed at my husband before, this moment would be the deciding factor.

"Excuse me," I say coldly, reaching for Blaze and picking him up off the table.

As I walk through the door and into the reception area, I hear Bishop say, "Physically she should be completely healed within the next 2-4 weeks. Mentally, you should give her as much time as she needs."

"Forever," I mutter, my back to the men.

"What was that?" Dee asks, stretching her arms out for the baby.

"I was just saying," I shoot a nasty look over my shoulder. "That in my professional opinion, stupidity is not something a person gets over, and sex should definitely come off the table when stupidity is on it."

Dee chokes on her laughter. Even Diogo looks more amused than annoyed, despite my best attempt to rile him.

"Indeed," Bishop echoes. "There is no cure for stupid." Then his sharp eyes pin me. "Nor is there a cure for stubborn. The only thing that helps for both is understanding the other person's perspective."

"Not a chance," I reply quickly.

Diogo stares hard at me, then says, "You're wrong, Doctor. Stubborn can and will be cured within the next two to four weeks."

TARAN

The reunion with my sister is both wonderful and gut-wrenchingly emotional. We cling to each other, holding tight for several long moments before pulling away, tears shimmering in both of our eyes. I laugh as I look at her. Diogo is right, we are so very similar. She's taller and curvier. Her hair has less red in it than mine, more of a rich auburn, but other than those differences we are very alike. Eyes are the same, bone structure, mannerisms. The years apart haven't changed us that much, at least not physically.

"Tell me what's been going on," Skye demands, stepping further into the apartment. "Where is my nephew? I've been dying to meet him."

"In here," I say with a smile, leading her into the baby room. She immediately goes to the crib, her eyes wide with awe as she takes in her brand-new baby nephew.

"He's so fucking beautiful, Taran," she whispers, her voice shaking.

"I know," I agree and join her at the crib. "You don't need to whisper. He sleeps like a champ and only wakes up when he needs something. He's demanding but economical with his time, just like his father."

She laughs and reaches into the crib to touch him, running her fingertips over the soft fuzz of hair on his head. Slowly the smile disappears into a more serious look. "You named him after our brother."

"Yes, we did. Hopefully we can give Blaze the life our brother was denied."

She shakes her head. "This is such a tough world to live in. Impossible to find a normal. The best we can do is drift with the tides and settle whenever and wherever we can."

"I don't agree," I say, though without any sting to my words. "You make it sound like we're at the whimsy of fate, but you know better than anyone that we make do with what we're given. We create the world around us from the ashes of dead cities. Try to make life into something better, maybe something even approaching happiness."

"I suppose you're right," she looks up but her gaze is distant. "I did what I could with my life in the Santa Fe Sanctuary. I compromised with the Warlord, made him fall in love with me, helped run the fortress and city once I'd become a trusted member of the harem. Now... now I'm back to having nothing."

She falls silent, contemplative.

"You miss him," I say, knowing her thoughts linger on the husband she was forced to leave behind.

She nods. "Every day I miss him." Her eyes grow misty. "And every day his face gets a little fuzzier."

I touch her back and sidle a little closer, wrapping my arm around her waist. "That doesn't mean you loved him any less."

"I just feel..." she trails off and shrugs, "... like I owe him better than to just move on and forget what he did for me. He saved my life."

"Maybe he did, but he wouldn't want you to waste your precious life burying yourself in his grave."

She sighs and looks down at me. "What if I didn't love him enough? What if that's why I'm able to move on with my life? Sometimes I wonder if I would have chosen Silas if I'd had any real choice?"

"Only you can answer that, but I can tell that you loved him to the best of your ability. Because that's what you do. You love wholeheartedly and without reservation. He was a lucky man and he probably died knowing it. We do the best we can with what we're given in this world. It's a fucking miracle any of us are capable of compassion and love any more. But the fact that we are just shows how strong human resilience really is."

A tear trickles down her cheek and she lifts her arm to wrap it around my shoulders. "Thank you, Taran."

We stand in silence for a few minutes watching the sleeping baby and immersing ourselves in the fact that we're both alive. Though the odds have been against us time and again, we've both come through tragedy time and again to rise up stronger and more determined to survive than ever.

After a minute I ask her, "Tell me about that scary looking bodyguard watching your back? He seems pretty devoted. I heard he wouldn't even consider letting you come into the Sanctuary without him. Does he think something will happen to you under our care?" I try not to sound offended, but I am a little. Being the Warlord's wife does come with some perks, one of them being safe passage for my loved ones.

She sighs deeply. "Yeah, it's him, not you. He's weird, intense and about as deadly and bloodthirsty as any soldier

I've ever seen. It's chilling to watch him handle the Primitives. He does not give any fucks about how deadly they are. Like he's daring them to bite him."

Even Diogo has the sense to respect the Death Kiss. I can't imagine not fearing the bite of a Primitive, and I have immunity to it. I don't know if that makes Skye's personal shadow very brave or very stupid. "What kind of a man willingly throws himself into danger like that?"

She shrugs. "I used to think he had a death wish. A Primitive once got into the city and trapped itself in the basement of an abandoned building. He went to dispatch the creature himself and I decided to accompany him. I don't know why I did it. I guess I sensed he had this attitude that the harem women belonged in the harem and I wanted to prove that I had the stomach for tougher jobs." She shudders as she recalls the memory. "It was horrible, not at all what I'd imagined. Before that moment, every time I'd had contact with a Primitive was in the heat of the moment, in battle. The creature was trapped behind a wall, weak and starving to death. Wolfe... he baited it. Held his arm out in front of it and watched with this cold expression as it threw itself against the wall over and over again trying to get at him. Finally, after a few minutes of torturing the poor thing he found a way to draw it out. He killed it so fast I was taken completely by surprise."

Picturing Wolfe I can believe Skye when she speaks of dispassionate torture. I've only ever seen his expression change once, when he was looking at Skye. I don't think he realized anyone was looking his way.

"Do you think he was torturing it for fun?" I ask hesitantly. I can't tell exactly where Skye stands on the issue of her protective bodyguard. She seems baffled by him, annoyed by his constant presence, but also resigned to having him near. But if he might pose a danger to her then I want to know. There's a big difference between killing out of necessity and killing for fun. If he's one of those people that loves the rush of death, then I don't trust him with my sister.

I remember back to when Diogo told me how much he enjoys the hunt, how he doesn't like going too long without killing. But Diogo was bred to kill. His entire purpose is to fight the enemy and rise to power. Is Wolfe any different? Am I being hypocritical for worrying about Wolfe's preoccupation with my sister?

"No, I don't think he did it for the joy of killing," Skye says thoughtfully. "Honestly, I don't think I've ever seen an emotion even close to joy or pleasure in that man. I believe he was studying it as he baited it. He was watching its reactions to his movements."

A thought occurs to me. "Do you think he does that often? Watches them?"

She nods absently, reaching into the crib to touch her nephew again, as though she can't get enough. "Yes, I've seen him watching them, studying the way they move. He once said he thought they acted like predator animals in a pack. Only more primitive, less calculating than a pack animal might display."

I think about what Skye is disclosing, the potential importance. She catches the look on my face and nods her head. "I know, if we can discern patterns in their behaviour it could be potentially groundbreaking in our war against them."

"He needs to talk to Diogo," I say firmly. "Tell my husband about his theories, if he has something concrete that might help. Maybe talk to Bishop and Christian too.

Any additional knowledge can only help in our quest for a cure."

Skye smiles grimly. "Wolfe doesn't play well with others, if he hasn't mentioned his theory by now then I doubt he cares to. I've never seen a person less interested in the lives of others. Except for Outsiders. Those guys don't give a shit about anyone."

I can wholeheartedly agree with Skye's assessment having spent some quality time as the unwilling companion to an Outsider when he dragged me from one Sanctuary to another. Though I'd seen some humanity in the man, for the most part he'd been a terrifying asshole who killed remorselessly and nearly raped me just to prove a point.

"I bet Wolfe would talk to Diogo if you asked him to do it."

She gives me a pointed look and rolls her eyes. "I hate asking that man for anything. I swear he's keeping a tally of everything he's done for me. I shudder to find out what payment will look like."

"I think you're being paranoid, he looks at you like you're some kind of baby animal that needs protecting. I don't think he would expect you to return any favours. At least not in the way you're implying."

"Who's implying anything?" she says darkly. "I know what he wants and it's just a matter of time."

I shake my head at her. "Well, I think you'll ask him for this one favour. The fate of humankind might depend on his cooperating with Diogo."

She laughs, "You've become a bossy little thing, haven't you? Fine, I'll talk to him, but only because you've made me responsible for the end of the world."

As we laugh, a sharp cry rends the moment. I reach into the crib and pick up my screaming son.

"I thought you said he would sleep through anything," Skye says accusingly, though her eyes take on a soft adoring look as she watches me handle Blaze. I carry him to the rocking chair and settle into the seat, pulling my top down to expose my breast. She watches in fascination as he latches immediately and starts sucking heartily.

"He woke up because he's hungry," I tell her. "I promise, we didn't disturb him unless he was ready to be disturbed."

She perches on the edge of the tiny bed I'd insisted Diogo add to the baby room. We chat about her making an appointment to visit the Doctor. At first she's hesitant and sceptical, she's been avoiding medical professionals since she was bitten for this exact reason. Once I reassure her that her secret will be safe with Bishop and that the testing is easy and painless, she capitulates and agrees to meet him. With that burning question out of the way we move onto lighter topics of conversation. As we talk Emery arrives. I'd been expecting her, but not until a little later. I'm pleased by the opportunity to introduce her to my sister.

Emery looks her up and down and, ignoring the guarded look on Skye's face, gathers her into a tight hug, holding her close. "Oh you poor thing, Taran has told me so much about you over the years, I felt as though I knew you, even when we thought you were dead. It's such a pleasure to finally meet you. Gosh, you look so much like my Taran."

I can see Skye's face clearly over Emery's shoulder. The combination of stunned and slow building happiness brings tears to my eyes. I'd lucked into finding family here in Sanctuary. Skye had found her own version of family in another Sanctuary. She'd been abducted and sold to a Warlord by the same outsider who kidnapped me. Fortunately, her Warlord had been a kind one and had made sure Skye found her place within his Sanctuary. Watching Emery hold her close and silently promise her a new family if she wants one is one of the best things I've ever seen.

After they finish hugging, Emery takes Skye's hand and sits with her. "Tell me what's going on in Old Tucson. Are you safe out there outside the wall?"

Skye grimaces and when she talks to Emery, opens up quickly. I realize that she probably feels more of an affinity to women, an instant trust. She'd became part of the harem family, embracing the group of women and being embraced by them.

"The situation gets worse with every passing day. We don't have enough food or medical supplies. People are dying of injury, disease, hunger, zombie bite and there's nothing we can do."

Emery rubs her arm comfortingly. "Ah, that is a bad situation. It sounds like the time before Sanctuaries became organized. People would kill each other over a handful of seeds."

Frustration wells within me as I imagine the suffering outside of the wall. "I wish we could just extend the wall, envelop Old Tucson and the all the people out there. It wouldn't solve all of our problems, like making resources stretch, but it would help relieve the manpower needed keeping the Primitives at bay."

Skye stares at me, her mouth slightly open. I can see the inner workings of her brain reflected in her eyes. I sit up straighter as I realize what she's thinking.

"Why can't we?" she demands.

I shake my head, thinking through the logistics. "Impossible."

"But why? The situation can't get much worse out there. This is the exact sort of solution we need."

"It would take months of demolition and rebuilding."

"We have the manpower and the desperation to make it work," she argues.

"It would put Sanctuary at risk, I don't know if Diogo would go for it."

"Your Sanctuary is already at risk. Every day more refugees arrive with fresh waves of Primitives on their asses. It's only a matter of time before they manage to pick us all off and hunger drives them to turn to your Sanctuary. Maybe you win the fight, but you lose a lot of citizens in the process."

She lapses into silence as I think about what she's saying. Fuck, I'm going to have to start talking to my husband again. The only person with even half a chance of talking him around to accepting this solution to the refugee problem is me.

Finally, I say, "I'll talk to Diogo."

"Thank you," she says, real hope shining through in her voice.

"Does someone want to tell me exactly what's been decided?" Emery asks bewildered.

Skye squeezes her hand and grins. "We're going to move a wall."

TWENTY-SEVEN

DIOGO

"Can I talk to you?"

Her voice is my version of heaven after starving for weeks for even a single word. I want to leap up and grab her, hold her against me and beg her to forgive me. I still don't regret my action against the traitor, Xavier Gunther, but I do regret that my violence against him and the lie I told her has caused her to lose faith in me.

I look up from where I sit on a bench, my hands buried deep in the moist soil of our new greenhouse garden. Instead of the individual pots I'd been planting before, I'm now modeling my mini greenhouse after the large city ones with long flat wooden containers to plant the beds in.

"Yes, of course you can talk to me." I don't point out that I've been waiting weeks for her to break down and start talking again. I would hardly deny her now.

She crosses her arms defensively over her chest, pressing the white fabric of her shirt against her fuller breasts and outlining her pert pink nipples. My mouth waters at the movement. I want nothing more than to reacquaint myself with her body. To worship and devour her until she screams in satisfaction. She doesn't look happy to be talking to me, but I don't care. I'll take what I can get.

"Have you considered knocking down a section of the wall and extending it around Old Tucson?" she says bluntly, staring at the wall behind me.

"I... hadn't," I say, lifting my hands from the dirt and standing.

The solution seems so simple, I don't know why I didn't think of it before. Actually, I do know why. Because the preservation of lives beyond my own Sanctuary is not a priority. Stabilizing and managing my own city is my only job. However, the influx of refugees and Primitives has caused some dangerous problems for us. Not least of which is the unauthorized use of our water resources for the refugee encampment. I've begun to worry about the growing likelihood of contamination.

"Why would we do that?" I ask just as bluntly. I want to hear her argument, her voice raised in passionate plea, before I give her my decision.

She looks at me shrewdly, her grey eyes calculating. I wonder which argument she'll go with; the humanitarian angle or appeal to the Warlord's logic.

"If you take in 10,000 refugees with the knowledge and power of the combined Sanctuaries of the east, then you will become one of the most powerful Warlord's on this continent. You will have more sway over resources and trade. You'll be in a more effective position when it comes to dealing with other Sanctuaries." She stops for a moment as though searching for another argument to sway me. She doesn't realize, I'm already swayed by her alone. Her ability to come up with an argument that she thinks will appeal to me is both cute and powerful. She will be my top negotiator when she takes her place as council to the Warlord.

"Is that all?" I prod her.

She glares at me and paces away. "No, not even remotely." Then she launches into another argument. "There are countless reasons to consider this proposal. Most of the people out there in Old Tucson represent the strongest survivors of their Sanctuaries. They were strong enough to flee and to stand their ground and fight. They are determined to survive. These are the people we need in our Sanctuary making it stronger."

I'm impressed with her argument and am about to say so when she switches gears, unable to help herself. "And Diogo," she looks at me, all hostility falling away for the moment. "We can't just leave them to die. I know that rebuilding a section of the wall is a huge, months long project, but it's the best idea we have. If it doesn't work, we could lose everything. Not just the refugees outside the wall, but eventually our Sanctuary if the Primitives turn their collective masses toward us. We can't let that happen."

I absorb her words with a swell of pride at her compassion and logical thinking. She's beautiful no matter what she's doing, but when she's on a mission, determined to better the lives of everyone around her, she's fucking glorious. An unstoppable angel.

"I agree," I tell her quietly. And for the first time since Stryker took her, she smiles at me.

I can't help myself, drawn to the warmth in her smile and her eyes I step toward her, reaching out. She steps quickly back, a shutter falling over her expression.

"I'm not ready yet," she says quietly. Her words, her body language, everything about her is a warning to back off.

"Not ready to forgive me," I say, trying to keep the irritation from my voice. I sigh heavily and run a hand through my hair forgetting for the moment that it's covered in dirt. "At least keep talking to me. Let me explain why I did it."

"No. I'm not ready yet." She shakes her head and backs further away. "I don't think I'll ever be able to forgive you, but maybe, in time, I'll stop being this angry."

"You're condemning me without a trial, Taran. Do you think that's fair of you?"

She swings her gaze up, showing me the full force of her anger and hurt. "You mean the Judge, the man that sentenced me to death?" she asks scathingly. "At least I got some kind of trial, what did Xavier get? A knife to the heart? A shot to the head?" I suppress a flinch at her accuracy as she keeps shouting her anger. "Even your farce of a legal system would've been better than nothing. No, you don't get to tell me what you think is fair."

I've spent weeks swallowing my own anger, accepting the full force of her blame, but this blind hatred, this prolonged grief over a man that she didn't even love is unacceptable. I'd allowed her to grieve for him once, she won't be allowed to grieve for him twice. I'm done with it.

I stalk toward her, forcing her to back up until she's touching the door leading to the floor below. "Are you pissed that Xavier didn't get a fair trial, or are you mad because I killed him myself? Are you having trouble with the idea that these hands that give you such pleasure are the same ones that disposed of your ex-lover?" The words are cruel, but as I watch her flinch and dart her gaze away, I realize I've touched on the core of her fury. She's angry with herself for loving a man capable of murder, a man capable of loving her back while simultaneously lying and withholding information. "You're angry about the lie, about what you think I did to you. Not what happened to Gunther."

I reach for her, taking her shoulders in a hard grip to stop her from running away from this truth. I lower my head so I can look her in the eye. "Do you think there's any chance he would've lived after what he did?"

She swallows hard and shakes her head. "No, of course not."

"He was a traitor, Taran, his execution was always going to be inevitable."

She chokes a little as she holds back tears. She lifts anguished eyes to mine. "It didn't have to be in a dark cell, surrounded by enemies. He was a human, he deserved human comfort before the end. You stripped him of his dignity, his right to a fair trial and his right to be executed in front of his people. Then you stripped him of his life."

"Yes, I did," I acknowledge her words. "I also deprived him of his ability to create a martyr. Our city was divided, it was on the brink of a civil war that would've destabilized everything and weakened us just in time for the Primitives to show up at our doorstep. I do not regret my decision, and if I could go back and do it again, I would."

She reacts explosively, her anger bursting out of her as she's forced to listen to the words she doesn't want to hear. She slams her fists into my chest and shoves as hard as she can. Of course, I don't move. Her strength isn't enough to cause me any harm. But her intent does. The idea that I've driven her to physical violence doesn't sit well, so I step back of my own volition, giving her some space.

"You lied to me!" she shouts.

"To save you pain," I shout back, grabbing her arms and giving her a small shake. "You didn't need to know that I was the one who killed him."

She shakes her head. "You told me you didn't lie, and I believed you. I've believed everything you said to me."

My hands tighten on her arms. "I never lied before you came along but saving you the pain of knowing I shoved a knife in your ex-lover's heart was worth a lie. The outcome was still the same, he was dead and you were alive and unharmed."

"Don't you dare blame me for your serious lack of morals!" She shoves at me again and this time I release her. I don't want to hurt her and the urge to slap her or shake some sense into her is starting to overwhelm my good sense. I don't want to hurt Taran, but I do want my wife back.

"I wouldn't change my actions," I tell her coolly. "Given the chance I would do it all over again, only I'd make sure you never found out. Do you know why? Because saving you pain will always be worth it to me. No matter how I get to that result, no matter how much of myself I have to sacrifice, your happiness will always come first."

She's breathing heavily, her shoulders heaving. The tears that she'd been holding back trickle down her cheeks. She looks at me with such hurt that it's impossible for some of my own anger not to drain away. She swipes at the tears with her sleeve and stares past me, over the rooftop out over the city. "Diogo... I can't do this. You lied to me and you killed someone I cared about. I don't think I'll ever be able to forgive you."

She turns away and reaches for the door intent on heading back down to our son. I've noticed that she cuddles him when she's feeling lonely, lost and sad, which has been a lot lately. I catch the edge of the door before she can disappear, calling out to her. She turns on the steps, her hand hovering over the railing, her tear-stained face tilted up to me.

"You may not have a choice, because I'm done living in a battle zone for a marriage. You can either forgive me and find a way to be happy in this marriage, or you will suffer the consequences of your anger. Because whichever path you choose, I'm done waiting, you will resume your role as my wife."

TWENTY-EIGHT
TARAN

I'm slow to wake from a desperately needed nap. As awareness comes to me I realize that I don't know what woke me
up. These days it would be the cries of my son that would
wake me from such a deep sleep. He'd been up and fussy
last night, so I put him down for a nap and then laid down
myself on the bed in the corner. But he's not crying now.

I sit upright, shoving hair out of my face. I push myself
out of the bed and stumble toward the cradle, reaching for
it. Blaze is gone, just his crumpled blanket shoved to the
bottom of the bed. As my brain absorbs the reality of my
missing son, I'm on the verge of panic when Diogo speaks.

"He's with Emery."

I look up. Diogo is standing in the doorway, his arms
crossed over his broad chest, his military uniform in perfect
condition on his tall frame. I blink several times and try to
shake the sleep fog from my brain. "Why is he with Emery?"
I've been talking to Diogo for a few weeks now, since he
agreed to discuss the wall extension to encompass Old
Tucson. There was no point after that in keeping my
silence, though the chill between us remains.

The hard look in his dark piercing eyes should be my first clue that he's up to something, but I'm slow to understand. In this first six weeks of Blaze's life no one has stepped in to undermine me or dared to take my child without my permission. In fact, in the past six weeks Blaze hasn't once been out of my sight. Panic begins to well up again as I imagine he must need me, must need to eat, or just be reassured by the presence of his mother. Diogo watches as these thoughts and emotions no doubt flit across my face.

I stand up straighter and glare at him. "I want my son."

"No." The way he says it, so easy, so autocratic, it infuriates me.

"Why?" I demand.

He waits a few seconds before speaking, as though searching for the words. Finally, he says, "You need to stop hiding behind our son and face the fact of our marriage. Or lack of one at the moment."

I gasp. "How dare you! I'm not hiding behind our son, I'm nurturing him, as I should be doing. As any good parent would. Are you suggesting I'm doing something wrong?"

He holds a hand up and takes a step into the baby room. "You've been an exemplary mother to our infant child. I'm not arguing with your dedication to parenthood."

"What then?" I ask angrily. "Why have you taken him without my permission?"

Diogo reacts with explosive anger, thundering, "I don't need permission to make decisions regarding our son. I had him removed so you can't use him as a barrier to our marriage anymore!"

I gasp and take a step back. Diogo has given me space these past weeks, allowed me to make all the decisions surrounding Blaze's care. That Diogo is reduced to yelling at me shows how serious he is. I try to remain calm, though my instincts are clambering at me to shove past Diogo and go find Emery and Blaze. I won't make it far though, and that alone keeps me rooted to the spot. Diogo won't hesitate in physically stopping me from leaving.

I clench my hands into fists and force myself to take several deep calming breaths. If there's anything I've learned from my husband over our time together it's that my anger won't sway his decision. If I want my son back in my arms I'll have to play along. "What are you proposing?" I ask as calmly as possible.

He shoves a hand through his hair and rolls his shoulders, cracking them and releasing some tension. His dark eyes search mine for a moment. "We're going for a drive."

I frown. A drive? Fuel is a premium in our society, difficult to come by, even harder to hang on to. What he wants to show me must be important for Diogo to decide we'll drive there. "Where are we going?" I ask, curiosity peeking through my annoyance.

"You'll see," he says shortly and turns, leaving me to follow him. I debate crawling into bed and going back to sleep. Not that I would actually sleep until Blaze is safe and sound in his cradle, but Diogo might get the point that I don't want to be in his company right now. If I resist, he'll probably drag me out of the apartment, forcibly carry me down the stairs and shove me in the jeep.

I sigh and stomp after him. "Fine," I tell him disagreeably. "The only reason I'm going with you is because I trust Emery to take care of Blaze. But once I've seen whatever it is that you seem to want to show me, I'm coming back here and you're bringing my son back to me."

Diogo takes hold of my arm as I pass him and gives me a little shake. "Enough," he says in a hard voice, bending close to my face for emphasis. "You will stop acting like a petulant child who's had her feelings hurt. I've given you six weeks to get this out of your system, now you'll give me a few hours."

When he puts it like that I do feel somewhat like a pouty child. Perhaps I could've given him an opportunity to explain his side more fully before now. Perhaps I could've softened enough to have an adult discussion. But I've been swamped with hormones, overwhelmed by new parenthood and confused by the emotions surrounding Diogo and Xavier. Unable to cope, maybe I did take the easy way out by burying my head in the sand and ignoring the difficult things I didn't want to deal with.

Still, Diogo murdered Xavier in cold-blood without a trial then lied about it. There is simply no excuse and there won't be an explanation good enough to satisfy the deep anger I feel whenever I think of my powerful husband taking vengeance on an unbalanced and weakened Xavier.

I pull my arm from Diogo's hold, painfully aware that he wouldn't release his grip if he wasn't ready. "Let's get this over with," I mutter, grabbing my jacket and heading out the front door.

Diogo's grim silence follows me down the 18 flights of stairs to the main floor where his jeep waits for us. Diogo's patience has definitely reached an end. He's no longer contrite or apologetic. He's pissed off. Part of me wonders if I was waiting for this, subconsciously pushing my husband toward this. Diogo can be a strong-willed beast. He's forced his will on mine over and over. I'm not surprised Diogo the Warlord is back and fed up with the icy silence that has become our marriage. I just wish I was better prepared for whatever he has coming my way.

He strides around me and opens the passenger door to the jeep. I slide in and hold my jacket tight around me as he slams the door shut and climbs into the driver's seat. I glance up at our home as he drives away, hoping it'll be there when we get back. Even though the unrest in the city has mostly died down, I still get jolts of discomfort when I think about our lost home and how close we came to losing each other.

"Where are you taking me?" I ask as Diogo is waved through the checkpoint and into Sector Two.

He ignores my question and continues driving. As we reach the massive gates guarding our city, I realize he intends to leave Sanctuary. My heart jolts in fear and I have to swallow the denial that leaps to my lips. Diogo is an accomplished warrior, he won't let anything happen to me. Still, it's difficult to forget that every single time I've stepped foot outside of this city in the past year, terrible things have happened.

As we drive through the gates, Diogo reaches over his shoulder into the back seat and grabs a rifle. He silently passes it to me. I take it hesitantly and look it over, running my fingers over the smooth steel.

"Just point and pull the trigger," he says gruffly.

"Why do I need it?" I ask, my voice softer than I'd intended, fear leaching some of the stridency from my tone.

He looks over at me, his eyes hard. "The first time I met you, you had a gun. You remember, Taran? How we met out here in the desert? You knew the value of having a weapon then. Now is no different. If I become incapacitated, you'll need it to defend yourself."

I lick my lips and nod. He's right. I've come to depend on Diogo to keep me safe from harm, when the reality is, if he's not around, it'll be up to me to fight my way out of a situation. I'd been all alone when Stryker took me, and though I hadn't been forced to actually defend myself, the entire scenario could've gone in a completely different direction.

We remain silence as Diogo races across the desert. It takes a few minutes, but eventually I realize where he's headed. My suspicion is confirmed when a rocky outcrop rising from the desert becomes visible. I hold my breath as he drives around the outcropping and stops the jeep in the exact location where I was attacked by Primitives one year ago. The place where Xavier had dragged me to after forcing me from the city. Where I first met Talon, the Outsider who would kidnap me and try to sell me to my sister's Sanctuary.

"Diogo..." I whisper, pain in my voice. I want to demand an explanation. I want to beg him to turn the car around and take me back to the safety of the city where I can set eyes on Blaze and reassure myself that he's unharmed.

I jump as Diogo's door slams, the sound reverberating through the vehicle. He strides around the jeep and jerks my door open. I sit staring past him at the clearing in fearful anxiety as if expecting the dead bodies of the men who died here to still be on the ground. Of course, they aren't. They would have either been buried or dragged away by predators.

Diogo loses patience waiting for me. He takes my arm and pulls me from the safe confines of the vehicle. I stumble against him and he rights me, holding me in front of him so I'm facing the clearing, one hand on my arm and the other on my shoulder, holding me immobile. I'm still clutching the rifle. For several long moments we stand like that looking at the scene of a horrific massacre. Only there's nothing left to look at. Just dust, scrub trees and rocks.

I'm not sure what Diogo's point is, why he brought me here, but as the past comes flooding back, I cringe against him. I don't care how angry I've been at Diogo, he's still my husband and he still represents safety to me. He remains large, solid and stoic at my back, silently reassuring me that he won't let anything happen while we're out here in the open, vulnerable to attack.

"Why have you brought me here?" I whisper.

At first, I'm not even sure he hears me as the quietly spoken words are taken by the constant desert breeze that plays havoc with dust, throwing it about and coating everything in sight. Diogo takes his time answering, before finally dropping his chin to my shoulder so I'll hear him when he speaks. He reaches past me and points to where the lineup of Outsider vehicles had been on that terrible day.

"Do you know what I saw when I arrived here?" he asks.

I shake my head, lost in my own visions of the past. Of those terrifying seconds when I'd taken refuge in one of the cars only to be driven into the open by a Primitive as she smashed through the window and came after me.

"A bloodbath," he says bluntly.

The Primitives had kept coming at us, uncaring of whom their victims were. Driven to spread the Death Kiss, they'd torn through our little group, murdering anyone that came into their path.

"Do you know what I didn't see?" he asks, his breath against my ear sending a shiver of awareness through me.

"No," I whisper.

"I didn't see you. Dead or alive, I didn't see you here. I turned that corner and flung myself out of my car and into a bloodbath with the single goal of finding my wife. I cut down everything in my path in the hopes that if I killed enough, I might be able to save you. I searched every single body on the ground, every severed limb, looking for you." I can hear the ache in his tone as he describes what he saw that day and an answering ache rises in my throat. "The thought of losing you destroyed me. I've never lost control the way I did that day. And when I finally found you, you were laying on the ground, a Primitive with her teeth in your throat. I thought I was about to die because no part of me wants to live in a world where you aren't alive."

I squeeze my eyes shut against the tears threatening to spill while a sob leaps to my throat. I take a deep breath and subtly move against Diogo, pressing my back against his front.

"If you'd died that day, I would've died with you. I would've laid down at your side, held you against me and I would've shot myself in the head."

I shudder, the tears now spilling free. Still I keep my eyes shut, trying desperately to hold the horrific images at bay. It's no use. I can't seem to keep them out. Every word paints a vivid picture of that day, the day we almost died together.

He continues speaking, coming to the reason for our sojourn into the desert. "You are my life, Taran. My Sanctuary and my happiness. I love you more than my sanity can take. If anyone threatens my Sanctuary, they will die by my hand. I refuse to apologize for that. Xavier put you at risk over and over. For that alone, I would've relished his death. But you were bitten as a direct result of him taking you into the desert against your will. For that, I would happily resurrect a dead man so that I can bury a knife in his heart over and over again."

I flinch and his arms tighten around me for a few seconds before he turns me and tilts my chin up. Finally, I open my eyes. Hot tears splash down my cheeks as I struggle to blink them away and breathe. I want to stay mad at him, I want him to suffer the way he's made me suffer, the way he made Xavier and countless others suffer. But I can't. He's just a man, and men make mistakes.

"I can accept your reasoning, but not your actions. You didn't have to kill him that way, nor did you have to lie about it," I insist. "You could've given him to Sanctuary and allowed the people to decide. You shouldn't be judge, jury and executioner. That's why I'm so angry, Diogo. You take lives without thought. You've become so used to the brutality surrounding your role as Warlord that you no longer value human life."

He stares at me long and hard, his own anger and frustration close to the surface. "You will forgive me," he demands. "I won't give you a choice."

The Warlord lays down his decree before taking me by the hand and escorting me back into the car. I shiver in apprehension as he strides around to the other side, his eyes never leaving mine. How does he intend to force my forgiveness? And will our marriage survive his heavy-handed ultimatum?

She's softening. It'd been a gamble, taking her into the desert, forcing her to face a terrible and bloody past. Taking her to the last place she'd seen her ex-husband alive. It hadn't been easy standing there with her, describing some of the most excruciating moments of my life as I detailed how I searched for her body among the torn apart corpses littering the ground. Her anger is still alive and well, but she is beginning to soften. To understand my point of view. No person, human or Primitive, man or woman, will get away with harming my woman, my wife, my Sanctuary.

Our drive to the city is as silent as it'd been on our way out, but this time the silence filling the vehicle is contemplative rather than angry. I suspect Taran is lost in memory and I'm sorry for that. I regret causing her even a moment's discomfort. But if forcing her to face the past is our way toward repairing a future then I'll do what it takes.

The city gates open for us, welcoming us home. I drive through and head toward Sector One, but not our new place. No, I drive toward the burned-out shell of the Tower. As we approach, Taran sits up straighter and leans toward the windshield, her sharp eyes taking in the devastation. She hasn't been back since the fire that nearly claimed both of our lives and the precious life of our son.

"Diogo, I'm tired," she says, almost pleadingly. She's beginning to understand that I'm taking her on a trip through our worst memories, showing her how fragile our happiness is. That she would be a fool to throw that away on a man like Xavier Gunther.

"I know," I tell her. "This will be our last stop before home."

Her lips turn down unhappily, but she nods her acquiescence and sits quietly as I bring the jeep to a stop as close as I can to the burned-out ruins of the Tower. She allows me to take her arm when I round the jeep to her side again, and willingly slides out onto the road. We take several steps together until our toes touch a twisted metal beam laying in the road in almost the exact spot where I used to park against the curb.

Together we look out across the devastation of twenty floors of apartment building burned to the ground. The acrid smell of burnt wood still permeates the air, flooding our senses and taking us instantly back to the night the rebels burnt down our home and stole our sense of security in Sanctuary. Taran crosses her arms over her chest, her gaze distant and unseeing. As I'd done in the desert, I stand behind her and hold her against my chest as I speak.

"Sending you through that window was the hardest most unselfish thing I've done in my life. Harder than the first life I took when I was a young boy. Harder than destroying my father. Harder than taking this Sanctuary and turning it into a fortress. In fact, if I was faced with making that choice again, I don't know if I could do it." I have to stop speaking for a moment as the memory of sending my pregnant wife out into the unknown darkness of a violent rebellion punches me in the stomach and steals my breath. "I thought I was sending you out into certain death, just a death slightly less certain than my own. Watching you crawl down the side of the building, your face filled with fear and despair... felt like severing my own limb."

We stand together not saying anything as she absorbs my words, the sentiment behind them, the very real probability that we could've died here, among the ruins of our old home.

"I thought I was leaving you behind to die," she says softly, her voice catching. "I thought when I looked up at you, at the anguish on your face, that it would be the last time I'd ever see you. There's only one thing that could've driven me from your side and forced me to leave you to die in a burning building alone."

"Blaze," I finish for her.

"Blaze," she acknowledges, then laughs unexpectedly. She turns to look up at me, her eyes shining with tears and humour. "I just realized, we named our son Blaze, as in fire. Our child damn near died in a fire and we named him after fire."

I chuckle, unable to resist smiling. I kiss the tip of her nose and her eyes widen at my move. She stares up at me, her gaze searching my face. I can feel her beginning to weaken. She may despise my methods, but her love for me is stronger than her convictions.

"I'm sorry I hurt you," I tell her, hoping she can hear the sincerity. Hurting my wife is the last thing in the world I would ever want to do.

She searches my face. "You're sorry for hurting me, but not sorry for what you did."

There's no point in answering her, she already knows

my response. She shakes her head, a shutter falling over her eyes as she pulls away from my arms and turns back to the car. She climbs inside and stares straight ahead, waiting for me to join her.

I wait a moment, wait for the wave of helpless rage to pass. I'm creating the opportunity and path for her to find her way back into our marriage on her own. I don't want to have to force her hand, to take away her free will again, but her stubborn attitude is backing me into a corner. I have one last thing up my sleeve before I give into the urge to force Taran back into my life and my bed.

THIRTY

TARAN

"I'm done with whatever this is," I tell him as he gets in the car. "Take me to Emery and Blaze."

He turns to look at me, not bothering to mask the glowing embers of his rage. Perhaps I could've used more diplomacy and less of a demanding tone. Sometimes I forget my husband is the Warlord; ruler of cities, destroyer of Primitives and kidnapper of wives.

He leans toward me, his arm sliding along the back of my seat. I cringe against the passenger side door, but he's such a big man he's still able to get right in my face. "You will see our child when I say you can. I'm not done with you yet."

The ominous words linger in the air between us. He doesn't say anything else, just stares at me, his gaze holding mine captive, his fingers tangling in my hair. I hold my breath and then release it in a long sigh. No matter how scary he is, I know Diogo won't hurt me. It's just not in him. I grope for patience of my own, reminding myself that he won't keep me from Blaze long. He loves our son, same as me. He won't allow our child to go without the comfort of his mother, and the sustenance only I can provide.

"Alright," I say softly, trying for a more conciliatory tone. "Where to next?"

"Home," he says shortly and turns to face forward, starting the vehicle.

Well that works for me, the closer we are to home the more likely I am to get back to my son and the routine I've spent weeks establishing. As Diogo wends his way through the city streets toward our new home I look around with a new focus. Blaze was born so soon after the violence of the rebel riots that I haven't had much opportunity to see the city rebuild. Sections have been burnt out, torn down, or abandoned. The buildings are silent sentinels to the unrest our Sanctuary has experienced. But out of the ashes there are signs of regrowth.

Many of the elites that were caught up in the rebellion have moved to different sectors, integrating with some of the poorer sections. Milla has moved in with Emery in the slums. As well as helping with incoming refugees, she's thrown herself into creating education programs and schools. While she's still bitterly disappointed over the death of her beloved husband, she's making herself useful to people who desperately need the resources she can offer.

A sliver of guilt slides through me. I used to be the Desert Wren, I used to stand for something. I helped the people of Sanctuary in the best way I knew how. Yet when Diogo took me, my life changed entirely. Instead of working for the greater good I became the wife of the Warlord. More of a symbolic figurehead than someone who can actually effect change. When Blaze was born I was able to focus entirely on him, bury my discomfort over being locked away for my own safety.

And just like that an epiphany hits me. I'm not angry at Diogo for killing Xavier. Okay, well I am angry about that, but I'm more angry over his unilateral decision-making. Yes, he is the Warlord. Yes, he is the man that makes the decisions. But he's also a man that professes to love me. Yet that love can be suffocating. It's barbaric and unhealthy. Diogo locks me up every chance he gets, he forced me into marriage, he forced me into a relationship I wouldn't have chosen for myself. And yes, while I have fallen in love with my husband, I am still the same Desert Wren I used to be. And she wouldn't have stood for the autocratic way in which the Authority has taken my autonomy.

Maybe I thought love would change Diogo, as I'd once thought it would change Xavier. Maybe I should have known better. People can fall in love, but they don't change. I'm almost as guilty for Xavier's death as Diogo. Though it was a chain of events I couldn't have predicted, my involvement with Xavier is what drove Diogo to kill him the way he had. I'm not naive enough to think I'm responsible for all of it, I can't control the actions of others, but I can control my own actions, and some of them led to Xavier's death.

That's it, maybe I feel responsible for what happened to Xavier. It was out of my control, but it was still my fault.

My feelings are such a riotous mess and I'm so deeply lost in my own thoughts that I barely notice when we arrive at our building. I snap out of it when Diogo's door slams. He opens mine and holds a hand out to me. I take it and allow him to pull me from the vehicle. We walk into the building together, his hand at my back. I wonder what else he has in store for me. I'm mentally and physically exhausted now from visiting two places that hold traumatic memories. I want to lay down and take a nap and I want to do it with my infant son.

We make it about halfway up the stairs before Diogo, apparently eager to get to our apartment, picks me up and carries me the rest of the way. I don't complain. In fact, the movement is comforting. He's done this for me so many times over the past year. Seen to my comfort and well-being. In a way, he is the perfect husband. But I'm beginning to realize that so many of the things he does for me are equally for him. He will see to my needs, protect me and keep me in comfort because knowing I'm safe gives him peace of mind.

If this how love is supposed to look? I'd always imagined when it happened it would be more of a partnership. An equal, or at least variable distribution of decision-making and power exchange. Instead, I'm living in a marriage that, while loving, is not equal. If my decisions are counter to Diogo's he will enforce his will on mine.

Instead of angry, these thoughts make me feel weary. I don't know how to make him see what he's doing to me. To us. To our small family. And I don't know how to counter him. How to express my needs without getting frustrated and angry. Perhaps if my parents or grandparents had survived, I would've grown into womanhood with more of a sense of who I am and what I need. With the ability to talk to my husband without my emotions getting in the way. While Emery did her best with me, we met each other while I was already deep in the rebellion, set on my course, and too stubborn to accept her gentle guidance. Now I'm keenly aware of my lack of family.

He sets me on my feet and opens our door for me to enter. I glance around. "Where's Grayson?"

"Why?" Diogo demands with a frown.

I look at him with exasperation. His constant jealously can be so overwhelming sometimes. I can't even speak the name of another man without him getting in my face. "I'm wondering because he's been my constant shadow since you made him my bodyguard. It seems weird to not have him around."

Diogo's frown remains. "He's with Emery and Blaze. I assigned him baby duty while we went on our tour. Perhaps I should rethink his permanent assignment, you sound as though you're getting attached."

Annoyance turns to anger. "Of course, I'm attached to him. He's my bodyguard and we've been through hell together on more than one occasion. Are you seriously considering taking another friend from me? Why? Because he's male, good-looking and good at his job? Well that makes perfect sense."

"Taran," he says warningly.

"No," I snarl, turning on him. "I've had enough of your insane jealousy and stupid rules. If you reassign Grayson I'll start following him around. I'll... I'll become his bodyguard, just to spite you. And because I don't want to lose another friend."

Okay, my argument is a little on the childish side, but damn it, I'm exhausted and tired of losing the people I care about. I know they aren't all Diogo's fault, but he moves us around like pieces on a chessboard until he's satisfied with the configuration. If his motivations were pure, his reasoning sound then maybe I could get on board with his autocratic declarations. But he's motivated by jealousy, which is not a good enough reason.

"You need to watch what you say, Taran," Diogo warns again.

I grit my teeth, telling myself to think before I speak. And then I speak without thinking, letting some of my anger loose in the form of some of the half-coherent thoughts I've been having. "Why should I watch what I say?" I shout, flinging my arms in the air. "You don't watch what you say. You say what you think and there's no Authority higher than you to tell you to watch your tongue. Well, now it's time for you to think before you speak, because if you keep letting emotions like jealousy rule your marriage you won't have a marriage for very much longer."

I almost cringe as the last word leaves my lips. Damn it. So much for being more thoughtful. I'd just let Diogo have it, giving him the verbal tongue lashing I've been working up to since I found out he killed Xavier.

At first Diogo looks taken aback. I wait, breath held, for him to release the fury that must be building after that diatribe. Then he does something completely unexpected. He laughs. He tilts his head back and releases a full-bodied laugh filled with humour. I can't help it. My lips twitch in response. No wonder he's laughing. Instead of calmly talking through some of the issues I have with him, I tell him to shut his mouth. If anyone else had done the same, told the Warlord to watch his tongue, they'd be counting the seconds left in their very short lives.

Diogo confirms this last thought when he finishes laughing and pins me with dark eyes, still filled with mirth. "Not a single person has dared to tell me to shut up. Well done, wife."

I'm not sure what he means by that. Well done, as in I've done it now? Or, well done, I'm finally getting through to him.

"Come," he says and takes my arm.

I'm so stunned by the unexpected turn our argument has taken that I go with him willingly, somewhat bemused and very confused. He pulls me up the stairs leading to the roof, and like it does every time I traverse these steps, my heart thumps painfully. The memory of our last home, now burned and gone, assails me. I've tried shaking it off, but the pain still lingers, keeping me away from the roof. As a result, I don't often go up. Since our marriage has turned cold, Diogo tends to go to the roof when he's home from work, while I stay inside. I'd only come up once in the past several weeks and that was when I asked Diogo about extending the wall to envelop Old Tucson.

"Diogo..." I trail off, not really knowing what I want to say. I don't want to go to the roof. Some of our best memories occurred on top of the Tower. Our most passionate moments, the declaration of our love and probably even the conception of our child given the amount of times we made love up there.

"It's okay, love," Diogo says, understanding infusing his tone. And he probably does understand. He loved his rooftop patio and greenhouse before I even became part of his life. It'd become something we could share, something we could glory in and grow together. I also notice the way he avoids calling me baby, he hasn't once since I yelled at him that Stryker had called me that.

We step out into the bright afternoon sun, warming the rooftop and casting glowing beams around a paradise right over my head that I hadn't even known existed.

"Diogo!" I gasp, pulling my hand from his and stepping out onto the patio, my gaze wandering in awe. "Did you do all this?"

"With a little help," he murmurs, pride suffusing his voice.

I stand quietly for a few minutes taking it all in. It's just like our old rooftop patio, but better. The greenery that constantly chokes abandoned buildings has creeped its way into every crack and crevice, but instead of cutting it away, Diogo has tamed it, using it for his own purposes and creating a canopy of lush green vegetation. I step through the arch he's built over the doorway and into the beautiful eden.

The greenery hasn't had quite enough time to crawl its way up the trellises Diogo has built to encourage the growth into usefulness. I can still see metal beams peeking through, but the overall effect of industrial and natural is breathtaking. Like a snapshot of our world. The way nature is reclaiming all that humans have built and destroyed one inch at a time. Yet, also capturing our determined struggle to fight for our survival. But instead of depicting the constant battle, Diogo's rooftop paradise shows an intertwining of both, human activity and nature.

This stunning creation isn't an accident. Diogo is far too intelligent to create art by accident. He set out to envision a snapshot of the world we should be living in. Not one where humans must triumph over nature, or vice versa, but a world where we can co-exist peacefully.

"I don't know what to say," I tell him, finally turning to face him.

His eyes are filled with the intense passion I've become used to from him but haven't allowed myself to experience in weeks.

The edge of his lip quirks up and he says, "You don't need to say anything, your face speaks plenty."

I nod and gaze around, my mouth dry with the need to cry, but with good tears instead of pained ones. I pick out different features and wander to touch and look my fill. There are metal beams built into the project giving the vines a place to wend their way overhead. I stare straight up, imagining what it will look like in a few years once the green canopy has truly taken hold. Diogo has brought in a stone bench set a couple of feet from the edge of the roof.

Built so we can sit and watch the city together, voyeurs set above the rest of the world. Separate, but still a part of everything.

"For you," Diogo says, coming up behind me. "All of this is for you, Taran. Everything I do is for you."

I nod, my gaze still on the sun-soaked city far below. Instead of the familiar pang of loss I'd felt coming up here before when I remembered losing our last home, I feel only peace. Diogo has built regrowth into our new home, a pathway between the old and the new. He's no good with words, often pisses me off when he drops his autocratic decrees. But his actions here are so much louder than the speeches of a Warlord.

Of course, he built this for me. I can see his intent in every part of the scene. The canopy to cast shade when the sun is hot. A tomato plant set next to the bench, symbolic of the first seed I'd planted so many months ago. The greenhouse, an exact replica of our last one, only bigger and longer. I wander toward it, wanting desperately to see inside. To see if he's built it the way I know he has.

I open the door and step inside, the warm humid interior embracing me like a long-lost hug. The scent of earth, greens and flowers spinning through my senses. I walk toward the back, dimly noting the rows of freshly planted boxes. I stop next to the stepping stool leading up to a beam set in the roof. Next to the beam is a hole, allowing sunshine and desert air in.

The tears finally fall, splashing against my cheeks and dripping down unheeded. I don't bother to catch them because they are cathartic, good and happy. They're the release of weeks of fear and misery. The terror that something new will jump out and kill everything I love and take away my new home. I turn blindly and step into Diogo who has followed me in. His arms envelop me while mine wrap around his waist. I bury my face into his chest and allow myself to cry for everything we've lost, everything we've discovered, and the things we've built, both together and apart.

"Can you find your way back to me?" he asks huskily, his voice strained as though he's also holding onto his tears.

"I don't know," I say honestly, tipping my face back to look up at him. "I'm beginning to realize that your killing Xavier isn't an anomaly, it's who you are. The violent Warlord is part of the package that includes loving husband and father, protective partner, and sensitive lover. I can't agree to accept one part of you while turning a blind eye to the other."

He stares down at me, his dark eyes fathomless. He absorbs my words thoughtfully and then says, "It doesn't matter what you can and can't accept. You are my wife and I won't let you go."

"Even if it means war instead of marriage?" I ask.

"It would be the sweetest war I've ever taken part in."

I can't help but laugh at that. "I would make sure that any war between us was far from sweet, Warlord."

He dips his head low, so his lips are hovering near mine. My heart leaps in anticipation and my lower belly floods with warmth. "You wouldn't have a choice, rebel," he says, his voice soft with an underlying core of steel that makes me instantly yearn for more. "I would tie you to my bed and force the sweetest orgasms you've ever known from you. I would stroke and lick every inch of you until you no longer remember your own name, let alone your reasons for fighting me."

I have to swallow the moan that leaps up my throat as

his words sap the strength from my lips. "All talk," I whisper against his mouth. "No action."

He bends so suddenly I gasp when his arms go beneath my knees and sweep my legs out from under me. As he strides through the greenhouse and toward the door leading inside, he says, "Consider this war started, wife."

I tighten my arms around him and grin into his neck.

No, husband, consider this war over.

THIRTY-ONE

DIOGO

"Umm, I didn't think you were serious."

Her voice holds the slight edge of panic mixed with the sweet sound of her excitement as I raise her hands over her head and tie them to the frame of our bed. As I wind the rope through her wrists, securing them to the metal, her breathing grows heavier. Sweet song to ears that haven't had the pleasure in more days than I care to count.

She twists her head to look up at her hands as I finish the knot. "Why do you have rope in your bedroom?"

"Our bedroom," I growl, moving down her body.

"The question still stands." Her last word ends on a squeak as I slip my fingers into her pants and jerk them down her legs.

I look up at her, pinning her to the bed. "If my wife wasn't going to come back to our bed willingly, I was going to make sure she got here another way and didn't have a way of escaping."

Her jaw drops open and she flounders for something to say. I take advantage of her confusion by dragging her clothes off. She tilts her hips a little, helping me. Unless I want to destroy her shirt, I can't get it completely off, so I unbutton it, trailing kisses from her neck down to her navel and then shove the shirt back on her arms. When her body is completely, gloriously exposed to me, I sit back on my haunches and just look my fill.

Taran's body has changed subtly, matured. Her breasts are fuller, heavier now, filled with the sustenance that will ensure life for our young son. Her waist has thickened a little and there are stretch marks across her belly and hips. I trace my fingers over them feeling the new softness to her skin. Her face changes a little, losing some of the passion that'd been there moments ago as self-consciousness takes over. She's shy about her new marks, though I think they are beautiful.

I'm completely enamoured of this gorgeous body, the new scars of her resilience mixed with the beautiful curves that have always been there. A rush of sadness and anger hits me that I wasn't around to watch her heal, to touch each mark as it settled on her body, to kiss away her insecurities. She held me at bay, punishing me for something that I couldn't and wouldn't change. I should have forced my way back into her life, forced her to realize she needs me.

"What's wrong?" she whispers, her eyes large and vulnerable. She twists her arms, tugging at the binding.

I shake my head, now is not the time to release my pent-up frustration at missing these past weeks. Later we can talk, later we'll discuss how to go forward and never allow such a thing to happen again. For now, in this moment, worshipping my wife is my only job.

"Nothing... love," I assure her. The word 'baby' nearly leaving my lips, further ruining the moment. Unburying Stryker and taking vengeance on his body flirts through my mind as I lower my head so she won't see my expression.

I decide to show her with actions how much I've missed her, how much I love everything about her. I start at her feet, massaging and working the kinks from them one at a time. I'm surprised by the sensual moan of pleasure that leaves her lips. I watch her face carefully as I work. Is it possible that her feet are yet another pathway to her sexual pleasure? One that I will absolutely be exploiting in the future.

I'd never bothered to take the time to explore a woman's body in great detail, never wanted to. They were for one thing only, a vessel for my immediate gratification. Once finished I no longer had use for them. Perhaps a cold way of thinking, but I didn't have time for distractions. Didn't care to explore relationships. Not before Taran. She is so far different from the women I've known that she may as well be an alien. She is tough, resilient, thoughtful, but fiery too. She holds me accountable.

Exploring her, seeking her points of pleasure is a task that I treasure. Not just for the further enjoyment of my cock, but for the sheer joy of losing myself in her. Immersing myself in the sensual world that is Taran.

I move from her feet up to her calves, pressing my thumbs into the muscles there, surprised to find them softer, less honed than they'd been. She is no longer climbing walls or running through abandoned buildings. Her new life is shaping her body, and I love every inch of it. She reflects our lives together and I'm more in love with her now than I ever thought possible.

She moans in ecstasy as I move up her body, caressing with my lips and massaging with my hands. She widens her legs as I reach her thighs after dropping light kisses on each knee, noting a tiny scar on her right one. Maybe she cut it during one of her wall climbing forays? I make a mental note to ask her later. I suddenly feel the overwhelming urge to know every part of her, hear the stories behind each and every mark, everything that makes Taran who she is.

I avoid moving to that sweet spot I want most. Torturing her, drawing out her pleasure is my reward for waiting. She squirms and moans with each touch as I dig my fingers into her thighs and work the muscles. I can see the glistening wetness on the dark red curls between her legs, begging for my tongue, weeping for my fingers.

"Diogo!" she gasps, unable to hold it in anymore. "Please, I want..."

I grin against her inner thigh, purposely rubbing my scruff-roughened cheek softly against her labia. She moans again and pants, trying harder to widen her legs to allow room for my shoulders, to guide me into her.

"Don't keep me waiting, it's been too long!"

I nip at her thigh, marking it. She jerks it away from my teeth with a gasp. "And whose fault is that, wife? You knew where our bedroom was, yet you chose the other room."

"He needed me!" she protests, her gorgeous grey eyes pleading for mercy.

"I needed you," I growl, nipping my way up her thigh to her pussy. She flinches, afraid that I'll bite her where she is most sensitive, but also afraid I won't. She craves my tongue, my kiss, my touch. Though this is a feast for my senses, a chance to reacquaint myself with her body, it's also a mild punishment. A way to show her that she is not in control, that I will give her what she wants when she gives me what I want.

"I still need you." I flick my tongue against the tiny clit peeking through the folds. She gasps and bucks up against me. "I will always need you." I position myself between her thighs, making myself more comfortable, as though about to gorge myself on her. "You took away that which I need most in this world." I lick her again, savouring her reaction, torturing her with conflicting words and actions.

"I'm sorry!" she wails, straining her hips higher, urging me to finish her.

"Perhaps," I tell her, sliding a finger through the dripping folds of her labia and then licking her delicious, sweet juice from my hand. Her eyes glow as she watches me. "And perhaps I'd better make sure you're truly sorry so it doesn't happen again."

"It won't, it won't!" she promises, her voice high and thready.

"No, it won't," I say darkly.

Then I fall into her, lapping her in earnest, no longer concerned with her comfort or her needs as I fill myself with the scent, taste and texture of her once more. Memory of our previous encounters rush through my mind, her naked body writhing in need, her moans filling my ears, her arms reaching for me and holding me tight.

She comes with a long keening wail and as she drifts back down, tries to pull her hips from my voracious mouth. But I haven't had my fill yet. I want everything, all of her, every drop she has to give. She yells my name, but I'm deaf to her pleas. I don't care if she's too sensitive to take more. She'll damn well take what I have to give until I'm finished with her. She tortured me with her silence and now I'll torture her with my love.

I eat her through another orgasm, my fingers thrust deep in her tight little pussy. I remind myself she's recently had stitches down there and gentle the thrust of my fingers. She doesn't seem to care though as her hips move wildly with me as she peaks again and again. Finally, I move back, allowing her a moment of reprieve.

She looks stunned, wild, and incoherent. Her red hair is flung across the pillow, her hands gripping the bars that they're tied to. She's helpless in my hands and loving every moment. I climb up her body, caging her with my arms. I drop my face to hers and say, "You are mine, Taran. No escape, not through silence, not through anger, not even through death."

Her eyes are wide and foggy as she rolls her head on the pillow. I reach down, line my cock against her and drive home. She howls at the intrusion and at first, I worry that I've hurt her, but she lifts her legs and wraps them around my waist, holding me tight in the death grip of her next orgasm.

"Diogo!" she shrieks, shuddering in my arms.

I try to be gentle. try to be mindful of the physical ordeal she's been through. Bishop told me she should be fine, should be ready to resume the sexual side of our relationship. It was one week ago that I'd talked to him about it. It had taken everything in me to give her that extra week, but for the sake of her health I had no choice.

Now, with the tight clamping of her pussy on my dick, I know I won't last. I've been too long without her. I ride her hard, pistoning my hips against hers, slamming myself deep into her body. Seconds later I grunt my pleasure in her ear as I release the pent-up semen. I collapse on top of her, uncaring that I'm squishing her. I need to feel the press of her naked body against mine.

She jerks her arms and whimpers. I don't move. I don't want her to move either. I just want to lay this way forever, trapped in the timeless moment of reuniting with Taran, mind, body and soul.

"I can't hold you, Diogo," she whispers.

I change my mind. Maybe she does need her arms. I

grunt noncommittally and reach over our heads, yanking on the end of the knot and untying her easily. It's not like she can go anywhere anyway while I'm pinning her to the bed.

She hugs me to her, surrounding me even more in her wildly sweet and earthy scent. I bury my nose in her hair and inhale. We lay that way for a long time, neither of us saying anything, content to be together for the first time in months.

I watch suspiciously as the Bishop guy pulls a needle and some other equipment from his desk. I narrow my eyes at him when he approaches. Despite my death stare he smiles widely and explains what he's doing. Or what he's about to do.

"I'm going to draw several samples of your blood to see if I can isolate the protein that makes you and your sister immune to the Death Kiss. I'll need you to hold your arm like this, on this little table here."

I'm sitting on a chair next to a table. He picks my arm up and places the elbow on the table and then extends the arm with the inside facing up. When he picks up the needle, I start to pull back.

"Where I'm from we don't stick pointy things in each other unless we intend to kill the other person with it." Taran giggles from across the room and I glare at her.

"Pointy things," she says and laughs even harder.

"Real mature, sister. Is there a reason you have sex on the brain?"

She blushes and stops laughing.

"I just love how you girls have picked right up acting like sisters even though you were separated for so long. You two are an inspiration." This from Emery, who is sitting on one of the exam beds, holding Blaze in her arms. She doesn't look up as she speaks, so I can't tell if she's being sarcastic or real. Probably both. Emery is a kind woman, but a blunt one too. She smiles down at my nephew and tickles him under the chin, trying to get him to grin back.

"Are you trying to tell us to behave?" Taran asks her with a laugh. "Good luck with that. When we were kids, we were best friends and partners in crime, but we bickered constantly."

I laugh, forgetting for a moment that I'm about to be stabbed in the arm with a giant metal needle. "Oh god, did we ever. You remember when we were playing zombies and cowboys out back at the old farm? It was so long ago, you were only nine or ten and I would've been twelve. We'd built a little fortress to keep the zombies out. We were stealing logs from the wood pile, and when grandpa found out, you completely blamed me. You had an entire essay memorized on how the whole project was my idea and any punishment should fall to me. I was so mad at you for being such a little punk, I threw a stick with a spider on it at you. But instead of being mad, grandpa helped us. He enjoyed playing with us like that, but he also made his time with us educational. I think he was trying to teach us survival skills. He used to do that. Have us build a fire to roast our food outdoors, but then do drills to extinguish the flames so we wouldn't attract unwanted attention."

"I remember," Taran says softly. "Grandma used to scold him, tell him we were too young, but he insisted we were smart and we needed to know."

"Thank god he did teach you how to survive," Emery

says. "Or I wouldn't have had the pleasure of meeting two such fine young ladies. But I'll tell you right now, if anyone throws a spider you both are getting your butts whooped. None of that nonsense around here."

We all laugh, and Blaze lets out a little burp then smiles. Emery coos over him, trying to get him to smile again. "What a good boy you are!"

Bishop squeezes my arm, wipes a swap across the vein with alcohol and places the needle against my skin. I tense up and try not to jerk away from him. Despite my unconventional upbringing and the past several years being married to a Warlord, I'm not really used to pain. My husband pampered me in every way, protecting me from all kinds of harm, while still trusting me to take care of myself. When I wasn't with my husband, Wolfe acted as my personal bodyguard. Even since leaving Santa Fe, he's made sure the worst of our situation doesn't touch me. He's made sure that I stay fed, watered, clothed and protected. I still don't know what his deal is, but I can't fault his protective nature.

As if sensing the fear in me, Bishop tries to distract me. "Tell me about your home in Canada."

"It doesn't exist anymore, either Canada or my old home," I say scornfully, untrusting of the man that holds so many lives in his hands. He seems kind and he has Taran's trust and respect, but I don't know him. Truthfully, I've spent the last few years surrounded by women, except for Wolfe and Silas. I don't quite know how to interact with men. And thanks to Talon, the man who kidnapped and sold me, I'm not sure I want to learn.

Still, this blood thing is supposed to be for a good cause. No one's said it out loud, but if he's able to figure out what makes us immune to the zombie bite, he might be able to produce some kind of vaccination or something. We won't be able to stop the zombies from attacking and biting, but we can stop anyone else from turning. Wait the Primitives out until they all die and then start civilization over again.

"Tell me about your old home and your family. I enjoy hearing you and Taran talk about happier times," Bishop says softly, pressing the needle into my skin. It's the weirdest feeling, having that bit of metal go into me. I feel a little queasy at the sensation.

"Skye used to do everything for us," Taran says, stepping closer to the bed and reaching for my hand, offering comfort. I have to resist the urge to pull away from her. Not because I don't want her touch, but because I've become accustomed to not showing weakness. Especially as a woman, living and fighting in a harsh and brutal world owned by men. Needing comfort is definitely considered a weakness. But her hand on mine feels nice, and does help me feel better about this process.

"My grandparents were older and there was no health care of any kind where we lived, so it was up to the oldest, Skye, to take on the brunt of responsibility," Taran continues. "They chose to settle down far from any cities in the hopes that Primitives wouldn't be attracted to settlements with only a few people scattered here or there."

"Did it work?" Bishop asks, filling the first vial with my blood.

"Yes," I respond this time, my eyes still following Bishop's hands as he replaces one vial with another. "We didn't encounter a single zombie until I was maybe five or six. Our parents were still alive then."

"I don't remember," Taran murmurs, edging closer, her hand tightening on mine.

"You were too small," I tell her. "And it was never the

right time to tell a child about the time a zombie attacked the house."

"What happened?" she persists, wanting the full story.

I shrug, as though it doesn't matter anymore, as though it isn't the most terrifying memory of my childhood. "We boarded ourselves up in the house. For days it beat relentlessly at the doors and windows trying to get in. Day and night, it never stopped trying to get at its goal. We huddled together in the living room, dad, mom, grandma and grandpa with you and me in the middle. Mom was pregnant with Blaze. We gathered every weapon we had in the house. A fireplace poker, an axe, knives. No gun though, grandpa hated guns."

"Yes, he did," Taran says, flashing a smile.

"You wouldn't stop crying," I told her. "The noise the Primitive made kept you awake and you didn't understand why we were all stuck together like that, why you couldn't go outside. You just kept howling and howling and making the situation even more miserable. I wanted to feed you to the zombie myself."

We all laugh.

"Did it go away on its own eventually?" Emery asks.

"Yes, eventually," I agree.

Actually, what had happened was it heard the goat bleating in the barn. The goat hadn't made a peep for the longest time, perhaps sensing the danger nearby. But it must've gotten hungry and started crying for its food. When the zombie heard the bleating it charged the barn, a far flimsier structure than the fortified house. It'd gotten inside in minutes and torn the goat to pieces. We'd had to listen to the animal scream as it was devoured. After that the zombie either forgot about our existence in the house or gave up and left. For weeks after we'd been too scared to go much beyond the front door, eating canned foods and rationing the firewood. Luckily, we'd had a good system for pumping well water for years or we'd have had to leave the house for water. Eventually we realized he wasn't coming back and there didn't seem to be any more in the area. That was the first and last zombie I saw until my parents died of flu a few years later.

I don't say any of this out loud. It's not important. We've all had hardships in our lives. No one comes out of this brutal, apocalyptic world unscathed. I eye the doctor. "What's your story, Bishop?"

Taran looks curious as well, but says, "You don't have to tell us if you don't want to."

He shakes his head. "No, it's fine, my dear. I don't mind talking about how I got here."

He takes the fourth and final vial of blood and gently pulls the needle from my arm. I sigh in relief as he presses a swab to the pinprick hole and tells me to put pressure on it. I comply with his instruction. After placing the vials in a tray and setting them aside, he walks stiffly to the nearest chair and lowers himself into it, leaning an elbow on the armrest. He looks contemplative for a moment before he begins speaking.

"It was such a long time ago," he says. "I want to get the facts straight and my memory isn't young anymore."

"Take your time," Emery says. "We don't have any place to be."

She can speak for herself. I have to get back to Old Tucson and make sure the fucking zombies haven't overrun the place in my absence. Though we've set up an efficient line, holding them at bay, they still pour in daily. Masses of them, trying their luck on the guns and knives that await them in the hands of the hardened soldiers, driven from their own cities to this Sanctuary. Still, I want to hear Bishop's story, so I settle in, my hand still cradled in Taran's as I listen.

"As you know, I was around to see the Fall. It was a mess of panicked people, Primitives taking advantage of the panic, cities, countries, everything falling apart. So many people died. Not just from the Death Kiss, but from each other. Neighbours turned on neighbours, police, military, anyone with weapons, they tried to keep the peace, tried to maintain order, but it wasn't possible. Not with that much fear and hysteria. No one believed anyone. Wild theories about the Primitives flew all around us. It was a terrible time. I would argue the worst, though I've seen many tragedies since then."

"You would have been young," I muse.

He nods. "Mid-twenties, fresh out of medical school, brand new to the military, where they were hiring doctors to help cope with their injured people on the front lines of the Primitive attacks."

"That must have been awful," Taran says, her voice filled with compassion for the horrors the young doctor must have seen and experienced.

He shrugs. "At least I felt like I was helping. I couldn't fight. Couldn't aim or shoot a gun to save my life. So I aided the men and women putting their lives at risk to save ours."

"Women?" I ask in surprise. "There were female fighters?"

Women don't usually hold positions in the police or military. Their wombs are considered too valuable. His words remind me of how tough it was to learn from Wolfe how to shoot and fight. Suddenly I feel proud of this new accomplishment of mine. I've always known I was tough, a fighter, but I'd never been given the opportunity to use weapons before now. Like my ancestors, like the women of our past, I've become a warrior.

"Yes," he says proudly, a twinkle in his eye now as he looks at me. "While men in the military still far outnumbered women, at the turn of the century, women were starting to hold many more important positions. Not just in the military, but in government and world organizations as well. Sadly, we've lost much of the ground women fought for."

I nod, gaining a new respect for the doctor. As much as I loved Silas, he thought that a woman's place was in the harem, in a locked wing of the Fortress where they couldn't be harmed by the world around them. His laws governing the city reflected his values toward women. Gentle, kind, but misogynistic. His views did start to change as his body failed and he had to rely on me more and more to help run his city.

"You were saying?" I encourage Bishop.

He smiles toward me and continues, "When it became clear that the fall of civilization as we knew it was near, we were discharged, told to go back to our families and await news on our next move. Of course, most of us knew that meant we were screwed and being told to go home and await the apocalypse in comfort with our loved ones." He pauses and rubs at the dark grey hair sprouting across his head. "I'd made friends with many people in the unit I was stationed with. People take kindly when you help save their lives. One of the higher ups warned me to get the heck out of Chicago... that's where I lived at the time with my wife and our young son. My parents and sister were a few blocks over."

"Did you?" Taran asks. "Take his advice and leave Chicago?"

He nods. "I wasn't about to turn down that kind of advice from a four-star general. He saved us, me and my whole family. I went home and packed them up and we drove as fast and as far as we could get before we ran out of gas. My dad was ex-military too, so between the two of us, we were able to set up a new home in the mountains." His eyes flick to mine. "Like your grandparents, we reasoned there would be less Primitive activity the further we got from crowds of people, their main source of food."

"Obviously you didn't stay in the mountains. What happened?" I ask, beginning to get a picture of what this man went through with his family. He doesn't even have to say the next part, I already know. The former United States wasn't as well protected as Canada. Not as many wide-open spaces to get lost in. They wouldn't have been able to hide far enough, deep enough before they were discovered.

"Over the years we were picked off one at a time. Rogue Primitives would attack while we were out in the woods looking for necessities. An Outsider took my sister. We never found out what happened to her." He trails off for a moment as we all imagine the possible horrors. Raped, sold, killed. A common practice still. "My wife actually died... a more natural death."

We wait, giving him time to grieve all over again for something he's probably tried hard not to think about for years. Or maybe he has. Maybe he still thinks about her every day. I don't know, I've never experienced all-consuming love. I loved my husband but I wasn't in love with him. The spark, the passion, whatever it's called, hadn't really been there for us. At least not for me. My brain flits to

Wolfe, but I shut that thought down before it can even happen.

"How did your wife die?" I ask as gently as I can.

He smiles in remembrance. "She was beautiful," he says. "A handful of a woman, both physically and otherwise. She was feisty and sharp-tongued. She once picked up the butcher knife as a Primitive broke its way through the back door and into our kitchen and stabbed it through the eye before it could touch any of us. She yelled 'not in my kitchen' and went right back to cooking, stepping over top of its twitching body."

A laugh bursts out of me at the image of the soft-spoken, mild-mannered doctor being married to such a brave woman.

"Died of cancer," he says sadly, the smile melting away. "At least that's what I think it was. There was no way to test her up in the mountains. No way to get her the medicine she needed. I suggested leaving to go find some, but she didn't want me to put my life in danger and I couldn't leave her alone like that. Too weak to defend herself and our son."

"Of course, you couldn't," Taran says reassuringly.

"So I watched her die, just waste away right before us. Her last words were to beg me to take Brandon, our son, and go to a Sanctuary city. By this time, Sanctuaries had arisen and were considered safer places for humanity to gather and begin rebuilding once more. When she passed, we left for Chicago, the nearest Sanctuary."

No one says anything as we picture what it must have been like back then. Then I ask the question that lingers on all of our minds. "What happened to Brandon?" Bishop has a wife in Sanctuary, a woman he must've met and married here. But he has no children that we've seen. Like every other story, his will end in tragedy.

"Died," he says, confirming my suspicions. "From infection. There were no antibiotics left in Chicago and he couldn't fight the fever. After I lost Brandon, I couldn't stay there anymore. I heard about a Sanctuary that was looking for a doctor and set out on a convoy headed west. I've been here ever since."

THIRTY-THREE

TARAN

We leave the doctor's office a little more subdued, a little more thoughtful, than we'd been before entering. Of course, I knew Bishop must have had a tragic story. We all do. Tragedy defines the people who call Sanctuary home. Everyone has lost someone. Death Kiss, disease, civil unrest. None of us have made it this far unscathed.

My eyes fall to my sleeping son, held securely on his godmother's arms. Even Blaze has experienced tragedy. His birth was a goddamn Greek tragedy. I smile grimly at the thought and wonder if I'll ever tell him of the circumstances surrounding that day, or if I'll leave the world to make its mark on him in another way. Because sooner or later, one way or another, he will fall victim to this damaged planet the way the rest of us have.

"Wipe that look off your face, brat." I'm startled from my reverie by Skye's clipped words. She takes my face in her hands and tilts her head down to mine. "He'll be fine. You and that giant crazy-eyed Warlord will make sure of it. Nothing will touch this child, trust me."

I smile, tears suddenly leaping to my eyes. I wrap my

arms around her waist and hold her close. "I've missed you so much. The years were too long without you."

She squeezes me back, quick and tight, before pushing me brusquely away. "It's time for me to get back to my Wol... to Old Tucson. We've had a quiet few days on the front but no one thinks it'll last."

I look at her worriedly, wishing she wouldn't go, but knowing that it would be useless to argue. Not only is Skye as stubborn as I am, but she's a noble, fierce woman too. She won't leave the people she now considers her people until she's ensured their safety.

"Stay safe, sister," I tell her and smile as she kisses Blaze and hugs Emery good-bye.

"Always," she says, getting into her ride with the fierce man who considers himself her personal bodyguard. He doesn't even let her come into Sanctuary alone. We finally gave them a car to use so they can come in for supplies and to visit. My understanding is that they share it with the other refugees, coordinating its use.

Emery and I climb into the car behind Skye's and Wolfe's, greeting Grayson, my constant shadow since Stryker died. The only time he leaves my side is when he's with Emery and Blaze. I'm becoming more comfortable with the idea of leaving my son with Emery since Diogo and I have reconciled. She's as much a grandmother to him as my own would have been. She adores him and takes him every chance she gets. I'm still sad that she decided not to move into the new building with us, but I understand her choice.

"How was the doctor visit, your sister finally give up some blood?" Grayson asks, pulling onto the road and carefully maneuvering us toward the new Tower. He's started driving like every obstacle on the street might attack us. The change in him since taking responsibility for the protection of both Blaze and myself has been heart-warming and a little funny.

"Yes," I say drily. "She doesn't trust many people, and it was hard for her to let a strange man poke a needle into her."

He rolls his eyes. "Doc Bishop is about as harmless as they come."

"Yeah, but she doesn't know that."

"She could beat the man up with a gentle breeze. No, your sister is just one stubborn lady. She negotiates with the Warlord like she'll have any choice in the matter."

"He respects her," I defend Skye. "He knows that she's good at taking care of people and making big decisions."

He snorts. "Sure, but she's still a nuisance."

"Hey, that's my sister!" I'm not surprised by his attitude. If Skye had been a man defending the lives of the refugees and negotiating on their behalf, no one would blink an eye. But since she's a woman, she has to work harder, think faster, and fight for her rights. "I'm proud of her."

He glances at me keenly and then capitulates. "Yeah, I guess she's intelligent and resilient. A little like you. Not hard on the eyes either. I would give it a shot with her if that bodyguard of hers didn't look like he's chewing on nails waiting for the opportunity to dismember anyone that looks at her."

I laugh at his description, but he's not wrong. Wolfe is a strange one, brutal and fierce, but with his own code of conduct, which no one can quite figure out. I decide to go in with Emery when he drops her off. "I'll just be a few minutes," I say, climbing out of the vehicle, with Blaze held against me. "I want to see how Milla is doing."

His lips thin into a line and he reaches for his door. "Not without me," he says, following us. He doesn't trust Milla.

As far as he's concerned, the wife of a traitor is a traitor herself. She could've turned her husband in. She could've switched sides or left him. But she stood with him, only coming to us when she knew there was no hope for her husband. This is part of the reason Grayson accompanies Blaze when he goes to visit Emery. He doesn't allow anyone to be alone with the child except for his parents and Emery. But especially not the wife of a traitor.

My feelings toward Milla are a little more mixed. I don't quite trust her, but I do feel for her. In her place I probably would've done the same. When you're at war, the lines between good and bad become blurred. In her mind, her husband was trying to step into the Warlord's shoes in order to bring order back to the city. Yes, his methods were often cruel, but then, so are Diogo's. I suppose the difference between us is I was on the winning side of the revolution and she was on the losing side.

She's lucky to be alive still. Diogo wouldn't grant amnesty for most people in her position. And while Milla knows on some level that she should be grateful, she still hates my husband. She's not a bad person though, so she tries with me.

We enter the house in single file, the smell of fresh baking bread teasing our nostrils.

"Emery?" Milla's voice calls from the kitchen. "Is that you?"

"Yes, dear," Emery says, pulling off her hat and coat and hanging them in the closet by the door.

Grayson looks around irritably and casts a look toward me. "Five minutes. The Commander is expecting you home this evening."

I raise a brow, sorely tempted to tell him that I'll do what I please. When Grayson is with me, I'm in charge and give the orders. Though technically, Diogo's orders do supersede mine. Still, it sucks to be spoken to like I'm a child.

"Fifteen minutes," I counter.

He shrugs and steps outside to guard the door without argument. Damn it. He just played me. He was probably always going to give me fifteen or so minutes but knew I would try to negotiate. Sneaky bodyguard.

As Grayson leaves, Milla comes around the corner into the living room wiping her hands on a cloth. As soon as she sees me the pleasant look on her face turns to a frown. "You," she says dully. Then her eyes fall to Blaze and she reaches for him. I give him up easily. As much as she resents my husband and is cool toward me, I can't fault her conduct with Blaze. She's perfectly sweet to him whenever she gets the opportunity to see him. I'm not surprised, she was never able to have one of her own, a fact that still bothers her.

"How is my little darling?" she asks, taking him from me and turning toward Emery, ignoring me completely. Emery opens her mouth to answer, but I shake my head stopping her. I may understand Milla's actions, her hesitance to warm up to me again, but I won't allow her to continue widening the rift in our friendship.

"He's fine," I answer. "A little fussy the past few days, but I was told by Bishop that this is to be expected. He's becoming more active, trying to move around more. He lifts his head now and kicks."

The sour look on her face melts away as she smiles brightly at Blaze. "What a smart boy you are!" she cries. "Starting to do things on your own. You'll be walking around on your own two feet in no time."

I smile wanly. "Maybe not for a while yet."

She sits with him and shrugs. "He's the son of the

Warlord," she says, somewhat bitterly. "I'm sure he'll grow up to be a strong young man, as tough as his father."

"And as unwavering and kind as his mother," Emery interjects before Milla can say anything more.

We drop the subject and I sit down in an armchair, watching while Milla opens Blaze's blanket and tickles his feet and belly with her fingertips. He giggles and grabs for her hand when she dangles it in front of him. She's as enthralled with my son as everyone else seems to be, which is why I trust her with the most vulnerable member of my family. It helps his case that he doesn't cry much and mostly sleeps and eats on a schedule. I've been told over and over again how lucky I am to have such a good baby. Instead of making me feel happy about my good fortune, their words of praise toward him make me fear having another. Blaze exhausts me, and sometimes he does cry and cry and I can't figure out what he wants. Does it get worse? Maybe I should mention to Diogo that we're only having one of these.

Of course, as soon as I have that thought I realize I definitely want more. One day. In the future. I can't get enough of his soft cuddly body, his warm baby smell and the way my heart leaps in happiness whenever I touch him. He's a perfect blend of me and Diogo, I can't imagine not producing another one just like him. Except maybe a girl next time.

"How are the schools coming along?" I ask Milla.

She's been organizing and formalizing the city's education system. Searching for people with knowledge in areas like history, reading and writing, botany, and survival skills. She's been campaigning people in every sector to help her clean out old abandoned buildings, reinforce them and then bring in supplies to start schools. After the coup attempt, when she began spending more time in the poorer sectors of the city, she became appalled at the lack of educational resources.

Her look becomes somewhat guarded as she lifts her head and glances toward me. "They're coming along really well. I've managed to find good locations for the schools in all of the sectors and I've organized teachers and classes in Sectors One through Six, Eight, Eleven and Thirteen. The others are a little more hesitant, less trusting. But I think I'm wearing them down."

"If anyone can do it, you can," I assure her, and I mean it. Milla is sweet, personable and determined. She's impossible to ignore with her energy and enthusiasm. I have trouble imagining anyone saying no to her for long.

"You know..." she says quietly, trailing off for a moment. She returns her gaze to Blaze, covering his little belly and chest with her hand. He grabs at her, curling his fingers around hers, a heartwarming new milestone in his development. "I didn't want Jorje to do what he did. I begged him to wait for news of Diogo, make sure the Warlord was actually gone before taking over the city. I was so afraid of repercussion if the Commander was actually alive."

"I can understand that," I say softly.

"I also hated the idea of him taking such a dangerous position." Her voice shakes in anguish and the tears start to fall. She leans back and dries them on the back of her hand. "It was bad enough when he was second in command, going on all those dangerous missions. But I saw how people were with the Commander. So many of them hated him for the decisions he had to make on a daily basis. Sometimes... sometimes I hated him too."

"Do you still hate him?" I ask carefully, not wanting to stop her confession, but needing to know if any part of my family might be in danger from her. Diogo might dismiss a woman, but I know better. I know what we're capable of, especially when someone we love is threatened.

She sighs, hiccupping a little. "I suppose not. I understand why he did what he did, it was what I was afraid of from the beginning. From the moment Jorje told me he'd made moves to ensure unrest in the city." She looks up at me guiltily, her eyes sparkling blue jewels. "I'm so sorry," she whispers. "I could've stopped it. I could've saved you from falling out of that building, I could've saved the Warlord. I could've... could've saved Jorje. He listened to me sometimes. I should've spoken louder, more often, told him to confess to the Commander. And then, and then... it was too late."

I shake my head. "It's not your fault, Milla. Don't put so much of this on yourself. It was terrible, all of it, but it's over now. And you're doing a brilliant job of helping this city rebuild itself even better than before."

She gives me a watery smile and nods her head. "Thank you." She wraps Blaze back in his blanket as his eyes begin to close and his tiny fists stop waving. "This little guy here is the perfect example of something amazing growing out of the ashes of our Sanctuary fire."

"Yes," I say simply, agreeing with her.

She sighs heavily and stands with him, handing him over. My time is up. She must have overheard Grayson giving me fifteen minutes. "Please come visit more often, I promise I'll behave myself."

"Thank you," I say softly, holding Blaze against my chest and revelling in his warm baby body. "I'll do that."

She turns away, then stops. Not looking back, she says, "I don't hate your husband for what he did. I understand why he had to do it. But I don't forgive him. Not yet. Maybe never."

THIRTY-FOUR

DIOGO

"Tighter," she demands. "I'm not made of glass."

I chuckle and tighten my arms around her waist, pulling her back into me. She tosses the spoon she'd been holding on the counter and leans back, tipping her head up and smiling. I kiss her on the tip of her nose and murmur, "The food is going to burn."

She laughs, the bright rich sound hitting me straight in the heart and then heading down to my groin. "When have I ever not burnt the food?"

She has a point. She's been practicing more, deciding that she wants a more conventional upbringing for our son, one where we sit down and eat meals together. Usually I end up taking over and finishing for her when she gets frustrated. I've told her that success in the kitchen isn't instant. She's never had consistent access to the utilities we do here; a fridge, a stove and consistent electricity. We enjoy our privileges, but we don't take them for granted.

She wiggles in my arms, reminding me of our momentary flirtation. "Turn the stove off, love," I say in her ear. She tips forward, thrusting her ass into my cock and turns the stove off. I groan and drop my hands to her hips, clenching them in her lush flesh. I'm instantly hard, desire for my wife rushing through me like liquid fire in my veins. I will never get enough of her. My need grows more fierce with every passing day, just as I knew it would from our very first meeting.

"I need to fuck you," I growl, dropping my head into her neck and nibbling my way from the base up to her ear, just the way she loves it. She moans her sweet music and I know I'm on the right track. I reach up under her shirt, delighted to find nothing between my hand and her breasts. The full, round globes fill my hands.

She squirms and tries to jerk away, tensing in my arms. "Diogo, Blaze hasn't eaten yet. I might... I might..." she doesn't finish the sentence.

"Might what?" I demand, not understanding.

She sighs and shakes her head. "I might leak," she says softly, embarrassment clear in her voice. I grin against her neck. I wish I could see her face. Her soft pale skin will be flushing a gorgeous pink.

"I hope so," I rumble against her, biting into the thin flesh of her neck and marking it. "It makes me so fucking hard thinking about it."

She laughs her relief and melts against me once more. I continue my sensual exploration of her breasts, lifting them and squeezing gently, plucking at her nipples until they become hard points pressed into the palm of my hand. I love the feel of them, especially when they're hard. Liquid drops touch the fingers that pull and tug at them, dripping onto my hand and then down her belly.

I've always been obsessed with my wife, but since the birth of our son I've become ravenously obsessed with her body. The lush fullness calls to the beast in me. I have to remember to go gently. But when she tells me to hold her tighter, fuck her hard, I'm helpless in her thrall.

I turn her around and drag her shirt over her head, baring her gorgeous breasts. Her face is flushed with both embarrassment and excitement. I drop to my knees in front of her, burying my head against her soft, warm belly, the weight of her breasts above me. I tilt my face back and look up at her, then I reach for her breast, straightening to take it in my mouth.

She gasps, her hand flying up to cover the nipple. "Diogo, no!" she says, her voice stunned but no less excited. I take her hand in mine and drag it behind her. I do the same with her other hand and hold them behind her back in a tight, unbreakable hold.

"You don't get to say no to me," I growl at her, but without the heat of anger. I understand her hesitation. She's a new mother, sometimes lost in a sea of hormones and new experiences. Having her husband drink her breast milk is likely taboo in her mind. Perhaps it might have been in mine too before I met her. But now, nothing will stand between us, especially not preconceived notions of how our marriage should be. Nothing will stop me from experiencing every nuance of Taran.

I take her nipple into my mouth, drawing it deep, savouring the touch of her hard nipple against the back of my throat. Her breasts are so much larger that they no longer fill my mouth the way they used to. The excess bubbles out, pressed against her chest from the ravenous pressure of my mouth.

"Oh god!" she howls, and I can practically smell the wetness spreading between her thighs as I devour her ultra-sensitive nipple. Milk spills from her and into my throat. The taste is good and I'm pleased that my wife is providing such sustenance for our child. I don't take much as I have no wish to deprive our son when it's his turn.

I move to her other breast and draw it into my mouth, this time attacking her nipple with a little more force, giving Taran the kind of love bite I know she enjoys. She keens wildly and tugs on her hands. I let them go and she buries them in my hair, holding me tight against her breast.

"Oh god, oh fuck, oh my fucking god!" she yells and I grin against her, loving her wild inhibition once she lets go of herself. "It's so good, it's too good, I think I can almost come from this!" she babbles.

"Not without me," I say, releasing her nipple.

I drag her down to the floor with me. She falls easily, her already weak knees giving out. I catch her in my arms and kiss her soundly, sharing the lingering taste of her own breast milk. She throws her arms around my neck and kisses me back with abandon, her knees parting over my thighs and her hips thrusting against my belly.

I shove my hand up her back and bury it in her hair, forcing her in for a deeper kiss, duelling her for supremacy as her tongue plunges into my mouth. I shove it back into hers and take over, sweeping the sweet recesses, touching her tongue, her teeth, everything.

My aching balls remind me to get on with things. As much as I love playing with Taran, driving her need higher and higher until she's ready to explode, there's nothing I enjoy more in the world than the feel of my cock buried in her sweet cunt.

Without warning I flip her over. She's forced to reach out and brace herself on the kitchen floor so she doesn't faceplant. I drag her pants off, tearing them in the process. I unzip my own pants, pull my cock out and kneel behind her, driving into her in one long, smooth movement. I grip her hips and hold her still, savouring the moment. The feel of her pussy squeezing my cock is the best thing in the world. Nothing compares.

She whimpers and wiggles, trying to get me to thrust again. I slap her ass, enjoying the way her hips jerk on my cock. She laughs and does it again, earning another slap. Her laugh turns to a moan and her pussy floods with a fresh wave of lubricant. I'm so fucking pleased with myself for turning my wife on to the point that she throws herself into the moment without hesitation, taking everything I choose to give her and begging for more.

I pull back and slam forward, filling her again, my balls slapping wetly against her. Over and over I thrust as she yells and claws at the floor, slamming her hips back into mine, seeking her own orgasm. Then I feel it, I feel the exact moment it hits her. Her pussy muscles squeeze me so hard she nearly forces me out. No fucking chance is that happening. I slam my way into her, tunnelling through her spasming pussy, taking every ounce of pressure she lays on my dick.

My balls tighten and tingle and then I'm over the edge with her, shouting my orgasm as I hunch over her back and fill her with my seed, my fingerprints dug deep into the flesh of her hips. We collapse together, her on the bottom and me on top of her, caging her with my much bigger body. Hell, she's so much smaller if anyone came into the kitchen just then they might not even see her. I'm careful to hold the majority of my weight off her back.

As we come down, she sighs contentedly, turning her face to grin happily up at me. I'm about to lay another kiss on her, a sweeter one, a thank you for being so fucking amazing, but a sharp cry has me jerking away. The single cry turns into many as our son tells us in no uncertain terms that we woke him from a pleasant nap.

Taran laughs and reaches for her clothes. She holds the torn pants up and gives me a mock frown. She doesn't bother actually speaking though, since we both know I live to get her naked as fast as humanly possible, which usually ends in the sacrifice of her wardrobe.

I drag my pants on as Taran forgoes hers in favour of her shirt, buttoning it up the front. When we're both half-dressed we walk to the baby's room together. By the time we get there he's throwing a fit bigger than his little lungs have the capacity for, his face screwed up and red, his fists waving in front of him, his blanket kicked away.

Taran picks him up and starts cooing and rocking him, while pulling a breast out of the half-buttoned shirt for him. As she sits in the rocking chair I had made for her, he latches on and starts sucking. Her eyes are on the top of his head and her hair falls around her face. Still, I can tell from the pink suffusing her cheeks that she's thinking about what I did to her in the kitchen and how much she enjoyed it. Poor girl, she's probably trying to reconcile her feelings toward both me and our son taking from the same source. Too bad, she'll just have to get used to the idea, because I'll definitely be doing it again.

I decide not to tease her about it, instead bringing up another subject entirely. "Heard from Grayson you plan on visiting Old Tucson tomorrow."

Her head snaps up and she looks at me in surprise. I'm not sure why she wouldn't realize her bodyguard would tell me everything about her, especially something as important as her leaving the city. She chews on her lip, thinking about how she plans on responding. The trip to visit refugees and check on the wall extension project is near and dear to her heart, but she also knows exactly how I feel about her leaving the safety of Sanctuary.

I decide to let her off the hook. She would have told me eventually, maybe over supper tonight. She was probably carefully planning out her arguments and then deciding on counter arguments if and when I refused to allow her to go. "I will be accompanying you instead of Grayson," I tell her.

She looks both shocked and relieved, then her gaze turns shrewd as she tries to figure out my angle. "Why?" she demands with a frown. We both know she doesn't mean, why am I going instead of Grayson, but why am I allowing her to go at all.

I think over my answer and then say, "You are the wife of the Warlord. You stand for the people. It was one of the reasons I wanted you for my wife, you are more diplomatic and soft-hearted. You can reach the citizens in a way that I can't."

She smiles with humour. "So glad I can be of service, Commander."

"You know that I also care for you more than is reasonable for a man in my position."

She rolls her eyes. "You don't even know the meaning of the word reasonable."

I chuckle. I do know the word, but not when it comes to her. My preferences for my wife are so far from reasonable that I spend an inordinate amount of time daily arguing with both her and myself on the correct course of action. Chaining her to the apartment, wrapping her in safety equipment and stationing a dozen personal bodyguards on her detail is, apparently, not reasonable. Although, perhaps if I'd done all of that months ago, she would learn to become less prone to being kidnapped.

"You were saying something about how amazing I am with people?" she reminds me, arching a brow.

"Yes, I believe it will be good for you to be seen in Old Tucson. You can forge connections over there, so once the refugees are integrated within our walls they will have a kind face and soft voice to rally around. It doesn't hurt that you look like your sister and they damn near think she's some kind of saviour angel."

She grins at me. "The tone of your voice suggest you don't agree."

"The woman is difficult," I grunt.

She laughs. "You used to think I was difficult."

"You're my wife and I love you, there's a difference."

"So, love my sister then," she rebuts.

I cross my arms and shake my head at her. She knows that's not going to happen. My heart is made of stone. Only two people in this world have cracked it, Taran and Blaze. The very idea of caring for her sister is laughable. The only reason I might go to any lengths to ensure Skye's survival is I know how devastated Taran would be if anything happened to her troublemaker of a sister.

"You will be expected to stay by my side the entire time we are outside the gates of Sanctuary," I tell her, ignoring her last comment. "You will not wander off, you will not go anywhere near the front lines, you will not speak with any of the soldiers working the perimeter of Old Tucson, and you will follow every command I give."

Her eyes follow the bulge of my arms as I clench my fists imagining all the things that could happen to her outside of Sanctuary. The very thought gives me worse heartburn than her cooking and makes me want to change my mind. I pile on several more rules before I'm satisfied my sometimes willful wife won't do anything I don't approve of.

The humour falls from her face and she asks quietly, "Is it so bad over there?"

"Yes, very." I watch her carefully, my beloved wife, the woman who I would gladly follow into death. I want to sugarcoat this for her, but there's no point. She'll see it with her own eyes tomorrow. "Not as bad as some refugee camps I've seen, but not good. They've created a front line with a trench where soldiers work to stave off the worst of the Primitive attacks. Men fall daily out there. Your sister fights as well, shadowing her man while he's stationed on the line."

"I didn't know Skye was actually fighting on the front lines!" she exclaims, her voice a mixture of horror and admiration for her tough older sister. I tend to agree with her, it's rare that's I've seen a woman as determined as Skye, as filled with passion and integrity. Except for my wife. Taran may not be much of a conventional fighter, but she fights for what she believes in. She spent years climbing the wall in what she believed was a fight for the justice of humankind.

"Some of the Primitives make it through the lines and into the ruins of the old city, picking off refugees as they go. Food and clean water are scarce, as is medical supplies and anything resembling societal structure. It's a mess out there. You need to be prepared to see some things you're not going to like."

She nods thoughtfully and then looks down as she moves Blaze from one breast to the other, helping him latch. "I knew it would be bad," she murmurs. "I guess I didn't realize how bad. This is probably why Bishop wanted to make a special trip out there."

"Indeed," I agree with her. "He cleared it with me days ago. He has supplies, food and blankets he wants to deliver."

"Emery too," Taran adds. "She wants to see the wall progress since she'll be responsible for overseeing food production on that side of the city once construction is complete. Has she talked to you about it? She has all kinds of wonderful ideas."

I have my doubts that all or any will be realistic but I keep my comments to myself. I like the way Taran and her friends are coming together to improve Sanctuary. It frees me to focus more on security, infrastructure and law and order.

"She's mentioned that she has several ideas she wants to run by me. I've told her to schedule a meeting."

Taran frowns. "Schedule a meeting with who? I don't think you've ever mentioned having a secretary."

I grin at her, flashing my teeth. "And that's how I get out of most meetings."

We laugh together, and for perhaps the first time in my life I feel perfectly content.

"Let me help you," I say, reaching for the armload of supplies Doctor Bishop is struggling to carry out to the car. We're loading two vehicles with food, blankets, medicine and other supplies.

"Thank you, Emery," he says kindly, tipping two of the boxes into my waiting arms.

"What is all this?" I ask, helping him place them into the trunk next to the bags of clothes and blankets I'd gathered from families from Sector Thirteen that wanted to help out with the refugee situation.

His voice drops as he gives me a quick rundown. "Some tubing and needles for IV's, antibiotics, painkillers, fluids, a few other things." He glances around quickly and I realize he's probably taking more supplies than he's been authorized to give, stretching our own city supply more than the Warlord would approve of.

I smile warmly and pat his arm. "You're a good man, Doctor."

He nods at my compliment and closes the lid on the trunk. We climb into the vehicle, me in the back with

Bishop and Taran in the front with the ever-imposing Commander. In the car behind us is a few more of Diogo's men who will act as our bodyguards while we're in Old Tucson. My heart pounds in exhilaration and fear at the thought. I haven't left this Sanctuary city since the day I arrived around thirty-five years ago.

I had been nineteen, and my parents and I were granted Sanctuary by the Warlord before Diogo. Since coming here I've lived under two regimes, not including Jorje Cruz's coup attempt. The old Warlord, Commander Pearson, hadn't been a military man. His title had been superficial, and his ability to govern showed it. At the time I had been too young to understand or care about the politics surrounding Sanctuary cities, but in the years after my arrival I'd quickly learned what made a successful Sanctuary, and what didn't.

Pearson had been diplomatic. He believed the city should make joint decision on everything, and put most things to a vote. The process had been slow and mostly ineffectual. Arguments, bickering and protesting had worn down any power he'd had. His power-hungry lieutenants had obliterated the last of the people's trust in Pearson's rule. It was only a matter of time before another Warlord stepped in and took over his crumbling city. Either that or a Primitive attack. Our wall hadn't been the best either, maintenance had fallen to the wayside and patrols were almost non-existent.

My parents hadn't been pleased with the direction the city was going in and we'd held discussions about moving to another Sanctuary. Either Santa Fe or Sacramento. But before we could decide, my father had been killed in a hunting accident. Broken-hearted my mother soon followed, allowing herself to waste away until death claimed her too.

For awhile I'd been resentful of her decision to leave me, but gradually, as time had distanced me from the tragedy, I'd come to realize the depth of my parents' feelings for each other and am proud of that connection. I was born out of love.

Before our new Warlord could come in and take over, I met someone. We married, for a brief time. It had been the thing to do. Marry and produce babies, for the good of the Sanctuary. But we quickly came to realize that we weren't a good match. We didn't hate each other, but we didn't love each other either. Our inability to get pregnant was the last nail in the coffin of my short-lived marriage.

Lack of children isn't uncommon in Sanctuary. Without regular access to food and medicine, fertility levels dropped. My periods had never been regular, so it hadn't been a surprise to discover that I struggled to get pregnant. And the one time I did fall pregnant, I lost it within weeks of the discovery. Again, I'd been pragmatic about the event. Miscarriages weren't uncommon either. Oliver, my ex-husband, moved out shortly after finding out. He believed that I didn't care enough, that I'd done something to lose the baby. I think it was an excuse to leave a marriage that made us both miserable. I'd waved good-bye and gone back to my simple life. Last I heard, Oliver had remarried and moved out of our Sanctuary.

When I was in my thirties, Diogo Fuentes had come in with his army, taking over in the blink of an eye. At first, we'd been horrified and fearful. His regime was harsh with so many rules and laws. Anyone that went against him was immediately executed. But then, like it always does, life settled into a pattern. We got used to the new Warlord's rule and shaped ourselves around him.

For my part, I hadn't been too disappointed. I slept

better at night knowing our walls were well defended and food was more plentiful under his guardianship than it had been under Pearson's. The commander's faults were in his arrogance, his refusal to listen to the people. By separating himself from the citizens of his Sanctuary, he couldn't hear us when we cried for food, when we begged for justice. He allowed striation to flourish, separating the poor from the elites.

Still, Diogo was better than nothing, and now, after meeting and falling in love with my surrogate daughter, he's opened his eyes to his city. Or perhaps he's just giving his wife the things that will please her. Either way, our Sanctuary is beginning to flourish under his dictatorship and has become a happier place for everyone. The reason doesn't really matter, as long as the results continue.

I stare straight up as we approach the wall. Truth be told, I rarely even come close to it. This is the barrier that keeps the Primitives out. It nearly killed me every time Taran climbed it and made her way out into the desert, making herself vulnerable to attack. Though she knew I worried, I held the majority of it back knowing how the lives of others would benefit from her efforts. It was her calling, and she did her job beautifully. I couldn't have been prouder if I was her own mother.

I gasp my awe out loud as the massive doors open wide and Taran turns in her seat to look at me. She grins and nods knowingly, having gone through several times now with her Warlord husband.

Our drive to Old Tucson only takes a few minutes. I grip the edge of my seat as we speed along the bumpy dirt path that's been forged from countless trip this way. The guard vehicle takes the front position and I can see men hanging from the windows, weapons sweeping the desert as they search for any approaching threats.

My heart thumps in fear and I almost wish I'd stayed behind with Milla and Grayson, who are babysitting Blaze at the house. I've never actually seen a Primitive up close, or even from a distance for that matter. The idea is absolutely terrifying. I've heard more than enough stories to know that I wouldn't stand a chance in the face of an attack. I'm not a fighter. I've never even held a weapon, let alone fired a gun or stabbed anything.

"Do you think we could be attacked?" I ask hesitantly. The question is directed at Diogo who's been out to Old Tucson several times in the past months. He intimidates the hell out of me so I don't often speak directly to him. Especially after I yelled at him to boost his wife out of a sixth-floor window while the building burnt down. Even though we both knew that was the best course of action at the time, I still worry he resents me for separating them during such a terrible event.

I shudder as I remember that day. How close I came to death, how close all of us came to it. The feeling of the building rumbling underneath me, the smoke blinding and choking us, and Diogo throwing his body into mine as the whole thing went down. I will never forget those moments. They play in my brain over and over whenever I close my eyes and try to sleep.

"Not likely," Diogo says reassuringly, his gaze meeting mine in the rearview mirror. I can read the truth there and relax a little, knowing Diogo doesn't sugarcoat. "The Primitives are going after the easy fresh meat of the refugees, and though they try the city defences once in a while, they aren't straying much off the perimeter set up in Old Tucson. We'll drive deep enough into the ruins that the likelihood of them getting in back there is almost none."

I nod, not surprised. Diogo wouldn't take Taran anywhere near the action, he simply values her too highly to place her in that kind of risk, though Taran has been through several battles and would point out that she can take care of herself. I smile gratefully and murmur my thanks. He may not be the son-in-law I might've hoped for, but we're growing on each other. I know when I leave this earth he'll still be doing his damndest to keep my girl safe. That's good enough for me.

"How many zombies do you think are out there?" Taran asks her husband.

He shrugs. "Dozens at least. Maybe hundreds. It's hard to tell since they seem to have some kind of attack strategy. We can't be sure how many are hiding and how many are hitting Old Tucson."

"Primitives."

"Pardon me?" I ask in surprise, turning to Doctor Bishop who'd spoken quietly, almost to himself, but loud enough that everyone in the car can hear.

"The word zombie holds stigma, it marginalizes and reduces the people that used to have value to us. Most of us have lost loved ones to the disease. We call them Primitives to differentiate them, but the word holds fewer negative connotations, it simply speaks to their state once they've been turned."

We all fall silent for a moment, and then Taran speaks softly from her place next to Diogo. "Thank you, Bishop. You are absolutely correct. They deserve what little dignity we can maintain for them."

My eyes burn as I think of the many lives lost to the Death Kiss. People we all knew and cared about. Bishop is right, we have no right to treat them like they're horrifying objects, they deserve more from the people that are still capable of loving and remembering them.

No one else says anything and the heavy moment passes. I lean forward in my seat, staring intently as we approach Old Tucson. I hold my breath and glance around fearfully, worried that this will be a weak point in the defences, but we pass easily through a heavily armed gate, moved for the purpose of our small envoy. Diogo lifts a hand to the men guarding the checkpoint. They nod and return to duty once they've pushed the heavy gate topped with barbed wire back into place.

I twist in my seat to look at them. They're some of the toughest most battle-hardened men I've ever seen and they look so young. Far too young to have seen so much. Then again, in this world, we grow up fast. Even reaching my age is an achievement, and not one I'll take for granted.

Our drive through Old Tucson is long and difficult. The debris in this section of the city is much worse than our Sanctuary where we've had years to clear fallen buildings and junk from the streets. The men in our guard vehicle are forced to get out frequently and move the obstacles before we can continue. After almost an hour of watching the men in front of us, Taran asks Diogo about it.

"Does it always take this long when you come visit?"

"No," he replies squinting through the windshield and then moving cautiously forward once the road is cleared again.

"Are you doing this because of me?" she asks shrewdly.

He glances over at her and then answers honestly. "Yes, your sister scouted out some safer locations much further back from the front line. I chose one of them, but there wasn't enough time to have a path completely cleared for us." He pauses for a moment and then says, "We should be there within minutes if I'm getting the landmarks correctly."

Sure enough, almost as soon as he says it we approach a building that looks as though it was once a small hospital. Skye steps from the front doors, shading her face and waving at us, a smile spreading across her lips. I smile in answer, though I'm sure she can't see me in the back of the jeep. She is breathtakingly beautiful. Odd, because she looks just like Taran, but somehow, while the same features on Taran give her an intense look, they make Skye utterly stunning.

She gives Taran and me hugs as we leave the vehicle and glances at Bishop with grudging friendship. I guess he's still not completely forgiven for stabbing her with a needle. Skye leads us into the building, speaking over her shoulder. "This place is buried so deep in Old Tucson, I'm not sure it'll be any use for what you're looking for Doctor."

"Bishop, please," he replies pleasantly, following her into the dimly shadowed lobby past a desk that looks frozen in time with items still littered across the surface. I look around in fascination. It's run down, but not too badly damaged that I can tell. "And it'll do just fine. With the expansion of the wall, your people will be able to spread out and inhabit the sections around here."

"Are you setting up a clinic over here?" I ask curiously.

"Yes," he confirms. "Though there is plenty of need within Sanctuary, out here is where the real emergency lies. There are acute injuries in need of urgent care."

"Are you moving?" I ask worriedly. I know I should be supportive but the idea of losing another friend is heart-wrenching. These days I cling to the few I have left. I think I must be developing some kind of anxiety disorder or something. I cling to those I love with an unnecessary fierceness.

My heart pounds in fear whenever I think someone I care about is at risk. Even living across the city from Taran and the baby is difficult.

Bishop smiles kindly at me, as though reading my mind. "I'll be over here a few days a week to help set up the clinic and work with anyone that has medical knowledge to organize them. Not to worry, I'm still quite happy in my own little clinic in Sanctuary."

I smile my relief and squeeze his arm. Again I tell him, "You're a good man."

He shakes his head. "The Warlord is a good man. He helped me come up with this plan and approved the particulars."

I glance toward Diogo, a little surprised the man who is notoriously stingy with our resources is willing to part with them so easily. He snorts and mutters Taran's name. Of course, his wife had a hand in the negotiations. I smile internally at their amazing dynamic. He is our tough, uncompromising leader. The man who makes the difficult decisions for the sake of all of us. Yet he bends for his wife, listens to her gentle wisdom and gives her passionate demands an ear.

"Yeah, yeah, you're all good men," Skye interjects, rolling her eyes. "Would you like to stand around in reception chatting all day or would you prefer to see what we've done with the hospital so far?"

I laugh and follow her lead as she walks at a fast clip pointing out various features of the makeshift hospital. There are twenty rooms, three that will be turned into acute care. She's had the place cleared of debris and is in the process of having people come in for cleaning detail.

"It'll have to be spotless and sterilized before it can be used. We don't want people dying of infection over here." Bishop glances into a room. "We'll need to replace the mattresses, but these metal bed frames were built to stand the test of time." He looks back toward Diogo.

"Make a list," Diogo growls to one of his men, who immediately pulls some kind of notepad from his pocket.

"This used to be a cafeteria," Skye announces as we walk into a large space lit up from dozens of windows. A bunch of them are smashed out, but enough still intact that the effect is still very nice. We all stand silently for a moment, staring up in awe at the beautiful glass ceiling. "I'm thinking of turning it into an atrium, where patients can come sit and rest in the sunlight while still being surrounded by the outdoors. We can pot some of the wild shrubbery and bring it in."

"We have a botanist over in Sanctuary that can help you choose the best varieties. Some of the flowering kind will brighten the place up." Everyone looks at Diogo in surprise. First of all that he would care about brightening anything up, let alone a hospital, but also his knowledge of plants.

Taran grins broadly and takes his arm in hers, squeezing him. He looks down at her, his usual fierce expression giving way to a moment of tenderness. My heart leaps as I watch them together. Clearly a private moment. Perhaps our Warlord knows more about the world than waging war and dictating the lives of others. Perhaps he has a green thumb.

We move to the end of the space, heading into the bowels of the building where Skye intends to show us the old 'boiler' room. I'm not sure what this is but I assume it has something to do with the functioning of a building this size. Engineering and mechanics were never subjects I easily grasped.

As we leave a shadow flits across the edge of my vision and I jump as a man steps out unexpectedly and strides purposefully toward Skye. I stare with my mouth open as he reaches for her, gripping her arm tightly and dragging her a short way away from the group.

"You didn't tell me you were leaving the camp," he snarls down at her, giving her a shake. "You don't ever leave the camp without notifying me."

She yanks her arm back, but he doesn't let her go. "You don't get to dictate my movements!"

"I'm the only one around here with any interest in protecting your stubborn ass," he insists. "Can't do that unless your ass is within reaching distance."

"Oh, fuck off," she snaps furiously, trying to pull away again. "I don't owe you anything."

"No?" he says, raising an eyebrow.

They argue in a bubble completely of their own making. I'm awed by the raw emotion surrounding the two of them. They clearly have very strong feelings for each other, but don't seem to have explored them. I look at Wolfe curiously as they argue. Now he's fallen silent while she tears into him, treating him to a vicious diatribe. What an interesting pair, both passionate, both strong and stubborn. He cares for her more than she seems to know, but it seems so obvious, his heart is on his sleeve. Whereas I can't tell where she's at emotionally. I know she's lost a husband recently that she cared deeply about. Maybe that loss is colouring her view of Wolfe's intentions.

"Perhaps we should calm down some," Bishop steps forward and interjects.

"He's only trying to protect you, Skye," Taran adds softly, then she gives the other man a sharp chiding look. "Though he could go about it a little differently."

I bite back a smile as the tiny Warlord's wife steps up to her sister's giant bodyguard and tells him he needs to calm down or take his pique outside. He eyes her like she's an annoying morsel that should be flicked aside, then he turns on his heel and stalks down the hall. I'm relieved at the release of tension.

Skye turns back to us, her face pensive. "Should we continue?" She glances up, her eyes flickering across everyone in the dimly lit hall.

"Indeed," Diogo mutters, his lack of amusement at the interruption clear. Taran takes his arm and we continue into the boiler room. I look around with mild curiosity as they discuss the possible sources for electricity and heating.

A shuffling sound behind me and a soft growling is the only warning I have. I don't even have time to turn around, but the others do and what they see has their eyes widening. Taran screams for me to move just as something lands on my back so hard I'm knocked to the ground. Pain shoots through my arm, the one that'd been broken in the building collapse. I'm stunned and completely unprepared for the agony that slices into the back of my neck.

Diogo reacts faster than anyone else, pulling his gun and a hunting knife. I flinch as a shot rings through the space, deafening me. The thing on my back slumps and I try to crawl out from under it. I look over, terror stabbing at me as I find my face inches from the dimming eyes of a small female Primitive, maybe even a child. Her poor little face has been completely desecrated. The flesh of her cheeks has been stripped bare, leaving behind congealed black blood and rotting skin. Her hair is a matted mess on her head.

As I stare at her, Diogo swings his blade, slicing her head clean off her shoulders. I shriek as it rolls away and scramble back from the body. My back strikes the wall and I stare around in horror as everyone stares back at me with conflicting looks of horror and pity.

I look up at my Warlord as he stands over me, his eyes hard chips of obsidian, his blade in one hand hanging down by his side and his gun in the other.

I reach my hand back, touching the wound on my neck. I begin to realize what everyone else has already concluded. I've been bitten. I'm about to take the Turn. Within seconds I realize this isn't a scenario that will end well for me. Not like it did for Taran and Skye. I don't have the immunity. I can already feel a fire igniting in my veins as my body prepares to change.

Taran screams and lunges toward me. I open my mouth to tell her to stay back, to keep safe, to remember that she has a baby to think about. Diogo swiftly turns and flings an arm out, catching her around the middle before she can plunge past him.

My left arm jerks of its own volition, as though I have no control over it. I scream in agony when my leg follows, hitting the concrete so hard it bounces. It feels as though my bones are breaking and shifting, rearranging themselves. Everything inside me feels like it's liquifying, like boiling lava is being poured over my internal organs, melting them down. I want to speak, I open my mouth to beg and plead for someone to end this before it gets worse, but nothing comes out. My mouth jerks and stretches wide and then even wider, and then something snaps inside, as though my jaw has become unhinged. Saliva spills from my mouth as I'm forced into a silent scream.

I look up at Diogo, silently pleading with him.

I don't want to die.

THIRTY-SIX

TARAN

I don't hear myself screaming, but when the room finally falls quiet my throat is raw so I know I must've been shouting at the top of my lungs. The sight of Emery, my beloved Emery, on the ground on her back, blood pouring from her is more horrifying than anything else I've ever seen. Diogo lifts his eyes to mine. I expect to find that bleak nothingness that is his signature when he's about to kill. Instead I see anguish, an expression that makes me fear even more.

I launch myself toward her, but Diogo catches me around the waist and holds me back. I'm helpless against his superior strength as I watch the woman who helped raise me slowly turn into a Primitive. Diogo half turns and gathers me against him, though he keeps his one arm free with his weapon raised and his eyes on her.

"I'm sorry," he says to me.

Those two words hammer home the reality of this situation. She's going to die, my best friend, my surrogate mother, is going to die, right here before my eyes. And my husband is going to do it.

"No, no," I yell. "We have to do something!" I look frantically around the room, but my gaze meets only concerned and saddened expressions. This can't be happening. Not when I'd finally been so close to happiness. I can't be losing another person.

"Taran... I'm so sorry, we did a sweep of this area, but it must've somehow gotten past our defences," Skye says softly, stepping toward us. She looks up at Diogo as she approaches. "I can hold her."

I shake my head, my hair whipping around as I try to drop to my knees, intent on crawling to Emery if I have to. Diogo transfers me to Skye, who holds me against her. I don't want to hurt my own sister, but I will fight her if she doesn't let go. I try to dig my elbow into her side but two of Diogo's men surround us, creating a barrier between me and what Diogo is about to do.

He points at another of his men. "You guard the hall, make sure there's no more headed our way."

The seconds tick by at a crawl as each one takes its toll on my beloved friend. Right in front of our eyes she twists and turns, shrieking like a banshee, her fingers turning to curved claws as she attacks her own face and scalp. Her head swings back and forth on the floor, her hat flying off.

Diogo kicks aside the body of the Primitive that had attacked her. I sob helplessly against Skye as he lifts the knife standing over her.

"Please, Diogo," I shout again. "Don't do it!"

He lifts his eyes to mine, his filling with hurt as I promise him I won't forgive him if he does this. A part of me knows this isn't true, knows he's just doing what he must to ensure survival for the rest of us. It doesn't matter. I'll say or do whatever it takes to get him to stop. Frantically I look around for something or someone that might help. Then my eyes fall on the Doctor.

"Bishop!" I yell, an idea coming to me. "Please, you can help her. You can cure her with my blood."

He thinks about it and shakes his head. "No, it's too crude, it won't work. With time and luck I might be able to find an antibody and if we're even luckier, maybe a vaccine, but it won't cure an already turned human. Besides, your blood types might not be a match, she could reject..."

"She's not a Primitive though!" I shout. "Not yet, but she will be if we don't help her. Please, even if it's a small possibility, we have to try, we owe it to her. She's done nothing but help and support all of us. She deserves better from the people she loves."

I shift my accusing stare to Diogo, piercing him until he moves his knife hand back to his side. A silent battle rages between us as I beg him with my eyes and he argues with himself over the wisdom of giving me what I want. Every instinct in his body is telling him to kill the turned human before she can turn around and kill someone else.

"Please," I beg, tears falling freely down my face.

Diogo growls his annoyance and glares at the doctor. "Is it possible?"

Bishop looks taken aback that the Warlord would even consider this plan of action. Then his intelligent brain kicks in and he thinks over the possibilities. Finally, he shrugs. "I suppose it's theoretically possible. I think there's a slim to almost zero chance this could work. I don't even know exactly what it is about Taran and Skye's blood that contributes to an immunity. I suspect a genetic protein marker, but I won't know until I've had time for further research."

Glancing down at the twisting screaming woman beneath him, Diogo says grimly, "We don't have time, Doctor. Tell me now, are you willing to try or do I put her out of her misery?"

Bishop looks down pityingly, his expression making it clear he doesn't think this'll work, but he says, "I'll give it a try."

Diogo leaps immediately into action, shouting commands at his men. "Cover her head, wrap something tight around her mouth so she can't bite. Tie her hands and feet, make sure she can't kick or scratch. You have thirty seconds. I'll hold her down."

I bring a hand up to cover my mouth, to stop myself from yelling at them to be careful with her. They don't have time to be careful, they have to get her wrapped and ready to transport. Each passing second is a move towards no return. We have to get her into a room and prepped for a makeshift procedure.

"Done!" Diogo's man snaps.

"Lift her up with me, I'll take her head and torso, you take her legs," Diogo commands. "Skye," he says sharply, "lead us to the nearest room that'll work for the transfusion. Bishop, you grab the equipment you'll need and meet us upstairs."

Everyone scrambles to move, obeying Diogo's orders. He didn't give me any so I stand looking around worriedly. Skye grabs my arm and says, "Come with me, we'll need to get you prepped too. No fucking way am I getting hooked up to a zombie."

"Primitive," I correct her, remembering Bishop's words back in the car on the drive over. "And she's still human. Still the woman that took me in and helped raise me. Gave me rations from her own mouth during lean months." I choke on my words and swipe at the tears.

Skye looks back at me with compassion as she hurtles down the hallway, towing me with her. Diogo and his men follow, struggling to hang onto a twisting Emery who is becoming rapidly infused by the superhuman adrenaline filled strength of a Primitive.

"I'm sorry," Skye says grimly.

I shake my head. It doesn't matter. Most people need to distance themselves from the things that were once our loved ones. It helps save pieces of our heart when they are inevitably taken from us. "Just help me save her."

Skye doesn't say anything, but she picks up her pace. I find a job to do when we reach the first set of double doors. I fling myself against them holding them open for our small party. As soon as everyone is through, I run to the next one, ensuring that no barrier will slow us down.

It probably takes less than a minute before we reach the top floor of the hospital. Maybe four minutes since Emery was infected. I feel sick with the implication. She'll be well into the Turn. Is there a way to turn her back? Is everyone just humouring me for her inevitable death? Should I just let her go and accept yet another death in the long line of people I've lost in my life?

No, I'm not willing to accept that this is the end for Emery. She doesn't deserve to go this way. Not after all the years she's sheltered behind the walls of Sanctuary, safe from this kind of harm, only to be bitten nearly the moment she steps foot outside of her home. It's just not fair, it can't happen this way.

"In here," Skye says urgently, flinging a door open.

We're faced with an empty metal bed frame, but the

room is clean and there's a table next to the bed. "Clothes," I mutter, stripping my coat off and laying it across the metal frame. Skye does the same, and when Diogo nods toward his men, they do the same.

"Tie her arms and legs to the bed frame," he orders. "Strap her head down too. Keep her mouth covered."

While they tie her down, Bishop comes rushing back into the room. His gaze is concerned and he's breathing hard as he drops his equipment onto the metal table with a clatter. He points at the bed. "Taran, you'll need to sit or lay down close to her."

I nod and approach the bed, but Diogo grips my waist and holds me back. He glares at Bishop and pulls his knife. He twists to place it against Emery's throat. She's struggling so hard she immediately cuts herself.

"Be careful!" I say to him, but he ignores me, looking toward Bishop. "Do it quickly. I won't tolerate much of this. She's too far into the Turn as it is, with each passing minute she gets stronger."

"Don't kill her," I beg him, turning to press my body to his. "Please, please don't kill her."

He drops a kiss onto my head and says, "I don't want to, baby. Believe me."

I nod against his chest and hold my arm out so Bishop can push the needle deep into the artery at my wrist. Getting a needle has never been my favourite sensation, but this time, for Emery, I'd be willing to take a thousand needles if it means she can come back to us. As Bishop works, I lean against Diogo and allow him to hold me protectively. He called me baby and I can't bring myself to mind. Suddenly it seems so trivial to get upset about his pet name for me.

We fall silent as Bishop pins Emery's arm to the bed and forces a needle into her vein, connecting us. When he finishes taping the needle to her skin he releases some kind of valve that allows the transfusion to begin. I look down and watch as the blood leaves my arm and makes its way through the short tube to Emery.

Only the muffled screams of my friend as she endures the agony of the Turn breaks the silence. The rest of us don't speak. As far as we know, nothing like this has ever been done before. A crude attempt to transfer immunity from one person to another. As the seconds tick by everyone in the room remains motionless, breathlessly watching and waiting.

I stand in the shelter of Diogo's arms, grateful for his strength. I don't think I could stand on my own right now. I continue to watch fixedly as the blood moves through the tubing. Her only chance of survival hinges on the success of this procedure.

I start to despair as she continues to shriek, twist and turn on the bed, the metal frame grating from ill use as she bounces on it. I bury my face against Diogo and wait. It feels like hours but is likely only minutes. Then something happens, something extraordinary. Emery relaxes. She settles into the bed and stops moving.

I hold my breath and peek past Diogo, worried that maybe we've killed her.

"What's happening?" Diogo demands, looking toward Bishop for an answer. I'm wondering the same. Is it working? Or are we killing her? I hadn't thought of the second possibility before, but maybe my immunity will kill Primitives instead of curing them.

Bishop shakes his head and approaches the bed cautiously. "I don't know."

He removes part of the cloth covering Emery's face, careful to keep it firmly wrapped around her mouth. It sticks a little to the deep gashes she's gouged in her forehead. I gasp. She's as pale as death, her eyes shut, the angry gashes livid against her skin.

"Is she... is she..." I can't bring myself to finish the sentence.

"Not dead," Bishop assures me, checking her pulse. He looks down at her curiously then lifts her hand, the fingers are relaxed, no longer curved to claw at herself and other people. "I've never seen anything like this before. I think it's probably unprecedented."

"Do you think it's working?" Skye approaches the bed too and touches Emery's arm. "She's so cold."

"Taran's blood is definitely doing something." He pauses, deep in thought and then continues. "If I had to guess, I would say the antibodies in Taran's blood that make her immune to the Death Kiss are attempting to overwhelm the Primitive disease, erasing it from her system."

"So fast?" Diogo sounds sceptical. "Don't these things take time? I've never seen anyone recover from disease this fast."

"Not necessarily. Necrotitis Primeval is fast-acting, turning its victims in a matter of minutes. There are very few viruses that have that kind of power. Most incubate within the patient until they overwhelm the immune system. Perhaps it makes sense that the cure, if this is a cure, will work almost as fast."

"You think she's recovering then?" My voice shakes as I ask the question.

"I don't know," he replies simply. "But you need to be prepared for any possible outcome. We've never seen anything like this before. It would be reckless to assume we're watching a recovery in progress. We might have simply slowed it down."

I refuse to believe there's no hope, especially when I've been through the impossible over and over again and survived. If I can do it, then so can Emery. I lift my eyes to meet Skye's and see a similar sentiment. She gives me a half smile and moves her hand down Emery's arm to wrap her fingers around Emery's, giving her comfort I can't. I feel a rush of gratitude that my bond with my sister didn't diminish over our years apart. We can still read each other.

"With your permission I'd like to unwrap her entire head," Bishop says to Diogo.

Diogo nods. "Do it."

His body tenses against mine and he holds me tighter as the doctor gingerly unwraps Emery's face. One of Diogo's men takes a step closer to the bed, raising his gun in case he needs to make a quick move to protect us.

As her face is revealed I feel my stomach lurch. In the seconds before they'd managed to grab her arms, she'd dug deep furrows across her forehead and cheeks, one of the first acts of a freshly turned Primitive, stripping the flesh from their own body. Her mouth is unwrapped next. Her lips are still pulled back in a snarl, but as the doctor continues to draw the cloth away, her jaw relaxes and her mouth shuts. She looks almost peaceful. As though she's sleeping off a sickness.

"How much blood do you need?" Diogo demands. "I don't want Taran to lose too much."

I roll my eyes but maintain my silence. I'm not even dizzy from blood loss, I don't think I'm at risk.

Bishop confirms my thoughts. "No, she'll be fine. The human body has about five litres of blood and can easily lose a litre without ill effect. I'm only going to take about half that from Taran."

Diogo narrows his eyes at Bishop. "Take a drop more than necessary and we'll be having a talk."

Skye laughs from the other side of the bed. "No blood drops, no hair, not even a nail clipping. Every precious piece of Taran must remain completely intact or her Warlord protector will be having a talk that you probably won't come back from."

The tension in the room releases and we all laugh, even Diogo. His eyes meet mine, a warm glow in them. He knows how overprotective he is. He struggles daily to find a balance for his obsessive need to keep me safe. He often goes overboard, but it's part of his personality. He's built to protect, especially those he has an investment in.

"Taran..."

The thin, shaky sound of my name coming from the bed has me jerking from Diogo's arms and rushing around him to Emery's side. He lets me go. I reach for her hand, wrapping my fingers around it the way Skye was doing on her other side.

"I'm here!" I say excitedly, looking up at Bishop.

Primitives don't talk and they especially don't say the names of the people they care about.

"I'm here," I say again, reassuring her.

She licks her lip, a trickle of blood escaping from her mouth. I wince when I see it. She must've bitten herself during the Turn. I reach up to wipe it away with the cloth lying next to her head. Diogo growls and snatches my wrist jerking my arm back.

I sigh and turn my head to look over my shoulder at him with a raised brow, giving him a look that clearly says, this is overboard Warlord, and besides I'm goddamned immune. If she bites me, it will be my third time. Hell, I'm practically collecting Primitive bite scars now.

He releases my hand but his own hovers over mine as I wipe up the blood and then gently touch her cheek where she hasn't scratched it.

"I... I can't move," she mumbles.

Hope rushes through me as she speaks again. She's making sense, not something a Primitive is capable of.

"You're strapped to the bed, Emery," I say softly.

"Why?" she asks. Her eyes remain closed and she seems to be having difficulty, as though struggling to stay awake.

"For your own protection," I tell her, not telling her it was for our protection too. She doesn't need to know that she would've attacked us if left unrestrained.

"Wh-what happ...." her voice trails off.

I speak before she tries to force more words than her current energy level is capable of. If Primitives are filled with adrenaline, then it makes sense that the loss of that adrenaline would leave a person feeling completely drained. Or at least that's my inexpert theory.

"You were bitten by a Primitive," I tell her gently, choking a little on the words. "It got you in the back of the neck."

Her eyes fly open and I'm shocked by the wild look in them. The blue irises are surrounded by red, completely bloodshot. Like a Primitive. I almost jerk my hand away, but then the wild look fades leaving behind confusion and fear.

"Am I... did I...?"

"No, you're going to be fine," I assure her, hoping like hell I'm telling the truth. "We used my blood to infuse yours with my immunity."

"W-worked?" She sounds surprised.

"It looks like it," Bishop says from beside me, reaching for my arm and gently removing the tape so he can pull the needle out.

"Thank you," she whispers, a single tear falling from her eye and trickling into her blood-matted hairline.

THIRTY-SEVEN
DIOGO

Taran sobs her relief in my arms, shaking from the release of terror she'd felt after Emery was bitten. I sheath my knife, relatively certain the danger has passed, and hold her tight against me. Emery has fallen asleep, her face set in exhausted lines. The poor woman had been on the razor's edge of turning into a zombie.

I've never seen anything like this procedure. Well, that's not entirely true. I've seen crude blood transfusions during times of battle. I've never seen anyone come back from the Death Kiss. Only Taran, and she hadn't started the Turn. I'm astounded that the procedure worked. That the blood from a healthy person can be used to cure a disease.

"How is this possible?" I demand of the Doctor as he removes the needle and tubing from Emery's arm.

Bishop takes a piece of gauze and presses it against the drop of blood forming from where the needle had pierced Taran's skin. "Hold it tight, until the blood clots," he says then looks at me. "To be honest, while I understand the fundamentals of how this procedure worked, I can't speak to specifics. We don't know enough about the Death Kiss for me to speculate."

"Try," Diogo growls.

He nods and thinks for a moment. Of course, he would've understood the implications as soon as Emery started getting better. "Well, it seems that Taran and her sister have a natural immunity to the Death Kiss. Since it's both of them instead of one, that would suggest the immunity is genetic. Likely there are other people in the world with the same immunity. Perhaps they don't even know that they're immune if they've never been bitten."

"Or maybe they do," Skye interrupts raising her hand to touch the edge of her scarf where it hides her scar. "There's such a stigma surrounding the Death Kiss that the likelihood of someone who's been bitten telling anyone is slim. I hid it for years, only sharing my experience when my husband saw the mark and knew it for what it was."

"That makes sense," Bishop agrees. "During my youth there was a deadly blood disease ripping through certain parts of the world. The chances of surviving this disease once it was contracted was very low. But a few did survive and when they tried to integrate back into their communities they were shunned and sometimes killed."

"That's barbaric," Taran says, and I smile. Of course my beautiful girl would hate the idea of people attacking each other. "What happened? Was the disease eradicated?"

"The crisis grew to the point that the World Health Organization was forced to step in and fast track a vaccine, which worked on most people. Unfortunately, there were many people that refused to take the vaccine and so the disease was not completely eradicated. And then Necrotitis Primeval took over as the most deadly disease in the world. I'm not even sure if ebola exists anymore."

Ebola. I turn the word over in my mind. Such a harm-less sounding word for something designed to kill so many people.

"Why would people refuse to take the vaccine if they knew it would keep them safe?" Taran asks.

Bishop hesitates before answering, as though gathering his thoughts. "Well, that's not easily answered, there are many reasons someone would refuse a vaccine. Sometimes people would refuse for religious reasons, sometimes it was a lack of education, or a lack of understanding in the science behind medicine. In the parts of Africa where Ebola had become especially prevalent, many people feared the vacci-nations would give them the exact disease they were trying to avoid. You see, vaccinations usually have a small amount of the disease that needs curing."

"The vaccination contained the disease?" Skye asks sceptically. "That seems like a bad idea. I would probably refuse it too."

The Doctor chuckles. "There wouldn't be enough of the disease in the vaccine to harm the recipient, simply to stim-ulate their immune system into fighting back."

"Do you think we can turn my blood into a vaccine?" Taran asks.

"We're still in early stages, but this," he waves toward Emery, "gives me hope that it's possible."

Taran smiles broadly and thanks the doctor profusely. "Can you imagine if we've just solved the Death Kiss?" she says excitedly.

I look toward her sister who still has a sceptical look on her face. I agree with Skye. This is a significant step forward in our understanding of the disease that has toppled our civilization, but the odds of actually curing it are slim. We caught Emery early, before the Turn could properly take hold. The more likely scenario is that in a few months or years our Sanctuary, with Doctor Bishop in the lead, will be able to produce a vaccine that will then have to be transported from city to city, then from country to country and then around the world. It'll make our fight easier, make it easier to pick off the Primitives if we're less afraid of turning. But they'll still be able to attack us. Most people who suffer a Primitive attack are killed by the brutality of it, not by the Turn.

I keep all of this to myself as Taran and Bishop talk. I can't dim her happiness as she imagines a future without this terrible disease ravaging our world. The fact is, even if the Death Kiss is eradicated, we're living in a very different place than the one that existed 50 years ago. Humans are brutal beings with an ingrained urge to fight. And those that don't fight, die. If there are no Primitives to kill, then I've no doubt human will turn on human as we fight for territory.

But these are problems for the future. For now, I need to get my wife out of Old Tucson and safe behind the wall. This attack has highlighted the dangers in leaving Sanctuary. Precautions were taken before we came, there should have been minimal danger. Yet danger found a way through the barriers and came straight for us.

"Can she be moved?" I ask, nodding toward the bed.

Bishop shook his head. "Absolutely not. She's far too weak. She could die in transport."

I nod thoughtfully and after a moment, start giving orders. "You can either stay here with her or come back to Sanctuary. If you choose to stay, I'll give you two days and then I want you back in the city working on this vaccine of yours."

"Of course, I'll stay," Bishop says. "If she continues to improve then we should be able to move her in a few days."

"Good. I'll leave two soldiers behind to guard the hospital."

"You don't need to do that," Skye argues. "I have men that can watch over them."

Stubborn woman.

"Bishop and Emery belong to Sanctuary and as such are my responsibility, besides you need your people on the line, not out here in the middle of abandoned territory watching for an attack that probably won't come." I turn away from her dismissively and take Taran's arm. "Let's go." I nod toward my men.

"What!" Taran gasps and tugs at her arm. "No, I'm staying with her."

I don't bother to waste words on telling her something she won't hear. I correct my earlier thought to include Taran, stubborn *sisters*. I heft a protesting Taran into my arms and carry her from the room, striding down the hall and out the front doors into the bright sunshine.

She clings to my shoulders and squints up at me. "I didn't even get to say good-bye."

"She wouldn't have heard you." I drop her in the passenger seat after one of my men opens the door to the jeep.

She glares at me through the windshield as I walk around the front and climb into the driver's side. I bite back a smile as I remember every other time she's given me that same look in this same car. My feisty little wife, always up for a good argument she won't win.

The second we're moving she snaps, "Maybe Emery wouldn't have heard me, but my sister would have. You need to stop forcing me to leave places before I'm ready. The danger had already passed, we could've stayed there a while longer."

I grin, the first real grin I've had in a while. I feel good. Really good. My wife is safe and sound at my side and we just took a significant step forward in eradicating a disease that has been killing humankind for half a century. I reach over and grip Taran by the back of the neck, dragging her toward me for a quick, hard kiss before turning my attention back to the road.

THIRTY-EIGHT

TARAN

Exactly two days later Emery is moved to Sanctuary. She is weak, and even that short amount of travel time is almost too much for her. Now she's laying in a comfortable bed in Bishop's clinic, an IV attached to a fluid bag dangling from her frail arm. Milla sits on her other side holding her hand and looking worried while I pace.

"Why is she so weak, Bishop?" I ask the doctor, turning as I reach the wall. I'm pacing because Blaze hasn't enjoyed the hours we've spent here, cooped up inside the clinic's windowless back room. He's fussing in my arms, waving his fists against my shoulders and occasionally wailing in frustration.

"I can't say for sure without the proper equipment, but I can speculate based on what we know of what Necrotitis Primeval does to the human body." He pauses for a moment, gathering his thoughts, the way he often does. Bishop isn't one to speak until he has something to say. "The condition of which she suffered is a brutal one, it doesn't just change the human body, but the transition takes place rapidly. Like I said, it's impossible to say for sure, but if I had to guess I would say her internal organs took quite a beating. Her blood type would have been changing over to Type N, which would have a massive impact on her physiology. On top of that you have the massive and constant rush of adrenaline being dumped into her system. The human body isn't meant to take that kind of a beating. There's a reason most Primitives don't live much beyond five years once they've turned, their bodies just can't take it."

"I thought they died early because they're driven to reckless behaviours," I point out.

He nods his agreement. "Yes, that too. Both contributing factors definitely shorten their lives, which is a good thing for us. It means there are much fewer of them out there. If they were able to reach full human lifespan potential they may have managed to overwhelm the few of us left over from the Great Fall."

I shudder at the implication and hold Blaze a little tighter. Despite the hardships we're forced to live through, we do get the chance to live, which feels like an absolute miracle when taking into consideration the odds we're up against.

"Well, when Emery recovers maybe you'll be able to use the information you're gathering in order to help get rid of this disease."

Bishop looks at me sadly and I know what he's going to say before he says it. "If she recovers, Taran. Her survival isn't guaranteed. If I'm right, then her organs took a beating that she may not be able to come back from."

I look over at Emery's peacefully sleeping face and my heart leaps into my throat. I fight back tears. She has to pull through, I don't know what I'll do if she doesn't.

Milla stands up, swiping at her own tears. "I'll be leaving soon," she says abruptly. Diogo is expected to come pick me up this afternoon, but we're not sure when. Milla is still not ready to face him. "Why don't you let me take care of Blaze for you so you can sit with Emery awhile longer? Dee and I intend to go visit one of the new schools in Sector Twelve. He'll enjoy the time outside."

I chew on my lip, debating whether I should let her take my son. She cares for Blaze as much as everyone around him, so I know he won't be in any danger with her. But I worry constantly when he's not with me. His rough entry into the world, combined with my position as the Warlord's wife makes him more vulnerable.

"I second that," Bishop says, standing up and reaching for Blaze, taking the decision from my hands. "Your son needs some fresh air and you need some uninterrupted time with Emery." Bishop looks into my eyes and says reassuringly, "He'll be fine. He'll have that personal bodyguard the Commander has assigned him."

I smile at that and agree with them, allowing Bishop to hand Blaze over to Milla. The bodyguard assigned to Blaze, Karl Harding, is even bigger and more intimidating than Grayson. He has a look that I've come to understand means the recipient of that look should start running, because the man is about to take them apart piece by small piece.

After Milla leaves with Blaze and Karl, Bishop mutters something about doing an inventory check and leaves the room. I'm positive he's just giving me alone time with Emery, but I'm grateful for his thoughtfulness. She's so well-loved, she's been constantly surrounded by people since she arrived back at the clinic. Even Skye accompanied her personally, wanting to satisfy herself that Emery's care here in Sanctuary is sufficiently up to her standards.

I sit with Emery, making sure to keep hold of her arm and hand so she has as much human contact as possible. I drift through a series of daydreams, imagining what life would look like if it were absolutely perfect. All of my friends and family would be alive and well, living in a Sanctuary without strife. We would get rid of sectors and open the city to refugees. But the refugees wouldn't be running from Primitives, because Primitives would be completely eradicated owing to the vaccination we're able to create using my and Skye's immunity. In a year or so I would get pregnant with my second child, a girl this time. She would look and act just like her Auntie Skye who would visit all the time and spoil my children.

Maybe... just maybe... we'd find a band of people living in the mountains, somehow safe from the Primitives. Among them would be my grandparents. We'd welcome them into Sanctuary with open arms and they would be delighted to see their last remaining family alive and well. They would meet their great grandchildren and settle down in an apartment in my building.

After a while, when her grief starts to fade, Milla would remarry... maybe Grayson or Karl. She likes the big tough guy types. They'd settle down and she'd discover that she could have children all along, she just needed the right partner. Skye would marry... an image of Wolfe pops up and then I reject it. Too scary, too intense. And I don't see him settling down in Sanctuary. No, she can't marry him. I need Skye to stay here forever. Maybe she can marry whoever Milla doesn't hook up with. Then I laugh out loud as I imagine Skye's reaction when I tell her she's going to settle down with Milla's reject.

"Wh-what's so funny?"

I look at Emery and the laughter dies. Her blue eyes are faded, the red in them now a dull pink. The lines in her face have become deeper grooves almost overnight. Her body is thinner, weaker. Though she looks haggard, I still think she's beautiful because she's my Emery. Once more I blink back tears as I explain to her about my daydream. She chuckles, a rusty sound that barely makes it past her cracked lips. I stand and pour a glass of water for her. I tilt her head and help her drink, catching the dribbles.

I sit back down and take her hand in mine again, appreciating the warmth against the palm of my hand. "I'm going to name my daughter after you," I tell her softly. "Emery is such a beautiful name."

"I'm flattered, but," she wrinkles her nose, "you can't break with family tradition. If its girl you need to name her something elemental, like the rest of you. Something really lovely, like... Rayne. I always loved the smell and the sound of rain. It washes away all the bad."

I smile at her. "Rayne it is then."

"Are you sure you want to do this?"

Diogo's voice comes from behind me and I twist in my chair to look at him. He's dressed in dark clothes from head to foot, leaving off his military outfit for the sake of his people. Tonight, he's one of them. His terrifying war mask, the skull of a Primitive, covers half his face so I can't see his expression, but I know from the sound of his voice that he's in a pensive mood. So am I.

"It's tradition," I answer simply and turn back to my little mirror, leaning forward to put the finishing touches on my own mask, which I've painted on. I'm wearing a ghoulish skeleton, with a red heart across the top of my cheek, just below the sweep of my lashes.

Diogo comes up behind me and drops a kiss on the top of my head. "Stunning, as always."

I smile up at him and then laugh as the lips in the mirror twist into a grotesque smile. I did a really good job of my makeup this year. "How's Blaze?" I ask Diogo.

"Turning into a little beast," he says with a slight smile. Our one-and-a-half-year-old son seems to have really hit his stride since learning how to walk, giving everyone some-thing to run after. Karl is at his wit's end chasing after a tiny human with absolutely no care for his own well-being. "He's with his babysitter and bodyguard," Diogo adds.

I smile at that, but don't bother asking which babysitter. It's become clear that everyone wants a piece of the Warlord's son. His own parents have to fight to get quality time with their own child, but I wouldn't trade this family for anything. We all fit together now.

I turn on my seat and give my hand to Diogo. "Let's go."

He pulls me from the bench and into his arms, dropping a light kiss on my lips so as not to mess up my carefully applied makeup. His lips hover over mine, lingering, breathing me in as I breathe him in. Together we stand that way, counting the seconds, minutes and years we've been together and all the ones yet to come. Gratitude can't even begin to cover what I feel when I'm with this man. Along with my son, Diogo is my everything. I can't imagine loving anyone the way I love this man. And he knows it, because every day I wear my heart on my sleeve for the world to see.

"Let's go," he repeats my words. "Get this over with so I can get you back here and see what's underneath those robes."

I laugh and pick up the skirt of my long flowing gown and the cape-like coat I'm wearing over top of it. Dee and Milla helped me prepare, kindly donating their own clothes in an effort to make me over into some kind of ethereal grim reaper. They said they were going for majestic, befitting the wife of a Warlord, but I think it's a little on the creepy side.

Grayson meets us in the hallway of our apartment building and nods solemnly. I'd asked him earlier if he planned on joining us and he'd told me that he was going wherever I was going unless otherwise ordered by Diogo. I'd probed further, wondering about his story. Lately it feels imperative to me to gather stories, find out who the people are behind the tragedies. Maybe one day I'll chronicle all of our journeys, piece together the timelines and try to make sense of everything.

Grayson didn't say much, just that he lost his family to a Primitive attack as a young child and was brought to Sanctuary as an orphan. He was lucky enough to gain the physical strength and skills necessary to become part of the elite guard, and then later my personal bodyguard. I smiled and joked that his job must be pretty boring these days. His reply had been a joke about my penchant towards getting kidnapped. While I have no intention of anyone taking me unawares like that again, I don't think either Diogo or Grayson are willing to let go of my tendency toward getting in trouble. They both watch over me like mama hens over their chick. He hadn't appreciated the analogy when I told him and I snickered over his disgusted reaction.

Together, our small group descends the stairs of our building and out into the cool evening. We join a crowd of people waiting for us outside. When they heard the Warlord was going to join them in their Day of the Dead walk they started crowding around the front doors of our building, waiting for us to emerge. I watch proudly as Diogo patiently takes the time to greet his citizens and ask them to join us in our walk. With each passing day he becomes more skilled at balancing his Warlord role with his role as a leader who understands his people.

We walk arm in arm through the streets, surrounded by a strange mix of both jubilant and solemn people. The Day of the Dead is a day of celebration, but it's also the day we acknowledge those that we've lost.

We pass easily through each checkpoint, which have

been opened for the public to pass freely through. I've been in discussions with Diogo over possibly getting rid of the checkpoints and merging the sectors now that he's restored order to the city and unrest is at a minimum. Bishop has been supplying me with arguments throughout history of how the separation of citizens is a bad thing, including a lesson on something called the Berlin wall.

As we walk, Skye calls my name and I wave to her through the throng. Breathing heavily as though she'd been running, she catches up to us and takes hold of my other arm. She's wearing a pair of tight black pants and a heavy masculine leather coat, one that I think belongs to Wolfe. Her face is painted with a sinister skull, similar to mine but starker and more frightening.

"Thank you for allowing us to join you," she says somewhat stiffly to Diogo.

He nods at her. "Now that that section of wall is down, joining Old Tucson with Sanctuary, your people will be given more ease of movement."

"They aren't my people," she denies, though she has definitely become their interim leader. They look to her for all things. She's become their advocate and, in some cases, their saviour. She watches out for their welfare and quite literally fights for their survival. Though lately she's been distancing herself from them, handing off more jobs to other people in her place. In my heart I know she's preparing to leave, but I don't want to ask her point blank. I don't think I'll be able to stand hearing the answer.

A few months ago, Wolfe left. None of us knows what happened and Skye refuses to say, but since his departure she's become more distant. When spoken to, she has a tendency to be abrupt and snappish.

We fall silent as we approach the flaming pyre next to

the open gates, which are heavily guarded in case the Primitives decide to come this way. I watch in awe as the flames reach up into the inky black sky throwing smoke and sparks. One at a time the citizens of Sanctuary step up to the flames and throw in the names of their loved ones. With each step we take forward my throat tightens.

As we reach the pyre, I remove the papers from the hidden pocket in my robe. Diogo goes ahead of me, tossing in the few names he's written down: Victoria Graystone, Garrett, Jorje Cruz, and Stryker. I was surprised that he'd added the last two to his list and told him when he was writing the names down. He'd told me that I've taught him what compassion looks like and that he now sees how this world can tear us apart and twist us into something we might not have been otherwise. He said that those men had been his friends and though they'd committed unforgivable crimes they still deserved to be remembered. I'd thrown my arms around him and hugged him tight.

As Diogo steps to the side I take his spot, feeling the heat of the fire sweep over me. I fling the names of my loved ones into the fire; my parents, grandparents, brother and Emery. We lost her almost two months after she'd been bitten. She didn't turn, but she was never able to recover from the injuries she'd sustained. In the end, her death had been almost a relief. Every passing day was agony for her as she continued to grow weaker and weaker until she could no longer eat or drink by herself. Then she stopped being able to speak until finally her organs shut down.

I've had many people in my life die, some violently, some from illness, and some, like my grandparents, simply disappeared from my life so I never found out what happened. None were quite like Emery. Every day I sat with her. I sang and I talked to her, I looked after her. She tried to fight, but after a long battle with little improvement she had finally passed away in her sleep when I wasn't there to comfort her.

A part of me died with her that day, a part that was young and hopeful, that could look at the world with optimism. I just didn't understand how we could be given so much hope when a miracle happened and my blood saved her, only to have her taken from us a few short months later. I still don't understand and maybe I never will, but for Emery I will keep fighting to see the brightness in every day.

Skye takes my place and tosses her own names into the fire. I'm not sure who she's mourning, but I can probably guess. We both lost our family at too young of an age, but she has also lost a husband and many friends when her Sanctuary fell. Now, except for me, she's alone. And as far as I can tell, completely miserable.

As we walk away from the pyre, surrounded by our fellow citizens, we fall silent, each one of us deep in thought as we use this day, the Day of the Dead, for what it's meant for; we remember. Finally, as we approach the checkpoint bisecting our sector from the area that separates Old Tucson from the rest of the city, Skye turns to say her goodbyes.

"When will I see you?" I ask her, hugging her close.

"Soon," she promises.

Something in my chest releases at her response. Skye won't leave without saying goodbye first. If she says she'll see me soon then she means it. She turns and heads back into Old Tucson with the other refugees. She could've driven into Sanctuary, but she chose instead to make the long walk with her people. I watch for a moment until she disappears from sight.

"Let's go home," Diogo murmurs in my ear, sending a

shiver down my spine. I take his hand and we continue on our path back into Sector One.

Karl meets us at the building with a sleeping Blaze held securely in his strong arms. He nods at us and heads up the stairs at a fast clip, intent on getting the baby to his bed. I smile at his protectiveness. His job isn't done until he sees his charge tucked into his bed and sleeping safely and soundly. The huge man never once complained about being taken off military duty and given babysitting duty. I couldn't have asked for a better protector for my son.

We make our way back up the stairs. Diogo picks me up about halfway through the climb and carries me the rest of the way. I don't complain. Our long walk to the city gates has taken up most of my energy. I tell Grayson that he can go home now, but he insists on seeing us right to the door before he signs off for the night.

"Goodnight," I murmur to him with a smile as Diogo sets me on my feet. I feel an overwhelming urge to hug my bodyguard. He has protected me every day for almost two years. He's put his life before mine and doesn't resent the job.

But my husband will likely object to me pressing myself against another man, so instead, I try to tell Grayson how I feel with my gaze. Risking his life and limb, I also reach out to squeeze his arm. Uncharacteristically Diogo remains silent through the exchange.

Then we're inside and alone. Finally.

"I'm going to check on Blaze," I announce, unsnapping the button on my cloak and pulling it off.

"Don't be long," Diogo replies, his voice a dark promise.

I grin and hurry into Blaze's room. As I look down at him, I'm overcome with emotion. Though this is the day to mourn our losses, it's also a day of celebration. Celebration for those lost lives, for the things they accomplished and continue to accomplish in our hearts. Thanks to my parents and grandparents I know what love looks like. I'd learned patience and compassion from Emery. And I've learned the depths of all my emotions and the passion I'm capable of with Diogo. These are lessons that will stay with me, even as the faces of the dead slowly fade into the darkness of memory. I will live to pass their legacy onto my children and grandchildren.

I brush the tears from my lashes, determined that there will be no need for more. I touch my fingertips to my lips and press them against the downy softness of Blaze's forehead. I leave his door open so we can hear when he wakes up. Lately he's been trying to climb out of his crib and I want to know right away if he falls.

Diogo has lit every candle in our bedroom, casting the room in soft shadows. I go into his arms, revelling in their incredible strength. He has taken so many burdens for this family, for this city and the desperate people pouring in looking for Sanctuary. His shoulders are broad and strong, able to take the burden. But sometimes he is also vulnerable. He feels the losses acutely. Not just the ones he cared about, but the deaths he's been forced to witness and unable to stop, the deaths he's personally ordered and the ones he knows will come. He is not the unfeeling monster I'd thought him to be when we first met.

Perhaps it's the emotion of the day, or our gratitude for being alive. Our lips meet in a passionate, almost desperate kiss. I go up on my toes to deepen the contact with my much taller husband. He lifts me against him, holding me tight and giving me what I need; his hands, his tongue, everything all at once.

He grips the collar of my dress and tears, and for once I

don't care. I reach for his shirt, pulling at the buttons. He pushes my hands aside and does it for me, rending the fabric right down the front while never once breaking our kiss. He pushes me back on the bed coming over top of me and caging my face between his palms, holding me in place and protecting me at the same time.

I reach between us, tearing at his pants and quickly freeing him. Our need reaches a fever pitch as torn clothes fall to the floor. Our battle is a silent one though, both of us aware of our son only one room over. In a single move Diogo is inside of me. I groan into his mouth, wrapping my arms around his neck and hanging on tight as he pumps into my welcoming body. He reaches down and grips my hips, holding them in place so he can thrust harder, faster, deeper. Our shared urgency takes over and we cling to each other through the storm of our passion until we both finish almost together.

Diogo holds me against him, my face pressed to his chest, his arm wrapped underneath me and over my shoulders, his other palm wrapped possessively over my hip. We don't find out for several more weeks, but this is the night our daughter is conceived.

I fall asleep with Diogo's whispered words of love in my ear.

A cold windy rain hits me, sinking through the layers I'm wearing. I glance toward Skye who stands with me on the line at the edge of Old Tucson. She's shivering in her coat and hat, her shoulders hunched and her hands stuffed in her pockets. Bishop stands on my other side along with a dozen of my men. Skye's people are maintaining the line while we work. Our visibility is diminished by the rain, but we've decided to move forward with our project anyway. Months of planning have brought us to this point, the turning point in our war against the Primitives.

An eerie silence has settled around us. Almost as though the enemy knows we're here and knows we're coming for them.

"They're out there," Skye mutters, as if confirming my thoughts.

According to her they ebb and flow, they run recklessly at the line in an attempt to drive the refugee camp back and pick off the survivors. With each failed attempt they learn. A fact that we've had to acknowledge and come to terms with. They're more intelligent than we gave them credit for.

The evidence points toward some part of their human brain remaining intact enough that the Primitive is able to tap into some form of reasoning behaviour. They are thinking, learning and communicating. We're beginning to see patterns in the way they attack nuclear power plants and the way they attack our city. On the outside, the attacks look suicidal, unthinking and entirely instinct driven, but now we believe differently. There's no other explanation for their ebb and flow attacks.

"On my mark!" I shout at my men.

They scramble to take their places. Some reinforcing the line while others flank the nearest weak points at the gate and the mess hall. We prepare ourselves for the onslaught. Skye pulls her knife and a gun, holding them loose at her side. Wolfe must have taught her the practice that works best in this kind of attack. Shoot to kill, then decapitate the enemy while they're down.

I do the same, the weight of my weapons against the palms of my hands giving me a sense of peace. I am a warrior, a protector and a Warlord. This is my place. Taking down the enemy that could rise up and attack my city, that could take down my family.

"Release!" I shout the next command.

We look over our shoulders toward the giant pen housing three quarters of our animal stock from Sanctuary. Goats, cows and sheep rush out and hurtle toward the back of the line. We leap into action, herding them across the line with shouts and the occasional discharge of a weapon. Mud from the wet ground is kicked up as they run.

I use my sleeve to wipe muck off my face. As the last animal moves out of the pen and follows its brethren out into the rainy afternoon, I turn and move to the edge of the line. Men from both Sanctuary and Old Tucson line up their weapons at the ready.

"Do you think it'll work?" Skye takes her place at my side again.

"We'll find out in a few minutes," Bishop says, stepping up to my other side. He's wearing the heaviest, warmest coat we could find for him. Intended to protect the old man while he waits with us for the results of our experiment. This is his baby and he wanted to be out here to watch the action and take notes for research.

Injected in each animal is a dose of the vaccine Doctor Bishop worked tirelessly to develop. We're using the city's stock to lure the Primitives into ingesting huge amounts of the vaccination. They are too far gone to be cured, but the vaccine might kill them. I don't know or care about the particulars, but Bishop has assured me that his experiments in the clinic have been promising. He believes once the Primitives take the vaccine that their bodies will try to fight the disease. Of course, like Emery who had weakened and died after getting a dose of immune blood from Taran, they won't survive the transformation back to human.

One of my concerns with this plan occurred when Bishop told me that the vaccination contains trace amounts of Necrotitis Primeval. "To stimulate the body's immune system to fight," he explained. I had been sceptical but then he'd given me a long lecture on the history of disease and vaccinations. I ordered him to stop talking, told him I trusted him with the safety of our city and allowed him to move forward with the plan.

The animals weren't harmed by the injections as they are only carriers for the disease. The only animal that we know of that experienced any kind of Turn is canines, and they were eradicated from Sanctuary cities long ago. Most people haven't even seen a dog in their lifetime.

At first the silence coming from the other side of the line is disappointing. We should be hearing something as the Primitives tear into their fresh meals and go into a blood frenzy. Then the first horrific sounds of an animal dying reaches our ears. Skye flinches and then rolls her shoulders and stands a little straighter. She knows, we all know, that this is for the good of humankind.

Taran was horrified by the plan and had begged us to think of another way. Logically she knows there is no other way, but her soft heart bled at the thought of this sacrifice. Some people are hunters and others are not. My wife is no hunter. I didn't point out to her that the animals would have been eaten anyway. Sooner or later, they would become food. They obviously would have been killed in a more humane manner, but Primitives are fast, the animals won't suffer long.

Soon, the sounds of dying animals fades into the rainy evening, then nothing.

"Brace yourselves!" I shout, anticipating that once the Primitives have eaten their meals, they will be immediately drawn to the next food source. Us.

Nothing happens though. The men on the line hold themselves tensely at the ready, their weapons drawn and pointed in the direction where the sounds came from. The mist is obscuring our view. Still nothing. Could it be possible? Did the vaccination work quicker than we thought?

We wait in silence, straining to hear something. When several minutes pass and nothing occurs, I give the order to advance. Almost as one we move forward, 50 strong, a mix of my people and Skye's people. We walk slowly, keeping formation, prepared to move quickly if a threat hurtles at us out of the dusky rain. But nothing does.

What confronts us when we finally arrive at the massacre sight is both terrible and wonderful at the same time. The animals have been torn apart until they're unrecognizable, teeth marks all over their flesh, organs and bones. Laying all around the dead animals are dead Primitives. Or so they seem. I bend to one of them and check for signs of life, but there's nothing. No pulse, no flicker of an eye, no snarl or growl. Just death.

And peace.

The zombie in front of me used to be a young woman, perhaps late teens or early twenties. Her blond hair is dirty and matted to her scalp where sharp objects have been thrust through her skin. Her clothing is in tatters on her body and her skin shows advanced signs of necrotitis, or rot, telling me she'd been a Primitive for a while, perhaps even years. But it's her face my gaze is drawn to. The ravaged features, probably once quite lovely, are still and peaceful.

The men follow suit all around me, checking on the Primitives and then shouting back to one another that they are all dead.

"The vaccine seems to have worked almost instantly," Bishop says, his voice taking on a musing tone. "Perhaps the adrenaline that constantly fuels them is the first thing that is stopped, which would result in instant death if they've been running on it for long enough. Or maybe they..."

"You can figure it out later, Doctor," I tell him and he falls silent.

I stand and Skye comes to stand with me.

"Now that we know the vaccination works as not only an immunity to the disease but a killer to those that are infected, we can work on eradicating the disease entirely."

Skye's voice holds awe in it, as though she can't believe this is a possibility. The threat of Primitives has been around for our entire lives. The thought that we may not have to live under the blanket of fear they cause is almost unimaginable.

"The other Sanctuaries will need to be told, the vaccination handed over to them," I say to her.

"I will take it to them and spread the word," she offers.

Skye has been making moves to leave Sanctuary for a few months now, so I'm not surprised by her offer. Taran will be devastated, but she'll understand. Skye hasn't been happy here in Old Tucson or even in the Sanctuary with her sister. There always seems to be a desperate air of misery around her. I don't know what she's looking for but it's not here.

"You are a carrier for the immunity," I remind her. "A very precious commodity."

She bristles. "Are you going to stop me from leaving?"

I think about it. I could, and I probably should. If anything happens to Taran, or my son, who also carries the immunity, then Sanctuary and the wider world would need Skye. But I won't stand in her way. Instead I will help ensure her success. "A party of the best men from here and from Sanctuary will be assembled and sent with you on your mission. You will be protected while you journey to the other cities and give them the vaccine."

She nods her head but doesn't say anything. She's not grateful, but she's not blind to the gift I'm giving her. She will face many dangers that her immunity won't protect her from.

"Make sure you say goodbye to your sister before you leave."

"Of course!" she snaps, insulted that I might think she'd do otherwise.

A sound stops our discussion, a scuffling in the darkness and then a strange animalistic noise. We brace ourselves lifting weapons and preparing to take down anything that attacks. But out of the growing darkness saunters a single sheep. Weapons lower and we stare in amazement as it wanders over to our group and stands, waiting to go back to its pen. The lone survivor of a massacre that may just be the beginning of the end of our apocalypse.

EPILOGUE
FIVE YEARS LATER

"Mrs. Fuentes!" I perk up as my name is called out in a small child-like voice. "Can you tell us a story?"

I smile warmly and settle onto my bench under the shadowy canopy of our rooftop paradise. A class of around twelve children sits in front of me, a blending of schools from Sector One and Sector Thirteen. Over the years we discovered what a benefit it was to have the children go on field trips and learn together. As the threat of Primitives grew less and less, we started taking groups of children beyond the wall, out into the desert so they can experience the bounty of our planet beyond Sanctuary.

Today they are on my rooftop learning about the value of greenhouses and hearing sensational stories of their mighty Warlord and his rebellious wife, the Desert Wren. I hadn't intended to discuss our past with them, but then I'd broken down and told a few stories. It's good for them to understand what sparked the rebellion and how we managed to resolve it.

I'm surprised and pleased that these children know of

my old nickname. Either they are taught about us in school or their parents are gossiping. But it's harmless, since our story has a happy ending. Or I should say middle, since our story is by no means done yet.

"Of course, I'll tell you a story," I say, sitting on the warm bench near the ledge looking out over our Sanctuary. Diogo built a higher fence on it so none of the children can climb up and accidentally fall. "Have you heard the story of Stryker and Abrielle?" A few nod, but most tell me no, I haven't told them this one yet. "Well, let me tell you then. Stryker was a mighty warrior, almost as mighty as our Warlord. He was happily married to the lovely Abrielle in the San Antonio Sanctuary..."

I tell them of Stryker's story, giving them every detail I remember, a story that I repeat over and over, along with all the other stories I've gathered. I tell them the sad along with the happy, though I do make sure I'm speaking in age appropriate terms. I have made it my mission to collect and tell stories, to encourage others to remember and repeat these stories. Paper is scarce, as is our ability to record information that isn't absolutely necessary. Thus we are using the tradition of oral storytelling, a practice used by many cultures before writing was developed. The oral tradition conveys generations of information that might otherwise become lost. I talk about Emery often, Garrett, Talon, Stryker, Jorje Cruz, Victoria Greystone, my parents, my grandparents, everyone.

I talk with the children, telling them stories and then listening to theirs, laughing and clapping with them. Time and again my gaze is drawn to one little boy with his cap of dark hair and penetrating grey eyes. His expression is so solemn, but I know he is just thinking, processing everything we say and turning it over in his intelligent little mind. I know this because I am his proud mama.

Blaze is now in his second year at the Sector One school. He loves his time spent with his teacher and classmates and is always eager to come and tell us all about his day. Diogo brags about Blaze's skills in combat and survival, things his father is teaching him, but I know that my son is a thoughtful and kind young man. He absorbs everything around him with a curiosity and intelligence that makes me ache with motherly pride and a little bit of sadness at his independence.

Soon the children are gathered up and taken back to their schools, an echo of 'thank you's' thrown back at me as they leave. I wave to them and tell them to be careful on their trek back down the stairs.

"Mama." I look down as my four-year-old daughter grips the edge of my shirt and scowls up at me.

"Yes, Rayne?"

"When can I go to school?"

I smile at her and gently remind her that she has one more year before she's old enough. She's been asking this question almost every day for two years as she watches her brother leave the apartment each morning with Diogo where he will be dropped at his school with his bodyguard Karl in tow. Rayne hates being separated from her older brother. And he is, of course, patiently wonderful with his demanding little sister.

I sit on the warm patio tiles and pull Rayne down onto my lap. Together we pull a pot toward us. A tomato pot that we planted only the week before.

"Look at the tiny little sprout," I point out to her.

"Your favourite, mama," she says happily digging her fingers into the dirt next to mine.

"Yes, my favourite," I say with a grin and drop a kiss on the soft red flyaway hair.

Together we sit out there in the warm sunshine planting more for our rooftop garden and talking about her desire to adopt one of the city animals. I laugh at her childish arguments. They need homes. Aren't they cold in the barns? Wouldn't the baby chicks be more comfortable set loose in her bedroom?

"But what about Skye?" I ask her, trying to divert her attention. "I don't think she would like to share her home with another animal. She's kind of a loner."

We both look up at the bird chirping in the foliage above our heads. The desert wren that comes back every year to visit and recreate her nest. The first time she came to us I'd been stunned and had exclaimed excitedly to Diogo that somehow our bird had found us. He was sceptical and dismissed my fanciful idea, saying it was a different bird. But I know it's her, my original Skye, my sweet little desert wren.

I know, because she came to me two weeks before I gave birth to my daughter. I was terrified about something happening. The stress of Blaze's birth left its mark on me, one that I will never get over. That stress caused complications in my second pregnancy. But the moment I saw that bird I knew I wasn't alone. We were two mothers who had found our Sanctuary. I spent every moment I could watching her build her nest and lay her eggs, taking comfort in the normal instinct-driven routine. Then it was time for me to give birth.

Bishop came to our apartment and, with Diogo at my side the entire time, I birthed our daughter in the comfort of my own bed. As we looked down at our brand-new daughter together, I couldn't help but feel an intense hope.

Hope for us, for humans, as we begin to flourish once more. Only this time we will do better, we'll learn from our mistakes and nurture a healthy and strong world that our children will be proud to live in.

"I don't think Skye cares if we have baby chicks," Rayne pouts. "She's just a bird."

"She's more than a bird, sweetheart, she's a symbol."

"What's that?"

I explain to her about my belief that Skye is a symbol of our healing planet, that she comes to us each year to show us that our natural world is still producing miracles, still surviving despite what humans have done to it and ourselves. Eventually she will learn in school about the rise of the Primitives and the hand that humans had in the spread of the disease. Most historians believe that Necrotitis Primeval could have been stopped in its infancy if humans had taken a different path.

For now, we compromise, and I agree to take her to the farm tomorrow so we can play with the baby chicks. A reasonable compromise to having chicken poop all over her bedroom.

Later, as I lay in bed with Diogo, our children safely in their beds, I make slow leisurely love to him, worshipping his body with my tongue and hands. With every sweep of my hands on his body I tell him of my love for him, with every kiss I thank him for my life and my children. And as I mount him and take him into my body, his hands on my hips, the entire world fades to just the two of us. Time stands still as we move together, coming together in an explosive climax. He catches my face between his palms and kisses me with the fierce love that has grown brighter and hotter with each passing year.

We hold each other after, no words between us. Only

our breaths mingling until they slow as we close our eyes on the gift of another day, the gift of Sanctuary.

THE END

Continue the apocalypse with Skye and Wolfe's story in
The Road to Wolfe!

He's going to leave without telling me.

I'm furious and I don't know where to direct my anger. I punch the side of the tent, doing no more than causing it to sway a little. When that doesn't work, I kick out at the table beside my makeshift bed and am slightly more satisfied when it crashes against the side of another bed.

"Why should I care?" I snarl into the gloom of the unlit tent. "He means nothing to me."

"We both know that's not true."

I whirl on the spot to find Wolfe, fully geared up, standing in the entrance watching my meltdown. Fury over-comes me and I stomp toward him. He doesn't even protect himself as I draw my fist back and send it flying into his belly. He doesn't move at all, just continues to stare down at me with his one good eye. Bright green, not even a flicker of emotion. Just nothing.

"You weren't going to tell me you were leaving," I accuse him.

"Who told you that?" he says mildly.

"It's obvious," I snap scathingly. "All your stuff is packed and gone, your bunk is empty and someone from the mess hall told me you asked for extra rations."

He nods unconcerned. "Also took some extra ammunition."

"Why?" I yell at him. We both know I'm not asking about the ammunition but his intention of leaving.

"It's time," he says simply.

"Fuck that!" I shout. I can't seem to lower my voice and we're starting to draw some attention. A few curious onlookers peek inside the tent flap, but as soon as they catch sight of Wolfe they scurry away. It would almost be comical, the fear he inspires in people, if I weren't so pissed off.

"How is it that you spend all these months practically stalking me, refusing to leave my side, and now, all of a sudden, you're ready to leave?" I come a hairsbreadth from saying *leave me*, but I swallow the words. He can't know how attached I've gotten, how much I've come to depend on his shadowy presence following my every move.

"It's time for me to go," he says again.

I slap him across the face and then gasp at my audacity. Not only did I do an incredibly childish thing by giving into my anger and attacking him physically, for the second time in the space of a few minutes, but I also slapped the deadliest man in the city, except perhaps for the Warlord next door.

He doesn't react at all and I'm left cradling my stinging hand, trying to wiggle some feeling back into my fingers. Fucker is made of stone.

"Fine," I say as regally as I can. "Get the fuck out of my sight, I don't want to see you again."

He moves so fast I don't have time to back up. His hand whips around my neck, circling it, tangling in the hair. He drags me up onto my toes as he bends down to my face. His lips hover over mine and I think he'll kiss me, but he doesn't. Instead of struggling, I stand stock still, shocked that he's actually touching me when he almost never does.

He speaks, his voice calm and level despite the swirling emotion sizzling all around us. "You're lying to yourself, woman. And as long as you lie to yourself, you lie to me, which I am now done with. I will leave here and you will come find me when you're ready for truth between us."

He continues to hold me that way, just standing and staring as the minutes pass. Like he's memorizing everything about me. Then he lets go and steps away. He turns to leave, heading for the door, and this time I know he's actually leaving and not coming back.

"Where are you going?" I demand, swallowing the hitch in my throat.

He pauses for a moment in the doorway of the tent, his

sharp gaze looking me over, once again cataloguing as much as he can before he leaves. Finally, he says, "Come find me when you're ready." He walks away from the tent, letting the flap fall into place behind him.

"What the fuck are you talking about?" I rush to the entrance and shout after him.

But he's gone.

"I don't understand," I whisper to myself.

But I'm lying.

⸻

** *Now available for purchase!* **

"Fuck," Riley grumbled, twisting to make sure she was correct. Nope, she didn't have the right tool.

It was late at night and all the guys had gone home so she couldn't call out to one of the other mechanics and ask them to hand it to her. Damn. With an aggrieved sigh, she pushed herself out from under the car. Shoving her long ponytail out of the way, she crawled toward the toolbox and rifled through until she found what she was looking for. Loud, thumping music filled the garage from where her iPhone was plugged into its port on top of one of the tool benches.

Turning back toward the '69 Camaro, Riley adjusted her lamp and prepared to slide back under. This baby was a thing of beauty. It called to her from the moment it entered her shop, which is why she was still working on it at 2:00am. If she did it up right she'd be able to turn a pretty profit on this little sweetheart and take Cilia on vacation. They desperately needed some bonding time.

The music switched off and a deep voice reverberated through the darkness of the garage. "I'm looking for Mr. Bancroft."

Riley froze for a few precious seconds before her head snapped up, judging the distance between a shadowed man and the gun in her toolbox. He stepped forward into the circle of her light, closing the distance between them. Riley's heart slammed against her ribs as his face became visible and she recognized the most ruthless man in the city. Soloman Hart, mafia kingpin, was standing in her garage, staring down at her with cold intent. He now stood directly between her and her gun. Not that she thought it would do any good against a man like him.

Riley felt incredibly small and grimy next to his large, well-dressed frame. She sat crouched on the concrete beneath him, wearing her usual tank top and grimy, oil-stained overalls with the top left to hang down. Her shiny, dark brown hair was pulled back in a messy ponytail and she wore no make-up.

He seemed to be looking her over, taking in every inch of her with interest. Her eyes narrowed in return. She was used to guys staring. She was a thirty-year-old female mechanic, working in a garage full of men. She looked younger than she was and knew she was attractive. Definitely fantasy material for some guys. Which is why she tended to work in the office and on cars in the back, well away from the clients. Very few people knew who actually owned the garage.

"How did you get in here?" she demanded, pushing herself up and standing to her full height, which was still several inches shorter than him. She crossed her arms in front of her chest and glared at him. She had a damn good security system or she wouldn't have been alone in the shop blaring music in the middle of the night.

He ignored her question and raised a dark, thick brow. "Mr. Bancroft?" The single question sent a chill down her spine, letting her know that the next words out of her mouth better be an answer, because Soloman Hart was not a man known for patience.

Riley pressed her lips together for a moment and wondered how best to answer him. The truth of 'Mr. Bancroft' was complicated. And Riley was starting to suspect she may be in some danger. The likelihood of a man of this caliber showing up in her garage for any reason was slim. Which meant something not good was going down. Soloman had men to deal with his car issues, he didn't deal with things like this himself.

She moistened her lips and then stopped when his sharp eyes followed the movement. Taking a breath, she said, "Mr. Bancroft is dead. He died two years ago."

His brows drew together in a frown that made Riley shiver from head to toe. Yeah, he didn't want to play games with her. His next words confirmed this thought.

"Don't fuck with me, little girl," he growled. "Everyone

knows Alan Bancroft is dead. I'm looking for the owner of this garage. Alan's son, Riley Bancroft."

"Okay," she whispered. "Why are you looking for Riley?"

Holy shit, she was going to die! The look on his face suggested that the last person that questioned him instead of instantly giving him the answers he was searching for had died a really extra terrible death.

Surprisingly, he answered, his deep voice clipped as he spoke. "Someone stole one of my vehicles yesterday. It was my favourite and I want it back. Thought it might show up here."

Shock flickered across her face. Who would be stupid enough to steal one of Soloman Hart's cars? Well, that explained why he would show up on her doorstep himself at 2:00am looking for answers. She ran the biggest chop shop in the city. Only very few people knew she ran the garage. She had a very good team of mechanics, mostly inherited from her father, that helped keep her safe behind the scenes. Few people even knew the name Riley Bancroft. Except, somehow Soloman did.

"Wh-what kind of car?" She asked hesitantly, hoping like hell it hadn't gone through her shop. She usually did her homework and found out where the vehicles came from so this kind of shitstorm didn't come down on her head, but that didn't mean things didn't get under her radar once in a while.

"Koenigsegg Regera." His voice held no inflection as he named one of the most expensive vehicles in the world. A car that would be one of a kind in the United States.

Riley took a few seconds out from her terror to be impressed. Damn. Soloman must like him some nice luxury racing automobiles. Too bad the man was such a cold-hearted, ruthless bastard. Under different circumstances she wouldn't mind getting under the hoods of his fleet, see what he had going on up in there.

She breathed a sigh of relief. "Nope, I definitely would've noticed one of those. Never even seen one in person, let alone had one in here."

He nodded, still studying her carefully as though taking in every minuscule expression that crossed her face. Finally, he said, "I'd still like to have a conversation with Mr. Bancroft."

Fuck. That was going to be a problem since there was no Mr. Bancroft. Instead, she nodded her head.

"Sure, no problem. I'll have him call you tomorrow." She'd get one of the other mechanics to call and reassure him that his car was never there and if it showed up he would be the first person they called.

He reached out and took her hand before she realized what he was about to do. He held her fingers in a grip that told her she shouldn't pull away from him. He had tattoos over his hand and knuckles. He looked down at the black, chipped nail polish and rubbed his broad thumb over the tops of her much smaller nails. She shivered at his touch. Based on his reputation and the few glimpses she'd had of him she'd always considered Soloman Hart cold, but his hand was surprisingly warm.

"What's your name?" he demanded, his voice deep and compelling.

Riley tried to pull her hand away, but he continued to hold her. She turned her body away and said in a haughty voice, "None of your business."

He stiffened next to her and she bit her lip, worried that she was about to find out what made this powerful man so feared among their underworld set. He chuckled lightly, running his thumb over her knuckles. "I think you'll find I can make it my business."

She shivered and dropped her eyes, still refusing to answer. She did not want this man finding out who she was. For more reasons that the obvious. When he was alive, Alan Bancroft had taught Riley everything he knew, but he'd kept her existence on the down low in case they ever needed to pack up shop and run. There was also the complication of her mother. Cilia Bancroft, shady accountant to the super rich, was a handful and best kept out of the notice of men like Soloman Hart.

"You can fly, little bird," he said quietly. He looked down at her, capturing her brown eyes with his bottomless dark eyes. "I will let you go for now."

"F-for now?" Riley asked hesitantly.

He released her hand and stepped closer, towering over her, his chest nearly brushing hers. Riley gasped at his unexpected movement and tried to move back. Her leg bumped against the car she'd been working on and she was forced to stand still next to him. Her head swam as his subtle, masculine scent enveloped her. It made alarm bells go off in her head. He didn't immediately move away from her.

"For now," he confirmed. "I think the day will come that we will see... a lot more of each other."

Her mouth opened and she stared at him. Was that a threat? He was looking down at her with something she couldn't entirely define. Speculation? Possessiveness? But how was that possible? He didn't even know her. Though she'd seen him before, they were just meeting officially for the first time.

His eyes brushed over her one last time and she had a keen awareness that she was being granted some kind of reprieve. But it came with a time limit. One that would eventually run out. Her heart slammed against her ribs.

"Do you know who I am?" he asked.

She blinked and then nodded slowly.

"Say my name," he demanded.

Riley gaped up at him for a moment and then, desperately wanting the dark man to leave, she gave him what he wanted. She licked her lips and whispered, "Soloman."

He turned and strode away from her, resetting the alarm before leaving the garage.

***

Soloman slid into the passenger side of his second favourite vehicle. Turning to his friend and bodyguard, he said, "Did you catch that?"

Roman nodded. He had been standing in the shadows near the door where he'd disabled the alarm and unbolted the lock to allow his boss entry to the garage. Though Soloman didn't need back up, the two rarely worked separately, especially since Soloman's climb to the top had earned many enemies. Both knew it was better to have a loyal man guarding each other's backs than to go it alone.

"I want her," Soloman said quietly, not taking his eyes off the passing street lights.

Roman grunted, but didn't say anything. He already knew. The boss rarely pursued women, beyond having them brought in for a quick fuck. That he even asked for this one's name was surprising. "I'll find out who she is."

Soloman nodded. "I want to know everything. There's something about her... I think I might keep her for a while."

Roman grunted. He'd get their information guy out of bed and working on the problem of the chick immediately.

Find out who she was so the boss could get laid. Soloman Hart wasn't used to being denied. No one needed to be around the man when he wasn't happy. Much better to just bring him the woman's information and then the woman herself all wrapped up and tied in a bow. Fewer people would die that way.

"And find out where the fuck Riley Bancroft is," he snapped, drumming his fingers restlessly on his leg. "I want my goddamned car back."

Now available for purchase!

ALSO BY NIKITA SLATER

If you enjoyed this book, check out some other works by #1 International Bestselling Author, Nikita Slater. More titles are always in progress, so check back often to see what's new!

Sinner's Empire

Book 1 - Sin of Silence - Preorder

Book 2 - A Silent Reckoning - Coming Soon!

Book 3 - Goodnight, Sinners - Coming Soon!

The Queens Series

Book One – Scarred Queen

Book Two - Queen's Move

Book Three - Born a Queen

Book Four - The Red Queen (Coming 2021)

Alejandro's Prey (a novella)

The Queens 4 Book Box Set

Fire & Vice Series

Book One – Prisoner of Fortune

Book Two – Fight or Flight

Book Three – King's Command

Book Four – Savage Vendetta

Savage Boss (a novella)

Book Five – Fear in Her Eyes

Book Six – Bound by Blood

Book Seven – In His Sights

Book Eight - Burning Beauty

Book Nine - Chasing Ecstasy (Coming soon!)

Fire & Vice 6 Book Box Set

The Driven Hearts Series

Book One - Driven by Desire

Book Two - Thieving Hearts

Book Three - Capturing Victory

Novella - The Princess and Her Mercenary

Driven Hearts 4 Book Box Set

The Sanctuary Series

Book One - Sanctuary's Warlord

Book Two - Sanctuary on Fire

Book Three - The Last Sanctuary

Book Four - The Road to Wolfe

Book Five - Skye's Sanctuary (Coming soon!)

The Sanctuary Series 3 Book Box Set

Loving The Bad Boy Series

Loving Vincent

Loving Jared

Loving Rico (Coming Soon!)

Standalone books

The Assassin's Wife

Because You're Mine

Mine to Keep (a novella)

Luna & Andres

Kiss of the Cartel

Stalked

After Dark

In collaboration with Jasmin Quinn

Collared: A Dark Captive Romance

Safeword: A Dark Romance

Chained: A Mafia Marriage Romance

Good Girl: A Captive BDSM Romance

Hostile Takeover: An Enemies to Lovers Romance

The After Dark Box Set

Visit ***nikitaslater.com*** for more information

and the latest updates!

ABOUT THE AUTHOR

Nikita Slater is the International Bestselling dark romance author of the Fire & Vice series, Angels & Assassins series, The Queens series and several standalone novels. Her favourite genre is mafia romance, the bloodier the better, though she loves to write about every subject under the sun. She lives on the beautiful Canadian prairies with her son and crazy awesome dog. She has an unholy affinity for books (especially erotic romance), wine, pets and anything chocolate. Despite some of the darker themes in her books (which are pure fun and fantasy), Nikita is a staunch feminist and advocate of equal rights for all races, genders and non-gender specific persons. When she isn't writing, dreaming about writing or talking about writing, she helps others discover a love of reading and writing through literacy and social work.